BOOK 2

A. LAWRENCE

That's the Spirit

Copyright © 2023 –A. Lawrence

This book is a work of Fiction. Any references to historic events, real people, or real places are used fictitiously. Other names, characters, places, and events are the products of the author's imagination. Any resemblance to actual events, places or persons (living or dead), is entirely coincidental.

All Rights Reserved –No part of this book may be reproduced or transmitted in any form without written permission of the author

Published by: Cloaked Press, LLC
PO Box 341
Suring, WI 54174
Cloakedpress.com

Cover Design by:
Carmilla M. Ravensworth
carmillacreates.carrd.co

ISBN: 978-1-952796-31-9

For Cindy, who read this book even when she was
scared.

Contents

CHAPTER 1: ROAR

Shay punched the mass of dim blue light.

Her fist slid through what felt like unset gelatin, all the way up to her elbow. The ghost slid away, completely unharmed, but left her arm covered in thick ectoplasm.

"Oh, gross!" She shook her hand, uselessly.

The ghost lunged at her. She fell against a bookshelf, the whole thing shuddering under her weight.

"Focus!" Jo yelled at her.

"Yeah, Shay, focus!" Duncan called from the kitchen, safely behind a line of salt.

"You're supposed to be helping!" Shay dropped to all fours and scrambled out of the way. The apparition passed harmlessly through the bookshelf she'd almost sent toppling.

"I could get a mop?" he suggested.

"You're the worst!"

It had been a normal day in Spellbound, until Shay turned the shop's sign to closed. Slime spread from underneath the door and formed into a human blob shape with holes for eyes.

Jo worked quickly, sealing off the shop portion of the house, but it didn't help when Shay was in the shop. Every time she made a move for the kitchen the blob herded her farther back.

"How did it get in, anyway?" Duncan asked. "Isn't the house warded?"

"It's supposed to be!" Jo skipped back a few steps when the ghost whipped around to face her. She held up a burning white candle. "Get out! You're not welcome here!"

The candle flared brighter in response to the force behind the words. The ghost cringed back. Jo tossed a sachet, causing it to flicker and fade.

"And it's gone." Duncan clapped. "Good work, team. Excellent job. Bonuses all around."

"You don't have the authority for that," Jo told him.

"You don't deserve one, anyway." Shay picked herself up, trying in vain to brush her jeans off. The ghost hadn't been kind enough to wait until after she swept.

"Excuse you, I brought the power of observation and witty commentary to this entire ordeal," Duncan said.

"Your powers of observation weren't great."

"If you're asking do I feel useless, I do," Duncan said. "But I'm also not covered in slime or dust, so I'm pretty okay with it."

"Get in the kitchen," Jo told Shay. "It's still here."

"It is?" Shay's voice cracked.

Jo ignored her. "Duncan, what does it want?"

"Why would I know?" Duncan asked. He sighed and rubbed the bridge of his nose. "I have no idea. To be gross? It's…mad. At Shay. It was part of the big ghost thing Shay punched apart and he's not in the right place anymore, so he's lashing out at whatever feels right. To be fair, I think he was angry before that."

"That was not my fault." Shay stepped into the kitchen and her shoulders relaxed. Between the wards and the salt, she was about as safe as she ever got.

She had taken down a giant conglomerate of ghosts a week and a half before, and it had scattered a bunch of powerful, angry, and confused spirits all over Teton Falls. Spellbound's voicemail was cluttered with customers who needed an exorcism. Jo said they weren't ready to deal with it.

The evening was proving her right.

"Hey, I'm not rationalizing it, I'm conveying emotions," Duncan said. "Feelings. Whatever. And not well. It's all hazy. Like…like I'm seeing everything through frosted glass."

"A frosted donut, maybe," Shay muttered.

"Rude, I'm trying to help you." Duncan poked her side. She slapped his hand. "Hey, ow. Uncalled for. Anyway, I don't know. I've been hearing a roaring sound. Heard it when it first showed up. I thought it was out on the street."

"Like a lion?" Shay asked.

"Fun fact, in most movies they use tiger roars, because they're louder," Duncan said. "But not, it's mechanical, like…a car with a bad exhaust, or…"

"A motorcycle?" Jo suggested.

He snapped his fingers and pointed at her. "Yes, exactly."

"Whatever it is, it's gross," Shay said. The ectoplasm evaporated with the ghost, but the crawling sensation hadn't left her skin, no matter how many times she wiped her hand on her jeans. "And—"

"Watch out!" Duncan yelled.

The ghost formed in the kitchen, faster than she thought possible. It lunged at her. The amorphous blob burned away to a black skull wreathed in pale flames. Twin points of bright blue fire shone in the sockets. It snapped sharpened teeth at her face.

It yanked her closer. One large arm wrapped around her throat. It was so cold it burned and stunk of leather. She kicked and struggled, but it held firm.

Shay couldn't breathe. Dark spots floated over her vision. Duncan grabbed her hand.

The kitchen fell away, the ghost along with it.

Shay sucked in a deep, cold breath of air. It smelled of lemons and wood polish.

They were standing on a landing. Dark stairs with plush red carpet spreading above and below them, disappearing into a thick fog. Sun shone through a window, motes of dust catching the light. There was nothing outside of the glass panes.

She'd only seen it twice, but she'd know it anywhere.

Finnias's landing.

Shay's heart constricted in her chest. She'd left him to float somewhere in a dark void. The mirror ghost said he was somewhere, but she couldn't be sure until she saw him.

She turned around but there was no one standing there, where he was supposed to be. Just an intricate red wallpaper. Gold diamonds caught the light.

"What the…where are we?" Duncan was still holding her hand. "Shay?"

"This is where Finnias died," she said. "Or it was significant? I'm still not sure. He should be here."

She stared at the spot where a pale, serious young man with dark hair and gray eyes had told her she could do anything.

He didn't magically appear.

"He should be here," she repeated.

"Shay—"

"No, he was standing right here," she insisted. "Finnias! Finnias, where are you?"

A whisper. She closed her eyes and strained her ears, trying to catch the words, but the low murmur didn't make any sense.

Duncan squeezed her hand. "Shay, we should go. Get out of here. Wherever here is."

"Shh." She waved her free hand at him. "I can't hear you. What are you trying to say? We can help you. We can find you."

"We have to go." Duncan yanked on her arm. Someone was walking up the stairs, like they always had, rising up from the mist, blurry and distorted.

She held her breath as a man about Duncan's age looked up at her with wide, blue eyes.

The world snapped back into place. She was in Jo's kitchen, being choked to death by an enormous ghost.

Jo threw an entire jar of salt over both of them. "Get out of my house!"

The ghost spun away from her, shrinking until it was a tiny blue flame that snuffed itself out. Shay sagged to the floor. She coughed, hard, spitting out ectoplasm burning on her tongue. "Oh. That. Tastes so bad."

"What the hell, Jo, could you lead with that next time?" Duncan sat down next to her, brushing salt out of his hair. "You okay, Shay Shay?"

"Could ask you the same thing." Her voice scraped against her throat. "How did it get in the kitchen?"

"I don't know." Jo sat heavily in one of the chairs around the kitchen table. She was normally pale, but she'd passed it all the way to gray. "What happened? You both froze up."

"I dunno, stuff got weird," Duncan said. "We were on a weird landing? Shay said it was Finnias's."

"It was," Shay said. "You remember that?"

"Uh, kind of not a thing I'm going to forget," Duncan said. "But the important thing right in this moment is that thing got through a line of salt. I thought the whole point of us staying here was that it was safe?"

"And free rent," Shay added.

"Okay, I'm sorry, back up." Jo held up a hand. "Finnias's landing?"

"The bubble thing I got pulled into when I grabbed his hand, his…death echo, or whatever. That's what it was," Shay explained. "A landing and a few stairs."

"Great." Jo knocked off her glasses when she rubbed her temples. They swung from the beaded chain around her neck. "Fantastic. Of course this is happening. And look what the ghost did to the floor. These are original to the house, you know."

Whorls of frost swirled across the hardwood.

"Okay, so. We have multiple problems and apparently zero solutions," Duncan said. "Why don't you ward the house again?"

"It's not my specialty, but I can try." Jo sighed, rubbing her left temple. "Arlo did it last time."

"You promised me my sister would be safe here," Duncan said.

"Sister is here," Shay said. "In the room. Listening to every word. And it's not like anywhere else is safer."

She didn't want to think about it. She wanted to change into her pajamas and hide in her bed for a few months.

"And sister didn't punch the ghost into little fiery bits so I'm a little upset with her, too," Duncan said.

Shay shrugged, trying to squash down any panic. She'd expected flames, too. "Finnias said it wouldn't work on every ghost, and that guy was squishy."

"Ew." Duncan made a face. "So, what are we going to do about this?"

"Max and I can ward Shay's room," Jo said, a little more confident. "I wanted to start teaching them, anyway, and tonight is as good of a time as any. It's not the best plan but it's what we have right now. Arlo's…well. I don't know when we're going to find him. I'm going to make some tea."

She put the kettle on.

Shay nodded. "I'm gonna go change."

The ectoplasm evaporated, but it left Shay's skin tingly and grimy. She headed up to her room. Jo had moved her to the tower room on the second floor. She even had her own bathroom. It was small, but it was tucked right next to her door.

She frowned at her reflection while she washed her hands. She had pale blue ghost marks on her jaw and neck, but she knew they'd fade quickly.

What made her frown was that her reflection did absolutely nothing strange. "Hey, mirror ghost. Are you there? We need help. Lots of help. We need to find Arlo and…and Finnias. You said you knew where he was. Care to elaborate?"

The mirror didn't do anything. No ghost was putting bags under her eyes or unraveling her braid before turning her face into a skull. She did that herself, combing her fingers through it before yanking it up into a ponytail, just to feel like she had a bit of control.

Her reflection followed her movements perfectly, like any ordinary mirror.

"Well, you know where to find me."

She headed back down to the kitchen, where she spent most of her free time. Her new room was amazing, but she didn't want to be alone. The living room was the congested artery of the house. There was too much antique furniture Jo didn't have the heart to throw out, but after turning the front room into a shop there wasn't space for it. It was coated in a thin layer of pastel doilies. Shay assumed Jo's grandmother had made them, but she hadn't had the chance to ask.

The cat usually took up the best spot on the couch, anyway. She gave Becky some scratches in passing. "You're a terrible ghost detector."

Becky purr meowed at her.

"Can't even pay the rent. Shameful."

The kitchen smelled liked cookies. Duncan was at the table with Gideon, who was frowning at his laptop, but he smiled when she walked in.

"Hey, Shay!"

"Hey…I don't know what rhymes with Gideon and I wasn't prepared I'm sorry." She sat across from him, tipping her chair a little too far back. "Whoops, sorry to you too, chair."

"The chair and I forgive you," Gideon said.

"Obsidian?" Duncan suggested.

He nodded. "Gideon Obsidian is my goth name."

"I like it," Shay said. "Where's Jo?"

"Finishing closing up the shop, I think, and she made cookies?" Gideon shrugged. "I heard you had a run in?"

"Yeah." Shay folded her arms on the tabletop and rested her chin on them. "Beardy McSlimeface."

"Beardy?" Duncan asked.

"At the end he looked kind of like a big scary biker dude," Shay said. "But with fire. And a skull. With really sharp teeth."

"So, the roar was a motorcycle!" Duncan clapped his hands. "Yes, score one for observation skills. Take that, Shay, I'm not so terrible at this after all, am I?"

Shay shook her head.

"Oh, c'mon." He nudged her knee with his foot. She kicked him in retaliation. "Ow! Hey! That was uncool. I take it back. I'd rather be terrible. I'd rather go hang out with Slimey and his cool motorcycle, stop spending time around nerds."

"You're a librarian," Shay reminded him.

"Libraries rock." Duncan spread his cardigan to show off his shirt. It was for the geology club, with "The Teton Falls Public Library Rocks!" written on it. "It's on a shirt. Can't refute it."

"I designed that shirt, that automatically makes me cool," Gideon said

"No, still a big nerd." Duncan gave him an annoying smile. "But maybe I like that you're a big nerd."

They'd been flirting for the last week, ever since she'd saved the town from being sucked into a ghost dimension. Or whatever terrible thing would have happened if Shay left the tear open.

Probably not as terrible as the flirting.

Shay didn't even want to think about how awful they'd be if they were actually dating.

"You're both nerds. What are you working on, anyway? Stuff for the library?" Shay had to admit that as far as subtle subject changes went, it wasn't her best work.

Gideon didn't comment, thankfully. "Oh, that's all edited and ready to go, thankfully. Sam did it. Surprisingly not a lot of evidence, all things considered.

Duncan shrugged. "Sucks for the big premiere.

"Yeah, I know," Gideon sighed. "I'll be honest, I think P.E.I.R.S. is on its way out, anyway."

"What happened to P.E.I.R.S.?" It was the first time Shay had heard anything about it.

"Well, besides the losing a guest star thing?" Gideon glanced over at Duncan, who winced. He'd been possessed by Finnias, at the time, and it wasn't his fault, but it still hadn't been the best way to end the night. "Basically, it comes down to Taylor not remembering where she got a bunch of our new equipment and Vic wants to make sure we're on the up and up. After the library thing we don't have anything on the schedule, but it doesn't even matter. My hunting days are over. I'm good. Ghosts are real. Way too real."

"That's fair," Shay said. "You can say we're too exciting to hang out with, it's okay."

"Nah, you guys are fine." Gideon shrugged. "Besides, you need me."

"Not going to argue with that," Duncan said.

"Anyway, turns out giving up my one real hobby freed up a surprising amount of my time," Gideon said. "So, I'm trying to figure out some things for you guys, help however I can. So. Finnias and the spirit charmer seemed to know each other, right?"

Shay didn't like to think about it. "Yeah, I mean, she knew him. He didn't really know…anyone."

"Right, the…amnesia thing. Still, I figure that they probably were haunting the same place before all of this, or at least if we find Finnias we'll figure out who the other ghost is," Gideon continued. "And Finnias was an older ghost. Like, died a long time ago, judging by what he was wearing?"

"Or was wearing a costume and got a real unfortunate party favor," Shay said.

"Maybe. If they knew each other when they were alive, and that was a long time ago, why is the spirit charmer active now?" Gideon said. "And what about the ghost that possessed Max? I think they're all connected, and that ghost said something that made you think he knew where Arlo was."

Shay liked to think about that even less. "Possibly."

"It's the best lead we have. I've been doing some digging," Gideon continued. "Now, I think I've found him. Finnas S. Woodrow. No word on what the S stands for, and I think it was an alias or maybe records are just spotty, so I haven't found much more out."

"Woodrow, huh?" Shay said. It was strange to think of Finnias having a last name. "How many dudes got big holes carved into their chests at the turn of the century?"

"Oh, I thought the hole was like, a metaphor, for his missing memories," Duncan said.

Shay shrugged. "Dunno. Didn't see how he actually died. Maybe we should wait for Max to get here."

"No, better we workshop it, I want Max to respect me," Gideon said.

"What about me? I'm a librarian, a researcher, I have a degree in it," Duncan reminded him.

"Yeah, but you think I'm cute," Gideon said.

"That's true."

Shay rolled her eyes. "And what about me?"

"You think I'm cool, obviously you already respect me." Gideon grinned at her and she stuck her tongue out at him. "Anyway, starting over, because you guys are on the verge of ruining my big reveal."

"I do love a big reveal." Duncan leaned forward. "I'm on the edge of my seat. Not literally, because Jo will turn me into actual donuts if I break her furniture, but metaphorically? I am there."

"Okay, here we go," Gideon spun his laptop around, to a website with a black background and a grainy old photo of a mansion. "I am confident he died in the Holt Manor Murders."

Chapter 2: Deadbeat

Shay stared at the house. She recognized it, now. The site of possibly the most significant event in Teton Falls history, according to any true crime podcasts.

"That's crazy," She finally said. Her voice was surprisingly steady. "The one mass murder event in the whole town and he gets caught up in it.

The Holt Manor was an old mansion out in the hills, nestled in a thick strand of pine. It was an enormous building, even by modern standards, with sweeping staircases, a ballroom, a library, meant to be some sort of back woods pinnacle of high society. Started in 1872 and completed in 1875, despite repeated warnings that the location chosen was cursed.

Thirty years later, every member of the Holt family and several guests were brutally murdered.

The murderer, and the murder weapon, were never found.

Occasionally, some author would come along and write a book about it, or an episode would pop up in a podcast. Teton Falls and its only claim to fame - the murder mansion.

"Huh, he's like a little bit of town history," Duncan said. "Did you know someone bought that place? I heard they renovated it."

"Who would want to renovate the murder mansion?" Shay asked.

"The house has been used by the city throughout the years, so there actually was already quite a number of extensive renovations," Gideon explained. "But it was bought two years ago, by a company called Fireglass Innovation."

"Which is owned by Stevens Realty Group," Duncan said.

Gideon stared at him. "How do you know that?"

"I'm a librarian." Duncan looked smug. "But seriously, I go to every town meeting, so I deal with the Stevens family a lot. They basically own the whole town."

"Wait, isn't that Taylor's last name?" Shay asked. The rest of the sentence hit her. "You go to town meetings?"

"Sometimes, I tell you I have a hot date, but I'm lying," Duncan said. "Local politics are very important, you know. That's how you find out that your apartment building is owned by the same jerk who's trying to gentrify the rest of the town and bought himself a wing in the library. The only solace we have is that our evil overlords think the library is very important. Probably because the wife keeps trying to make Teton Falls into some culture hub."

Shay frowned. "Has she…been to our downtown? Like…ever in the past five years?"

"Well, maybe when the town isn't horribly haunted she'll get her way and we'll all possibly want to go downtown." Duncan shrugged.

"Back to the matter at hand, they were selling the house you and Max found the first mirror in," Gideon said. "And they owned the theater. And the Governor's House. And the old coffee shop you guys were trapped in."

Shay nodded for lack of anything better to do. "Well…I guess not Taylor would have an easier time possessing someone whose family owns the whole town."

"Whole valley," Duncan agreed.

The oven timer chimed, and Jo walked into the room. She pulled out a sheet of cookies from the oven, warm air wafting into the kitchen. If Shay wasn't already chubby, partly from eating too much of Nana's cooking, Jo's propensity to bake or make food every time something mildly inconvenienced her would have done her in. Shay had no idea how Jo was still skinny.

It must have been the stress.

"Do you always have a bunch of cookie dough in your freezer or is it a recent thing?" Duncan asked.

"It's for emergencies." Jo slid each cookie onto a cooling rack. "What were you guys talking about?"

"About Gideon having a conspiracy theory about the Stevens family being secretly evil," Shay said.

"Or not so secretly," Duncan said. "Y'know, the whole gentrifying the town thing."

"Listen, they bought the Holt Manor two years ago," Gideon repeated. "And now a ghost that is clearly from the Holt Manor murders shows up. I don't think it's a coincidence."

"Okay, no, I'm agreeing with you," Duncan said. "Our rent was ridiculous. We had a two bedroom apartment. We didn't even have air conditioning. Or heating that worked."

"You can stay as long as you need to," Jo said. "Just help with groceries."

"Done," Duncan said. "I'm never leaving."

"Back to the Stevens…" Gideon was being very patient for someone dealing with Duncan on a tangent.

"Right." Duncan nodded. "Back to them. Not much we can do, I think I mentioned the super rich and politically powerful part. But hey, at least we know why the spirit charmer picked Taylor, now."

"And she's pretty," Shay said. "What? She seemed vain."

"Good point," Gideon said. "I don't know where all this is leading to, but with the spirit charmer still out there and all of this happening, I figured I'd do some research. I'll keep looking."

"Good looking," Duncan said. "And you're good looking."

Gideon grinned. "No, you are."

Shay groaned. "Please stop. Okay, so, the richest family in town is doing ghost things now? Why? They already own everything."

"Not everything," Jo said. "But close. That's a good lead, Gideon. I appreciate what you're doing."

"Sensing a but," Duncan said.

"It's just…" Jo sighed. "We need help."

"You think?" Duncan's eyebrows rose.

"We're apparently up against…all of that. I don't know what I'm doing, and…and I know Arlo isn't going to walk through the door, but I can't find him and…" Her voice cracked and she cleared her throat. She finished getting the cookies off the tray and poured water from the kettle into her largest tea pot before she continued. "I can't keep waiting for someone to show up with answers. I need to help both of you, and I can't, so…we need someone else."

"Yeah? Anyone else know about these…abilities?" Duncan asked. "I think we're all a little lacking in that department."

"You're a little lacking," Shay muttered.

Jo ignored her. "I don't know. I barely know anything about it. I was taught nearly everything I know by my grandma, but all she told me is that someone with the ability to touch ghosts would come, and I had to help them. Which is…not exactly giving me the tools I need to do just that. We need to figure out a plan of action. I can't find Arlo, but that ghost can. The one who possessed Max."

The only sound for a few moments was the oven ticking as it cooled off.

"He could have been lying," Shay said. "But if he knew Finnias, maybe he was involved in the murders, too. Do you think the landing is the one at Holt Manor?"

"There's one way to find out, but since it involves breaking and entering, I don't like our odds," Duncan said.

"I think if we find Finnias, we at least have, y'know, a clue," Shay said.

"Oh yeah, let's go out and start yelling for him, I'm sure he'll come back," Duncan suggested. "Maybe put a shirt that really smells like him on the porch."

"Let's try something new where you're not a jerk and try and help me figure things out," Shay said. "Mirror ghost—"

"Isn't even talking to you right now, right?" Duncan said. "Besides, I'm pretty sure that it was messing with you. And I don't want to be possessed again. It sucked and ever since then I keep picking up on weird ghost energy and I hate it. Whatever. Regardless, I don't want to be a ghost hotel. Even if I would get five stars. No vacancies. Just me in the penthouse."

He tapped the side of the head.

"We can find another way to communicate with Finnias." Jo placed a plate of cookies and tea in the middle of the table. "It's a good idea, Shay. If we can find him, if he really does have a connection to that other ghost, I can probably locate him. It's not guaranteed, but it's…it's something."

"Which leads perfectly into the other point I've been researching," Gideon said. He clicked on another tab on his laptop.

"Spiritual Connections?" Shay asked. "Connecting you to loved ones who have moved on. Gideon, really?"

The website looked professional, or at least compared to what she thought a website for a spirit medium would be. No giant spinning crystals, sparkles, or ominous sound effects. There was a picture of an unassuming office building, a few people wearing black t-shirts against a white brick background, and a bunch of information too far away for her to read.

"Let's see. A team of spiritual mediums who forge connections between their clients and those who have joined the afterlife. Spiritual Connections uses séances and spirit boards to speak to your loved ones that are no longer with you. Palmistry and aura reading are also available." Duncan snorted. "Aura reading? C'mon, Gid, I was very recently thrown into a death bubble and even I don't believe in that."

"A what bubble?" Gideon sounded alarmed

"I mean, not my death, I'm fine," Duncan said. "It was a…vision, I guess. Real weird stuff.

"What I'm hearing is, you believe in visions and not auras?" Jo asked.

"Yeah, okay, when you say it like that I do sound like an idiot," Duncan admitted. "So, auras. That a thing? Yay or nay."

"They're a thing," Jo said. "And if the person I'm thinking of is still there, she can see auras."

"Wait, you know them?" Shay asked.

"I do. Some of them," Jo said. "They are actual mediums. It's not a bad idea for Duncan to meet them. They can probably help more than I can."

"You know a bunch of spirit mediums and you didn't think 'hey maybe this new medium should meet them'?" Duncan asked.

"I'm not sure you are a medium," Jo said. "A medium feels the energies and emotions of spirits, some can even channel them. Someone really empathetic can use the same ability on the living. You do something else. You weren't channeling Finnias. It was a full-blown possession where you gave up control but gained a lot of beneficial side effects. When you feel out a ghost, you don't seem to be…doing it the way I've seen most mediums work, if I'm being honest."

"I guess," Duncan said. He pulled a hand through his hair, making it stand more on end than it usually did. "Y'know what, let's go with Shay's idea. Let's find Finnias."

"With any luck, they should be able to help us," Gideon said. "Maybe at least give us some direction, right? I might have…already made an appointment. Vic went there once, I watched the video and she seems pretty legitimate."

"Vic's opinion means nothing to me, but if you think so…." Duncan sighed. "Yeah, I guess it couldn't hurt. Maybe they'll have more insight into these…ability things."

"They have to have a name, right? Not just abilities?" Gideon asked. "Y'know, Jo's a witch, so Shay's a…ghost puncher."

"No," Shay said.

"Shay's right, as far as I'm aware," Jo said. "Being a witch isn't the same. But I don't know, I don't have the same…look, I was raised in the craft, I don't know anything about abilities other than what little Arlo has told me, and I don't think he knew much. All I know is they make you extremely vulnerable."

"That's not comforting," Duncan said.

Jo gave him a measured look. "I'm not trying to be comforting. This is dangerous and you need to know. You need to be prepared."

Shay didn't want to think about the dangers. She'd had enough danger and excitement for one lifetime already.

She snagged her phone from the charger. Max already said they were coming over, she let them know about the new plans. "Max will be here soon. They're going to love this. We tried a seance once. Nothing happened but Max got scared and almost lit their Nana's basement on fire. Good times."

It had been a fun night, before she'd known ghosts were real. They'd turned off all of the lights and lit a candle, holding hands around it while Max read the instructions off of a website. They'd sat in the dark, the light catching highlights in Max's hair, their dark eyes sparkling when they laughed. They knocked the candle over when the flame stuttered and they'd had to hurry to clean up the spilled wax.

"What time is the appointment?" Jo asked.

"Eight."

"Great, plenty of time to show Max how to work wards," Jo said.

"Gotta lock out the bad vibes," Shay said. "Good vibes only. All other vibes are illegal."

"Sure," Jo said. "Now, whatever medium you talk to, you're going to need to a first and a last name. I don't know if an alias will work."

Gideon shrugged. "At least we know where he died? And when. Exact date."

"Maybe even how," Shay said.

Duncan shook his head. "Still betting on metaphor. Five bucks."

"It should help," Jo agreed.

"And we have a strong emotional connection or whatever," Duncan pointed out. "Y'know, if all else fails, there's always other people we can try to get in contact with who might have some answers."

"Arlo isn't dead," Jo snapped, not quite slamming her tea cup down onto its saucer.

"Of course not," Duncan said. "I meant our dad."

A hot, slow anger burned into Shay's chest, but she squashed it down. "Since he texted me about college options in Portland this morning, I'm pretty sure we can give him a call without anyone's help."

She'd told her parents about getting the job at Jo's shop and about absolutely nothing else. They thought she could do better than retail. The last five months disagreed with them.

"Shay, you know I didn't mean him," Duncan said. "I meant… well, you know. Our biological dad."

"Maybe, still a deadbeat," she countered. Gideon and Jo were both looking down at the table as if the paisley tablecloth pattern held the secrets of the universe.

"Who might actually be our dead dad? If he's dead then he didn't leave us," Duncan said. "He just…he did leave us, but there's this whole shuffling and mortal coil involved, so we can't hold him accountable there."

Shay wanted to lash out. She wanted to say something cutting and horrible, release the fire burning in her lungs.

The tension was a presence all of its own, a haunting that had been following them from place to place, house to house.

Duncan had been eight when their dad left. She'd been two and didn't even remember him. There were hardly any pictures, squirreled away into storage spaces out of her reach.

If Duncan wasn't angry, she didn't have any place to be. "You know what? Sure. Fine. I'm gonna wait for Max."

It wasn't safe, but no one stopped her when she left. She sat on the porch stairs and took a deep breath of cold air.

CHAPTER 3:
ILLEGAL VIBES

Shay pulled her sweater sleeves over her hands to ward off the chill, sitting down on the steps.

The sun sank behind the houses but light still filtered across the sky, highlighting the clouds in pink and orange. Below a cold blue permeated the air. Halloween decorations up and down the street burned it away with bright oranges and green. In two days, kids would be crowding the sidewalk, begging for candy. Jo said they would be open late, catering to trick or treaters and the last-minute holiday crowd.

In less than a week the jack o' lanterns and skeletons would be replaced by Santa and reindeer.

If Shay figured out how to survive what she imagined to be the most haunted night of the year.

The door opened and she sighed. "I don't want to talk, Donuts."

"Good thing I'm not Donuts, and I don't want to talk, either," Gideon said. She looked back at him and he waved. "Hey. Mind if I join you?"

"Knock yourself out," she scooted over and he sat next to her.

True to Gideon's word, they didn't talk. The fire in the sky faded to blue. Leaves rattled down the sidewalk. The wind chime hanging from the porch sounded like old bones clattering together.

"Almost Halloween, huh?" Gideon said.

"Yup." She leaned against her knees. "Guess we'll have to take the skeletons off of the roof."

"You could make them festive, a Santa hat here, and few bells there…" Gideon chuckled.

"I bet Jo would go for that," Shay said. "Unless this was all Arlo. Honestly, I can't tell. Do you think we have a Krampus statue? Seems on brand."

"And a fog machine." Gideon nodded. "Nah, but I bet she puts up a big tree and tons of lights. You into that kind of thing?"

"Oh yeah, I'm a decorating master," Shay said. "Last year I made a star out of a gum wrapper and put it on one of those car air fresheners. Masterpiece. Plus, my dorm had that new car smell."

"Sounds amazing."

"Yeah." Shay felt a little better. The timer turned on the lights around them, purple and green spiraling up the posts and around the guard rails, fake candles flickering in the pumpkins. "My parents aren't into Halloween, but they go super hard for Christmas. The second we clean up Thanksgiving dinner everything starts to go up. It probably would sooner, but they have tons of dumb kitschy fall stuff."

"Your parents sound fun," Gideon said. Shay snorted. "Okay, sarcastic fun. They're in Portland, right? Why did you guys move out here?"

"I could ask you that," Shay said. "We're from here, actually. Mom used to write books and dad taught down in Pocatello, but they were both offered positions in Portland when I left for college so…bye, I guess. They said I could move in with them, but I picked Dunc. And here we are."

"You really care about your brother, huh?" Gideon smiled a bit.

She snorted. "No. You care about him. I care about Max."

"That's fair," Gideon said. "I do care about him. And Max is pretty great."

"That's oddly sweet but also really gross," Shay said.

"Good." Gideon grinned at her. "Do I have your sisterly seal of approval? Can I ask him out?"

"Honestly, I'm surprised you haven't." Shay made a face. "Yeah, fine, I guess. You know, he made me go to the dumb theater to be his wingman and he didn't even need it. You're clearly enchanted by his use of hair product and dumb jokes. Disgusting."

Gideon laughed, loudly. "I guess I'm glad you approve. While those things did draw me in initially, your brother does have surprising depth—"

"Ew!" She slapped her hands over her ears. "I don't even want to hear about Duncan's depths! Ever!"

Gideon downright cackled and the horrible tightness in Shay's chest loosened when she laughed, too.

"All right, but I do like him for more than the hair products," Gideon said. "And the jokes. He is pretty funny, though."

"Looks aren't everything," she said.

She heard Max's ancient explorer sputtering down the road before she saw the headlights.

"About time!" She hopped to her feet and ran down the sidewalk.

"Bye I guess!" Gideon called after her.

"See ya!"

Max pulled up to the curb and the roar of the engine cut off. Max barely got out of the car before she grabbed them in a hug.

"Oof!" They hugged her back, tightly. "Geez, I saw you two days ago. Sorry I'm late. I had a thing."

"Two days too many." She stepped back and gasped. "Was that thing a haircut?"

"Aw. Yeah." Max touched their hair. It was shorter than it had been, especially in the back. The headband was gone, letting their hair fall over their forehead. Not being surrounded by hair made their face softer. "You know me. I can never commit to growing it out, and it was getting long in the back and I kept thinking it was like…spiders or little ghost hands when it touched my neck…is it bad?"

"It looks amazing," she said, and meant it. She ran her fingers over the back of their head where it was shaved. "Ooh so soft. No more little ghost hands for you."

"Just little Shay hands."

"Rude." She smacked their shoulder, lightly. "Maybe I won't let you have any cookies, fancy hair person. I'll eat them all myself."

"Jo made cookies?" Max frowned. "Why? What happened?"

"So much." She grabbed their hand. "C'mon, Gideon has a whole presentation, and she's going to teach you how to do wards. And after that, a fun field trip."

"I get to learn magic?" Max brightened. "Finally! I thought she wasn't going to teach me anything. Hey, Gideon."

After exchanging greetings and explanations, Max frowned. "But why now? The wards were working before, right?"

"As far as I'm aware," Jo said. "I assume it was some sort of ripple effect from the tear. Most likely they've been weakening for a while now. I still don't understand how that ghost got into the kitchen."

"I crossed over the salt line, maybe that's how?" Shay suggested. "Maybe I did something?"

"I can't rule that out." Jo frowned.

"But I get to help?" Max asked.

"More like I will be directing and you'll do most of the work," Jo admitted. "I've been stretched a little thin. Honestly, it's all about intent, and I think you probably have very strong feelings about protecting Shay. Gideon could help, too."

"I'd be glad to," he agreed readily.

"Great, I'll have you get Duncan's room, just in case."

"Can I watch?" Shay asked. "In my room. Not Dunc's."

Duncan's room had all of his figures in it, and she was not in the mood to be stared at by that many plastic eyes.

"Knock yourself out, you can check for ghosts," Jo said. "How about you do that now while we get some things together? Not because your room is probably a mess you don't want me to see, of course."

"Yeah, of course. It's totally clean," Shay said. "Spotless, even. I know the rules. Yeah."

She dashed up the stairs two at a time, calculating how quickly she could fold laundry. Not quickly enough. Shoving it into drawers and hoping she could close them would have to do.

She did manage to get them shut and get her dirty laundry into her neglected hamper. She was getting all of the things she'd thrown on the desk in order when a cold breeze distracted her.

She frowned. The curtains around the window seat were closed. The lights from the porch weren't even visible through the pink and frills. It was possible she'd left the window open a crack earlier.

She took two steps towards the window.

Something moved under the cloth, stopping her short.

The curtains expanded like they were breathing and settled around the shape of a person.

Shay walked backwards, slowly and carefully. If she could get to the door, she could get down the stairs, and Jo and Max could take care of whatever was in her room.

The curtain expanded again, fluttering up. There was nothing underneath. They floated back and a face pressed against the fabric, outlining the indents of the eyes and an open mouth.

Shay's foot came down on a creaky floorboard.

The face snapped towards her.

The door slammed shut.

She scrambled for it, yanking her sleeve down over her hand before trying the knob. It might as well have been a lump of ice. She spun to face the curtain. It was straining against the rod, the first ring plinked off and rattled on the floor. And a second.

"Okay, ghostie, I've got a secret weapon," she said. It hadn't worked against the biker ghost, but it had to work now. She balled her hands into fists. She willed the fire to appear.

Nothing happened.

The curtain yanked itself off the rod and the ghost barreled at her. She punched it. Cloth engulfed her hand, tightening around her arm and yanked her closer. The ghost's face was right in front of hers, fabric pulled tight against it, frozen in a scream.

She tried to cry out, but it felt like her jaw locked shut. She couldn't back away.

The door opened so violently it banged against the wall. Herbs and salt hit her in the back and scattered on the ghost. It shrieked and lunged back, the curtain falling around her.

Max hurried to unwrap her. "Are you okay?"

"I...I think so?" Her voice shook and her hands trembled. She rubbed her wrist where the fabric had dragged across her skin. Max pulled her into a hug and she breathed out, slowly. It was fine. She was safe.

"Ugh." Jo kicked the curtain. "Shay, do you mind if I burn this?"

"Knock yourself out." She never wanted to see the curtains again. "I…I couldn't banish it. Like I did before, with the fire and the…it didn't show up. Again."

She stared at her hands. That was twice in one night. Before she'd been able to shrug it off, at least a little bit.

She wasn't sure anymore.

"Okay, we'll figure it out." Max led her over to the bed, checking her wrist. There were a few blue marks from the biker ghost, but otherwise she didn't think she was hurt. "You're okay. We'll get your room safe, all right?"

"Yeah." She nodded.

"And if you don't want to go to the seance—"

"No, no, I want to go." She wasn't so sure that was true anymore, but she didn't want to stay in her room, either. Or get in Jo's way.

She wanted to find Finnias.

"Okay." Max smiled, it was a little strained, but they were clearly trying to make her feel better.

She managed a weak smile in return. The ease of conversation before evaporated, leaving their words stilted and unsure. She had been fine, just minutes ago, but the scare had her remembering the manic glint in Max's eyes while they were possessed, the way they'd forced her down the hallway.

It wasn't their fault.

"Let's get this room cleared out," Max said.

Jo set up a little cauldron and lit a piece of charcoal, heaping more herbs that hadn't been thrown at a ghost on top of it. She opened the windows, pulling down the other curtains when she did.

"I'll leave this burning for a while, just to be safe," Jo said. "All right, Max, you have the guardian?"

"Yes. I definitely remembered I had it." Max pulled a shiny black rock carved into the shape of a wolf out of their hoodie pocket.

"Aww it's cute."

"It's our house guardian," Jo explained. "Normally it protects the whole house, but I think we need it here more than anywhere else. We'll do a few other things, too. I'm trying to cover as many bases as I can."

She was spritzing water all over the window seat and the floor. She noticed Shay staring and shook the bottle. "Silver infused. Should clear the rest of the nasties out."

"I trust you," Shay said. At one point in time, she would have thought Jo was a little off her rocker, but she hadn't been wrong yet. Shay wasn't about to start questioning her methods.

"We can't have illegal vibes, after all."

Shay grinned. "None at all. That would be criminal."

"Do I want to know?" Max asked.

"No," Shay said. "What are you doing?"

"Showing the guardian around the place and making a ward," they said. They walked slowly around the edge of the room, holding the little figurine, trailing their fingers across the wallpaper. The curls of ivy glowed under their fingers, forming a line around the entire room.

"It's pretty." The light was golden, it felt warm, like coming home.

"What is?" Jo glanced down. "The…cauldron?"

"The light," Shay said. Their expressions wouldn't have been any different if she started shouting in tongues. "Am…I not supposed to see the light?"

"Not typically, no." Jo frowned.

"I was imagining a band of light," Max said. "Like you told me.

Jo tapped her lips, deep in thought. "I might have to do with your ghost sight, or—"

"Hey!" Duncan yelled up the stairs. "Are you guys done? Gideon is! We have some ghosts to chat up!"

"Or something we can worry about later," Jo said. "Finish the wards. Shay, you put the guardian where you want it."

Shay took the statue. It was warm and surprisingly heavy. She placed it on the top of her dresser. "Is there anything I have to do?"

"No, I'll take care of it," Jo said. "And clean things up."

"Thanks, Jo," she said.

"No problem." Jo glared at the wad of fabric. "I always hated these curtains."

CHAPTER 4: HORSING AROUND

"One day, I'm going to get my license, and you guys won't be able to shove me in the back seat anymore," Shay said.

She'd been shoved behind Gideon in his nondescript hybrid SUV thing. It was marginally roomier than Duncan's rust bucket of a compact and smelled better than Max's clunker, but it was still a back seat.

"Yeah? What are you going to drive?" Duncan sat next to her, saying Max had longer legs, but she was pretty sure it was because of what he'd heard about the curtain.

"I think there was talk of a pirate ship, once," Max said.

"Alas, what Teton Falls lacks in public transportation, it sadly doesn't make up for it in waterways." Shay sighed. "The dream is dead."

"You could get a horse," Gideon suggested. "Then you wouldn't have to worry about your license."

"Aren't you afraid of them?" Shay asked.

"Wait, really?" Duncan leaned forward.

"No." Gideon sounded a little too defensive.

"Sure." Shay kindly dropped it. At the rate they were going, she'd be able to tease him for a long time. "That's okay, it won't fit in Jo's house, and she'd get so mad about the floors. Original to the house, you know."

"Besides, it might die," Duncan said. "But I guess we'd have a ghost horse."

"I would legitimately be afraid of that," Gideon admitted.

"You…wouldn't have to feed it?" Max suggested.

"Horses don't have a back seat for me to stick you tall folk into," Shay said.

"I'm perfectly average height," Max mumbled.

"They do if you get a carriage," Duncan suggested with a grin. She glared at him. "Yeah, yeah, hold your horses. Or lack of horses."

Shay shoved him and he shoved back.

"Hey!" Gideon's shout was sudden enough to have them both sitting to attention. "Quit horsing around!"

Duncan cracked up. Max groaned in agony.

Shay took pity on them and changed the subject. "How did you get us an appointment so close to Halloween, anyway? Have you been planning this all week?"

"Kind of," Gideon admitted. "There was a cancellation, so they were happy to fit us in. We'll be meeting with a Rose Madelyn. She sounded nice on the phone, at least."

"At least," Shay said.

They drove to the edge of town, where businesses and half empty strip malls stretched between empty lots and abandoned houses. The mall was a large patch of darkness in a weedy lot, a sprawling testament to urban decay in a weedy parking lot. The last big box store had closed the year before and nothing else had lasted. Teton Falls and the closely neighboring Doveton barely had the population to support it when it was built in the eighties. It was a little bit of a miracle it lasted nearly thirty years.

Something pale and glowing glided across the cracked asphalt, light trailing behind it in streamers. It didn't seem to notice them. She looked away.

"This town is a dump," she muttered. Everyone made noises of agreement.

"My mortgage is cheap, at least?" Gideon said.

"Where do you live?" Max asked.

"I have one of those townhouses in Aspen Grove," Gideon said. "The multicolored ones. I have two bedrooms I'm not using if Jo ever kicks you out," Gideon said. "Or Max, always room for you. My roommate moved out a few months back, company might be nice."

"Is that why you moved here?" Shay realized she actually knew very little about Gideon besides being a former ghost hunter and thinking Duncan was cute for some reason. "Cheap rent?"

"I mean, it didn't hurt," Gideon said. "It was for a company called Cutting Edge. They weren't cutting edge enough for me to work remotely, and eventually they weren't even advanced enough to stay open, but I got a client base so I can't complain. And y'know? It's not bad here. I like the outdoors stuff."

"Came for the job, stayed for the death cults and the Mormons?" Shay asked.

"And the country music." Gideon switched the station, an amalgam of pop and alternative rock, over to a man warbling something about the good ol' days over the twang of a banjo. Shay and Duncan protested. "Don't worry, we're here."

They pulled into the parking lot of the office building from the pictures — tall and brown. It seemed familiar. Shay frowned at the exterior, trying to remember where she'd seen it before. "Wasn't this a school? A super haunted closed down school?"

"Yeah, they turned it into office buildings a few years ago," Max said. "The building was historic, but the inside was fair game. There aren't a lot of videos, I mean they redid it before everyone had a camera in their phone, but some of the accounts are pretty intense."

"And there's the murders." Gideon parked the car.

"Can't forget the murders," Max agreed.

"What murders?" Shay jolted upright in her seat from her slouch. "No one said anything about murders. I think if you're taking the ghost touch girl to a place you should probably disclose any and all murders."

"Two girls were murdered and their bodies were found in the basement," Max said. "It was a pretty gruesome find, too. They'd been there for a while."

"And obviously it's a cold case," Gideon said. "It was back in the seventies, so…watch out for bellbottoms?"

"I do that in general, yeah," Shay said.

Duncan cringed. "Ah yeah, I remember reading about that. There are a lot of murders that never got solved. And freak accidents. Y'know, we should start a true crime podcast. The Teton Falls Murder Club. Serving up homicides with a side of ghosts.

"I'm too pretty for podcasts," Max said.

"I sadly can't argue with you. Whelp, no time like the present." Duncan climbed out of the car and everyone else followed suit. He stared up at the building. "This…this feels very bad. How can anyone stand to work here?"

"The murders supposedly didn't take place here, just uh, the body disposal," Max explained. "If we're lucky, any ghosts would have been displaced by the spirit charmer. Shay, do you see anything?"

Shay squinted up at the building. There weren't any spectral lights shining through the dark windows, but it didn't mean anything. The curtain ghost rose unbidden in her mind and she shuddered. "Not right now, but I'm with Dunc. I don't like this place."

Even though there were lights on the second floor, something about it felt abandoned, empty.

A ghost was like an empty house.

At least, that was what Finnias told her. She'd thought it was a metaphor, at the time. She wasn't so sure anymore.

"Okay, good." Max put a hand on her shoulder. She jumped a bit. "Sorry, I thought you…Hey, Jo gave me some stuff, we'll be okay. I promise."

"Thanks, Max." It helped, but she couldn't shake the heavy feeling something wasn't right. Maybe she was getting paranoid and it was the cold bite of the evening air worming its way into her jacket. "Let's get inside, it's freezing."

"Duncan, you coming?" Gideon asked.

Duncan was still standing on the sidewalk, staring up at the building.

"Dunc?" Shay asked. There was no response. "Donuts?"

She put a hand on his shoulder and he started, his face terrified for a moment. He blinked and the fear smoothed away. "Woah. Sorry. I spaced there. We were talking about murder?"

"We're past murder and more concerned with the cold," she said.

"Oh. Okay." Duncan nodded. "Got it."

"Are you okay?" Gideon asked.

"Yeah! Yeah, I'm great," Duncan said. "I mean, kind of…off? I think I caught whatever the kid who sneezed on me had. Anyway, heebity jeebity time. Let's go get some creepy crawlies."

"If you're sure…" Gideon's eyebrows were drawn together in concern, but followed Duncan into the building.

The lobby was marginally warmer, but humid. The building had been hollowed out, the lobby open to the second floor, lights hanging from an industrial ceiling. Glass fronted offices, all of them dark, filled the bottom floor. A free-standing staircase rose next to a fountain made of a huge, frosted piece of glass, water dripping down it and plopping rhythmically into a large basin below.

"This is not what I expected," Shay said.

"I guess when they found out they could do anything with the inside, they ran with it." Gideon shrugged.

Shay thought about running her fingers through the waterfall while they walked up the stairs. It was very green, and probably slimy. She just barely kept her hand on the metal railing.

"This is fancy," Duncan said. "We should rent office space here."

"Office space for what?" Max asked. "The podcast we don't have and never will?"

"I was thinking more…when there's something strange, in your neighborhood…"

"No," the rest of them said in unison.

"Wow, geez, gang up on a guy," he muttered.

The second floor had a glass wall in front of a series of rooms, all with cushions and long, low couches. The back was shrouded in curtains. The door had "Spiritual Connections" in big, swirling silver letters. It was repeated on the bricks above the front desk no one was sitting at.

"Something tells me this is the right place," Duncan said. Shay swatted his arm and he elbowed her back.

Gideon tugged on an old bell pull next to the door. Liquid chimes sounded deeper in the office. A few minutes later a black woman around Duncan's age opened the door. She was a little shorter than he was and curvy in a soft pink sweater and yoga pants. Her face was soft and generous, her skin a warm brown. Her dark hair was thick and wavy, braided back on one side, the rest flowing around her shoulder. She had an enormous and elaborate silver ring on one finger. Her nails were long and acrylic, silver with a white design on them. They flashed in the dim light.

"Miss Madelyn?" Gideon asked.

"Call me Rose," she said. She had a soft, honeyed drawl, transplanted from somewhere east of Texas. Shay wondered what had brought her all the way to Idaho. "Gideon, right? Come on in. Are these the friends you mentioned?"

"They are," Gideon said. "This is Shay, Duncan, and Max."

Rose ushered them all inside and closed the glass door behind them. It was noticeably warmer in the Spiritual Connections part of the building.

The entryway had blond wood floors. There were more glass enclosed rooms hidden away by curtains. It was more of a series of human sized terrariums than an office. Shay tried to not picture the mediums as hamsters and failed.

"Don't throw a rock in here," Duncan said quietly to her.

"What was that?" Rose turned back to them.

"Just uh, nice office space," Duncan said while Shay struggled to not laugh.

"Thanks," Rose said. "We're a little short staffed right now, but we'll make sure you're taken care of. Right this way."

She led them into one of the curtained rooms. It was softened with gauzy drapes hung all over the room, even over the ceiling, giving the impression they'd stepped into a large tent. The entrance was covered in long strands of beads that sounded like rain on a tin roof. A fountain burbled in the back. It was pleasantly lit by several drop lamps in jewel tones. Strings of fairy lights formed little galaxies above their heads.

There was a dark, low wooden table surrounded by cushions in the middle. In a circle of thick, white pillar candles was a spirit board made of dark wood with silver letters.

"Take off your shoes," Rose instructed, which was Shay's instinct, anyway. She crouched down to untie her boots. "Put them in the cubby next to the door. We have slippers if you want them. I'll be right back with some refreshments."

"Oh, you don't have to-" Gideon started to say.

Rose held up one hand. "I simply find having a cup of tea with someone helps me to get to know them before I start calling spirits for them."

"Oh." Gideon blinked. "That makes sense. Do you need help or…?"

"No, I'll be right back, get comfortable."

They all sat around the table, leaving the spot in front of the spirit board open for Rose. Shay settled between Duncan and Max.

"She kind of reminds me of Jo," Shay said. "Just her whole vibe. And the refreshments thing."

"Not caring too much for this thing." Max eyed the board.

"It's way better than the one I used at a sleepover once," Duncan said, picking up the planchette even though Max motioned for him not to. "Check this thing out, it's super heavy."

He handed it to Shay, despite Max making a noise. It was heavier than she expected. It was carved with flowers set with purple gems, winking as she turned it back and forth.

"Want to hold it?" She offered it to Max.

"Put it back," they whispered at her. "I don't like those things."

"They're toys," Duncan said. "Besides, no ghosts in here. Shay doesn't see any."

"I can't see all ghosts," Shay said. "I mean, probably. Otherwise this would look even more like a fancy aquarium. Do you know how many people in the world have died?"

"...Oh, yeah, now you tell me." Duncan glared at her. "Here I thought you were full of ghost omnipotence."

"Considering I didn't even believe in this stuff two weeks ago I think I'm doing pretty good," Shay reminded him. "Besides, don't you have your own ghost radar? Maybe rely on yourself for once."

"Owch," Duncan said. "Cold. My ghost radar might be broken. I don't know."

"Have we all thought about how it's probably not very smart to have me at a meeting where we're actively calling ghosts or...?" Shay winced at the various degrees of startled and guilty expressions around her. "Oh. Okay. So, we haven't. Awesome."

To be fair, she had been so focused on finding Finnias, she hadn't thought about it, either.

The curtain rattled and they all went quiet. Rose set a tray down, passing them each a saucer and pouring them all a floral smelling tea in plain white teacups. No one took water instead, not even Shay. She was pretty liberal with the honey, but Jo was going to make a dedicated tea drinker out of her, yet.

"Let's get started." Rose sat at the head of the table. "With you, Gideon. We talked a little on the phone, but I wouldn't mind hearing about it again."

"Okay." Gideon nodded. "I work in graphic design, mostly freelance. I'm a photographer, too. Mostly landscapes, but I do weddings sometimes. I moved out here a few years ago for a job but ended up staying."

"Teton Falls sometimes has that effect on the right people." Rose nodded and turned to Max.

"Oh um. I'm Max. But uh, you knew that. I work in a daycare. Do some amateur video."

"I work in a bookstore," Shay said. "And tag along for amateur video shooting."

"Which brings us to me," Duncan said. "I'm a librarian at the public library here in Teton Falls. I love long walks by the river. And I have a cat."

Rose narrowed her eyes. "You aren't being honest with me."

Chapter 5: Stick the Landing

Shay glanced at Duncan, who shrugged.

"You, especially." Rose pointed at him. "Something is happening with you."

"You have been weird lately," Shay said.

"I'm always weird," Duncan said. "But thank you, I'll remember next time you need something.

"I meant I'm worried about you, don't be a jerk," Shay said.

"You don't worry about me, I'm the big brother, I worry about everyone and everything all the time forever, got it?" Duncan's voice was sharp. He took a deep breath. "Sorry. That came out…how about we have this fight in a much less awkward situation. Let's do what we came here to do. All you need to know is I was possessed recently.

Rose's eyebrows went impressively high. "Were you?"

"I was. You said something was up with me, and now you know," he said. "But that's not why we're here. We need some questions answered, and since we believe our father knows the answers, so we would like to attempt to contact him."

Shay bit her lip to keep herself from saying anything. Duncan was right, and she knew he was right, no matter how angry she was. And if the man was dead, he'd had no choice in leaving them.

Or betraying them.

It still made her sick, but she stayed where she was. Max took her hand and she squeezed theirs gratefully.

"...All right," Rose said after a long, measured pause. "I'll need his name."

"Walter Rowe," Duncan said. "He would have been about thirty when he died."

Shay's stomach twisted. Duncan guessed their dad died soon after he left them. Which meant he'd only been twenty-two when Duncan was born. Only a year older than her. And he'd disappeared when he was only a few years older than Duncan. He had been an ancient figure in her head, but if he died, he'd been younger than Jo.

"That's all I need," Rose said. She stood up and lit the candles. She dimmed the lights and lit incense. Shay expected lavender, but it smelled of cinnamon.

Rose sat back at the head of the table and held out her hands to Gideon and Duncan, so abruptly business-like it was jarring. "It works best if we all hold hands. We'll get comfortable first. If you feel uneasy or cynical, please leave the room. This could be pretty intense. Yes or no questions are easiest to answer. Normally, I'm able to converse with the spirit, but if I become unable to ask, Duncan, you're in charge of asking questions. When you're done asking, we will ask the spirit to depart before we break the circle."

"Right." Duncan nodded.

They all held hands. Duncan's hand was cold with anxiety. Shay's own fingers were icy and her right hand was still blue with ghost mark.

They sat for a few moments, probably an attempt to get into the mood. Shay just felt worse.

"Are we all ready?" Rose asked. Her eyes reflected the candles. They all nodded. "Great. Remember, don't break the circle until I give the okay. Now. Let's begin."

She closed her eyes and bowed her head. Shay wasn't sure if she was supposed to do the same, but Rose hadn't said so she watched her for any sign. There was no spectral glow in the room that Shay could detect.

Not yet, anyway.

Rose was quiet for a while. Shay was tired of holding Duncan's hand. She balanced on a razor edge between anger and full-on panic. She didn't want to talk to her dad.

And yet…she did. She'd never met him. She didn't remember him at all, any early memories mixed up with memories of Connor O'Brannon. A scratchy beard, laughter, being held up high. Would he even recognize them? Would he even care?

Would he have wanted them to stay Duncan and Shay Rowland?

She didn't know, and it was tying her up in knots.

"Walter Rowe," Rose said, after what felt like an eternity. "We ask for you to join us today. Duncan, your son, requests your presence. Please come and reside with us for a while."

Nothing happened. The candles burned, their flames perfectly still. The water babbled somewhere behind them. Incense smoke curled up towards the ceiling in thin spirals.

"Walter Rowe, please heed our request," Rose's command was louder.

Still nothing. No ripple of wind, no sudden sense they weren't alone. Shay stared at the candle flames, willing anything to happen. She blinked and the lights remained behind her eyelids, little teardrops of bright neon against the dark.

Rose let out a long, slow breath. "I'm sorry. I'm not getting anything."

Shay hated when her heart dropped. Her own disappointment. She should have been vindicated, or angry. Anything other than sad.

"Nothing?" Duncan sounded as bad as she felt. He cleared his throat. "Oh well. Um. Okay. That's fine, I mean, it was kind of a long shot, anyway."

Rose took his hand in both of hers. "Sometimes a spirit can't be reached because they've moved beyond. If he's not answering, there's a possibility it's because he's in a better place."

"Yeah. Sure." Duncan sighed. "A better place. Like Vermont! Being a ski bum. Thanks for trying."

"I'm sorry, Duncan," Gideon said. Duncan gave him a tight smile.

Rose narrowed her eyes. "Now, do you want to tell me what's going on? There's something you needed to ask the spirit, and I have a feeling it had to do with whatever is happening to you. Same with her."

She pointed at Shay.

"We uh…" Duncan looked at Shay like she was going to give him some guidance. She had nothing to offer. "We've had some recent ghost troubles. Our friend thinks it's because of our dad, so we were hoping to contact him. Ask him a few things."

"What sort of trouble?"

Duncan shrugged. "The aforementioned possession. Shay had problems with a mirror."

"Right. And who is this friend?" Rose dropped Duncan's hand and frowned at Shay. "What bookstore do you work for?"

Shay was pretty sure saying the name was not going to go well. "Spellbound?"

"I knew it." Rose sighed. "Did Jo send you here to ask something impossible? To gloat?"

"Uh…no?" Shay wasn't sure where this was coming from, but she was having words with Jo when they got back. "I don't think so. She said you guys were legitimate."

"Did she, now?" Rose narrowed her eyes.

Shay winced. "She mentioned you guys knew each other but didn't really go into it."

"We have history," Rose said. "You should ask her about it sometime. If all you wanted me to do was try and contact your father, then I would ask you to-"

"No, wait," Gideon said, quickly. "We had one more. One we know is definitely a ghost. His name is Finnias S. Woodard. It might be an alias. He died in 1909."

"That's quite an old ghost," Rose said.

"He's the one that possessed me," Duncan clarified.

"Ah." Rose nodded, like that explained everything. "Finnias, you said? And I assume you had the strongest connection to him?"

"Uh, I guess," Duncan said. "But maybe Shay."

"Me?" Shay asked. "But he didn't…I mean. I guess?"

She'd held his hand. Felt his heart beating.

He'd helped her close the tear.

He said she could do anything.

"Let me see." Rose looked at Shay in a way that made her feel like she was being x-rayed. "It might be best if we're not connected when I call him, anyway. If the two of you could switch places?"

"Sounds good to me," Duncan said.

They traded places. Rose took her hand. Her nails and ring dug lightly into Shay's skin. She smiled. "Don't be nervous, hon. Ghosts can be scary, but they don't want to hurt you."

Shay almost laughed.

At least Finnias hadn't actively tried to hurt her.

"Same rules as before," she said. "Now, Shay, I want you to focus on Finnias. What he looked like, if you know. Your connection to him.

She wasn't sure what kind of connection they could have had. He was kind of a smug jerk, but he'd helped her. They had known each other for all of six hours, but he'd been willing to give up everything for her. The truth of his past, his memories, all of the things that mattered to a ghost. All to save her life.

She wanted to see him.

She had questions, but more importantly, she wanted to know he was okay. That she'd done the right thing.

If she could do anything, then she wanted to drag him back.

"Are you ready?"

She nodded, not sure what she could say.

Rose closed her eyes again. The candles flickered before she spoke, almost imperceptibly, like a door had opened deeper in the building. Anticipation welled up in Shay, tightly woven with anxiety.

"Finnias S. Woodard. We request your presence at our table. Please, come and speak to us."

Shay remembered she was supposed to be focusing on him and closed her own eyes.

She wasn't sure what she should be picturing. A white shape? A ghost with a hole in his chest?

She settled on how he'd looked in life. A pale, serious looking young man. Dark hair, styled back. Serious gray eyes, almost an unnatural color. Sharp cheekbones, taller than her, slim in a pinstriped vest and white shirt. They'd been holding hands, standing on the plush carpet of the old landing.

He'd been whole, the sunlight from the window picking up silver threads in his gray vest. She concentrated on the angles of his face, the curl of hair falling over his forehead, refusing to be swept back with the rest. His pulse, rapid and scared under her fingers.

She opened her eyes and was sitting on the staircase.

Duncan was sitting next to her, still holding her hand. No one else followed them.

"This wasn't what I was expecting," Duncan said. "Shay, what did you do?"

"Why is it always my fault?" Shay asked.

"Because it probably is?" Duncan let go of her hand and stood up. "He's not even here. Why are we? And…where is all the mist?"

Mist had always covered both sides of the staircase, but now she could see them clearly. Above them was a hallway. Below was a wooden floor and the soft murmur of conversation. Shay stood up, slowly. "This isn't right."

"You think?" Duncan asked. Shay grabbed his arm and tugged him over to the window. She didn't recognize anything. It was winter, the sun streaming through leafless branches close to the building. Evergreen trees surrounded a wide lawn covered in a thick blanket of snow.

Footsteps on the stairs.

"…We should go," Shay said.

"Where?" Duncan asked. "Up the stairs?"

The figure walking up the stairs was clearer than ever. A man in a vest and dress shirt, the same one Shay had seen before. His blond, curly hair was swept back from his forehead. His mustache was meticulously curled. He had a jacket over one arm. He put a hand where Finnias's shoulder would be and lifted the arm with the jacket.

He turned to her, his neck at an unnatural angle.

"Now, y'all aren't supposed to be here," he said in honeyed tones.

She knew that voice.

She stepped back so fast her heel hit the stair, hard enough that she sat down. "It's you."

He loomed over her. "It's me."

"Shay!" A distant voice yelled. Shay thought she recognized it, but couldn't place it. The voice was louder the second time. "Shay!"

The man lunged at her.

Shay was back in the dim room, still holding Rose's hand. The candle flames flickered and stilled.

"I'm having trouble connecting with him," Rose said. "There's…some interference."

Shay turned to Duncan, who was wide eyed and pale. His grip on her hand was painful, but she didn't try to pull away.

"Shay?"

She realized Rose had said her name a few times. "Yeah?"

"I asked if you wanted to try using the spirit board."

"I…" she was shaking, but she couldn't pull her hand away from Rose's, she hadn't said it was okay yet. "Yes?"

"You're very pale." Rose frowned.

"I'm just…a little spooked," Shay said. "Can we take a break?"

"Of course." Rose let go of her hand and she barely resisted the urge to curl it to her chest, staggering up to her feet.

Shay excused herself to use the restroom.

She stared at the mirror, but it was just her. Tapping on the glass didn't do anything, either.

"You suck," she said. "And you're a liar. Finnias isn't anywhere. I bet Arlo isn't even trapped. He probably retired to some beach in Italy where he sells flip flops to tourists or something."

The mirror offered no rebuttal.

"Maybe not Italy but…somewhere warm, and…and nice. Where it's sunny and there aren't any ghosts."

If such a place existed.

The door opened and she whirled around, but it was Max.

"Woah, sorry." They held up their hands. "Just checking on you. Were you talking to the mirror?"

"I was trying to." She stuck her tongue out at the mirror. "It wasn't a great conversation. Completely one sided. All self-reflection."

Max ignored her weak pun. "Still no mirror ghost?"

She shook her head. "Nope. And no Finnias. Unless the spirit board is magical or something, which it isn't. She probably got it from some Etsy store."

"Yeah, probably," Max said. "I don't like it, but…if it helps? I mean, it's a tool, and you should use all of the tools in your toolbox, and since it's a professional and not a bunch of kids in a cemetery, I guess it's okay."

"That was one time, Max." She laughed. It sounded wrong, like it was frozen by the cold deep in her gut. "And nothing happened."

Max snorted. "We almost got arrested."

"Okay, but nothing spirit-y happened," she said. It had been years ago, before she knew ghosts were real. "I don't think cemeteries are haunted, anyway. Unless someone died in cemetery. But hey, at least they wouldn't be going far."

"Wow, Shay." Max laughed a little. "That's uh. One theory."

"The only correct theory," she said. "A cemetery is where your bones go, not where your life was. Though I guess a grave digger or someone who worked there would be a candidate for haunting, too…"

"Back on topic—"

"We could go to a cemetery and find out."

"A terrible idea," Max said.

Shay grinned. "Rose could bring the spirit board."

"No, nope, absolutely not, here I am, doing my best to be open minded about this thing, and here you are, torturing me—"

Shay started laughing and Max replied with an indignant huff.

"Sorry." She felt better, the memory of the voice fading. "I torture you out of love. And to make sure you stay humble. Since you're the best, so your best is twice as best as anyone else's."

"As long as you remember it." They placed their hands gently on her shoulders. "I just…wanted to make sure you're doing okay? You were pretty shaken up. Is it about Finnias or…or your dad?"

"I—"

She needed to tell them. About the staircase, about the man there, how Finnias was strangely absent.

Someone pounded on the door and they both jumped.

"Hey!" Duncan yelled through the door. "Are you two done bonding or whatever? We're starting up again!"

"Yeah fine whatever!" Shay yelled back. It would have to wait. It could wait. They'd have time after. "Yeah. I'm okay. You could even say I'm…board. Really only works if I spell it out. But it is a spirited attempt."

"That was bad, even for you," Max said.

"Yeah, not bringing my A game," Shay said. "Luckily, it's a game."

Max replied by opening the bathroom door for her and gestured her out into the office.

CHAPTER 6:
S-E-T-O-U-T

The lights dimmed when Shay walked into the room. She nearly stepped back into Max before she saw the remote in Rose's hand.

"Are you feeling better?" Rose asked.

"Yeah, ready to ouija it up." She wasn't, really, but she had no idea how else they could contact Finnias. She couldn't exactly tear a hole through the veil and hope she found him.

"I prefer to call it a spirit board." Rose pulled it closer to their side of the table. "Everyone else, sit back. This part is for just Shay and I to try. Spirit boards aren't dangerous by themselves, but you shouldn't take them lightly. Do you know how they work?"

"The ideamotor effect," Max said. "Even if you're trying to not move, you still move a little bit. That's how the planchette appears to move on its own."

"Correct," Rose said. She rearranged the candles around the board. "Often spirits aren't able to manifest, but they can speak to our subconscious, and that's what causes words to be spelled out. It can also be used as a form of divination, a lot like pendulums, or tarot."

"So…it's not possession?" Gideon asked.

"Full on possession is fairly rare," Rose said.

Duncan nodded. "Good to know."

"More often we are influenced," Rose explained. "I like to consider spirits a guide."

Shay wasn't sure what information spirits would have for the average person besides what happened when someone died, and she doubted they knew what lay beyond. Most ghosts were just memories, after all. Remnants. She kept her thoughts to herself. Rose might have meant the energy of the universe that Jo kept talking about, or an entirely different kind of spirit.

Rose positioned the planchette on the board. "We'll each put our fingertips on this and spell out 'hello' and Finnias's name. See? It's not scary."

"Right." Shay wasn't scared that the spirit board would work.

She was honestly more afraid it wouldn't work, and she'd be left floundering. She stared at the planchette, wondering how all of her uncertainty was supposed to be alleviated by a hunk of resin.

The planchette glided smoothly under their hands.

"We have a spirit board here for you to communicate with us," Rose said. "We are speaking specifically to Finnias, or any spirit who may know where he is. Please, if you have anything to share, let it be known—"

Shay was focusing on staying still, but the planchette slid sideways under her hand like someone had yanked it.

"S-H-A-Y," Rose read aloud. Shay's heart pounded. Whatever was with them, it knew her. It had to be a good sign. "Yes, Shay is here. Do you have anything to say to her?"

It moved again, spelling out the next word.

"M-I-R-R-O-R." Rose glanced up at Shay. "Does that mean anything to you?"

"But the mirror ghost hasn't been talking to us," Shay said.

"The what?" Rose frowned. "Wait. R-A-V-E-N. What on earth…?"

"The Raven's Nest," Shay stared at the planchette. Rose couldn't possibly know about the old café, where she'd officially met Finnias. Shivers crawled their way up her back. "The mirror at the Raven's Nest."

"Of course, that's where you pulled Finnias out," Max said.

"Great, we can break in, I love being a criminal," Duncan agreed.

"I don't," Gideon said.

The planchette yanked itself out from under their fingers. The candles stuttered and the temperature dropped.

The planchette scraped across the board, invisible hands pressing it down as hard as they could.

"…G-E-T O-U-T." Rose's eyes widened.

The planchette kept moving, spelling out the two words over and over again, faster and faster. The board swung across the table, knocking over candles. Shay barely grabbed one that fell off the table entirely. It spilled hot wax on her fingers.

"Ohhh I don't like this," Max sounded a little squeaky. With a groan the whole table moved, sliding across the room, taking cushions with it. It hit the glass wall on the other side with a loud crack.

"C'mon!" Gideon grabbed Shay's arm and pulled her to her feet. "Time to go. Let's listen to the nice ghost."

"On it." She snagged her shoes and shoved them on, not bothering with the laces.

Duncan shook the door handle.

Nothing happened.

"Locked," he said.

"Again?" Max's voice full on cracked.

"The door doesn't lock." Rose crossed the room to grab the handle and shake it herself. The beads in front of it clacked and clattered, but the door barely moved. "What did you do? What on earth did you ask me to call?"

A wind rippled around them. The curtains swayed, billowing into the room and for a horrifying moment she thought it was the ghost from the house. Gideon steered her towards the middle of the room when she froze up. Max took the candle from her hand and lit it with a lighter. They held it up, the flame steady despite the breeze.

The curtain didn't form a ghost. There was no shimmer of the poltergeist that belonged to the spirit charmer, either.

This was something else.

"Let us out!" Max swung the candle back and forth, the light trailing behind it.

The room grew even colder, turning Shay's breath to white smoke.

Pillows, candles, and the tea tray rose into the air, twisting before they shot into the room. One of the cups hit her, but her jacket took the brunt of the blow. Porcelain shattered against the walls. Max swung the candle and a saucer barely missed them, veering off to hit the curtain behind them.

The door opened and Duncan staggered out into the office. They piled out, barely getting out before the door slammed closed behind them. They all hurried to the exit. The hanging lights swung and flickered, sending shadows spinning around them. Shay reached the door first and pushed it open.

The lobby was eerily silent.

The water wall was a solid sheet of ice.

The door slammed shut behind her. She grabbed the handle. The cold burned her fingers and she let go with a hiss.

"Shay!" Max's voice was muffled. They rattled the handle uselessly. "Shay, get out of there!"

"But you—"

"We'll be fine!" Duncan yelled. "Go!"

She nodded and ran down the stairs. Mist coated the floor of the lobby, billowing around her ankles when she dashed to the entrance.

She hit the door running.

It didn't move.

The ice cracked and shattered, tumbling to the floor and scattering across the tile.

Shay put her back to the door, trying to calm her drumming pulse, to keep her breathing from becoming a desperate gasp.

The lights flickered out, leaving her with only the emergency exit light above her head, bathing her in a red glow.

The ice lifted into the air, glinting like rubies.

"Aw, beans."

Shay ran for it. Ice pelted the glass like gunshots.

She ducked behind one of the bigger planters in time before ice shredded the plant above her and smashed the side, dirt spilling across the floor. She screamed, covering her head with her hands.

It was over in an instant.

She leaned against the planter, breathing hard.

Something cracked.

The tiles next to her spider webbed. The surviving plants shriveled up and blackened. She scrambled to her feet and the cracks spread under her feet. One of the hanging lights crashed to the ground, glass shattering. The walls creaked and groaned.

The emergency light flickered out.

Spectral light blazed from the staircase. Pale mist tumbled down the steps.

A man formed from the light, stepping out of it and down the steps, his shoes clicking on each one. Rust coated the railing where he slid his hand along it.

He was tall and thin, wearing a vest over a button up shirt. His hair was swept back and he had a curled moustache.

She knew him.

The man on the staircase, and the ghost that had possessed Max.

He shone so brightly it didn't matter if the lights were off. The mist burned away and mold crept across the floor. She took a few steps back. The planter next to her crumbled and dirt spilled over her shoes.

The ghost reached the bottom of the stairs.

He turned to her.

His eyes darkened to gaping holes, dark lines spreading from them across his face. When he grinned at her his teeth were sharp.

A breath and he was directly in front of her.

It hadn't worked against the biker ghost, or the ghost in the curtain, but it had to work here. She lifted her hands and willed the fire to appear, for at least a spark, something that would save her.

Nothing happened. He leaned closer, close enough to see the fractured skull beneath his translucent skin.

He grabbed the collar of her shirt and lifted her into the air. She choked in surprise, fingers scrabbling against his icy sleeve. The back of her shirt dug into her neck, and armpits. She kicked but her foot met nothing.

"Hello, Shay." His voice echoed from far away. "It's good to finally meet you properly."

"Let me go!" She pulled on his sleeve.

He dropped her. She barely got her feet under her but her legs gave out a second later and she sat on the ground. He was a well-groomed young man again, wiping his hand on his vest. His other hand was still hidden under his coat.

The last time a ghost had been aware enough to talk to her, it had been Finnias.

The door flung open and Max ran down the stairs.

"Shay, get down!"

She lunged to the side. Max threw salt in a wide arc. Little green fires sprouted from where it hit the ghost. He snarled, his eyes going dark again.

"That was incredibly rude," he said. "We're trying to have a conversation here. Maybe I should possess you again."

He surged forward but Max had a candle ready, thrusting it in his face. Duncan and Rose made it down the stairs and held up candles of their own.

He smirked.

"Guys, I don't think—" Shay didn't get to finish.

The flames went out.

"What?" Max stared at the blackened wick.

"Oh crap," Duncan said. The ghost was on him a second later, picking him up and slamming him into the floor like he didn't weigh anything. He whirled and lifted a hand. Rose choked and staggered back.

"Duncan!" Gideon ran to him but was tossed back effortlessly.

Shay staggered to her feet and charged the ghost. She yanked a sachet out of her pocket and slammed it against his back.

It didn't do anything.

She shoved, but the ghost was a pillar of ice. She was powerless against it.

"That won't work." He grabbed her wrist and yanked her closer. Fissures spread down the sleeve of her jacket, the leather cracking and peeling so quickly it was audible, the end of the sleeve unravelling. Dark spots spread across her skin and the cold ached in her bones.

He froze and turned his head to the side.

He let go and she staggered back, holding her hand to her chest, terrified to look at the damage.

With one last smile he was gone.

The lights came back on. All of the lights were hanging from the ceiling again, swinging gently. The planters were intact. Water dripped down the wall fountain. The tiles were solid again.

Her jacket sleeve was whole, and the only thing showing the ghost had been there at all was a blue ring around her wrist where he'd grabbed her.

"What...what just happened?" Duncan sat up, rubbing the side of his head. "Ow. I think I broke every single one of my ribs. Shay, you good?"

"I...I think so." Her legs gave out and she sat on the floor.

Max was at her side in an instant, taking her hand gently to check her wrist. "Let me see."

"I'm okay," she said.

They moved her hand from side to side. Luckily, it wasn't the wrist that she'd hurt punching the enormous ghost. No tenderness, no grating.

"We need to leave," Rose reminded them. "Now would be great."

"Right." Max pulled her to her feet. They kept a hold of her hand, walking out the exit together.

CHAPTER 7:
SOUL EXPERT

Thay climbed into Gideon's car and Max shoved in next to her, Rose taking the other side without any actual discussion.

She didn't mind being stuck in the middle, for once. She linked arms with Max and leaned against them. The cold still clung to her, despite her best efforts.

"Back to Jo's?" Gideon asked, starting the car. The heat came on full blast, along with country music. He quickly turned it off.

"Yeah," Duncan said, twisting in his seat. "Rose, you good with that?"

Rose shrugged. "I'm not going back in there for my keys."

"Fair enough." Gideon pulled the car out of the parking lot.

"Now you're all going to explain to me exactly what happened to my office," Rose said.

"It's kind of a long story," Duncan said. "Full of twists, turns—"

Rose cut him off. "Summarize it for me."

"I can touch and see ghosts, Duncan can something something," Shay said. "And we shared a vision thing? With the ghost?"

"Safe to say it wasn't a vision," Duncan said. "Pretty sure that's the guy who murdered Finnias. Maybe murdered everyone in the Holt Manner Murders. Yikes."

"He's the one that possessed Max," Shay said. "I...I recognized his voice. I-"

"What vision?" Max cut her off. She realized they had barely talked about Max being possessed. That she hadn't really processed it at all.

At the same time, Rose said. "Okay I might need a little more to go on."

Shay let Duncan explain. He was better at telling stories and she was tired, leaning against Max and fighting to keep her eyes open. The adrenaline and subsequent crashes from three ghost attacks in one night left her drained.

And she hadn't been able to do anything against them.

Her hands were curled up against her knees and she made fists until her fingernails stung her palms. Finnias said it wouldn't work on every ghost, but the last one had been bright enough for a siphon. She should have been able to do something about it.

The fire hadn't come.

She'd been useless. Less than useless. If the ghost hadn't vanished on his own, she had no idea what would have happened.

Without the fire, she was a sitting duck.

"So yeah, I think we accidentally summoned a possible mass murdering ghost and we're all lucky to be alive," Duncan said. "The end."

"Why didn't you tell me?" Max asked.

"There was a lot going on?" Shay said. "I don't know, I didn't think we were actually there until I saw him, y'know? I thought it must be some residual thing."

"Same," Duncan said. "He was really clear. Is that how you see them all the time?"

She nodded.

"Wow. I'm sorry, Shay. That sucks."

"Yeah, it does." She didn't know what else to say.

Max put a hand over hers. Their fingers were brands against her skin. "You okay?"

They kept their voice low.

"I don't know." She hadn't even been able to push the sachet into the ghost. A ghost that had threatened to possess Max again. She wasn't even sure that they'd heard him. She could only hope they hadn't. "I couldn't do anything."

"Neither could I," Max said. "Guess I'm not much of a witch after all. And when he came at me I…I kind of choked, and…"

She nudged them with her elbow. "You're just barely learning, and…and he's a really strong ghost. And I'd be scared of him, too. I am scared of him."

"Yeah," Max didn't sound particularly convinced. "I…I don't really remember. When he, y'know. Possessed me. And you…"

Hadn't told them anything. Hadn't even let them apologize, though there was nothing to apologize for. They hadn't done anything wrong, just had the bad luck of running into a horrible ghost.

"I couldn't do anything." She purposefully misunderstood. She felt awful about it, but she couldn't talk about it. "And I don't understand why."

"We'll figure it out." Max dropped the issue, and she hated how relieved she felt.

Rose's voice cut through their conversation before she could reply. "So, you're the ones who made all of these…problems? And now you can't do anything about it?"

"Technically it was the spirit charmer and we saved the town but there's been some fallout," Duncan said. "Shouldn't someone warn Jo you're coming?"

"I'm driving," Gideon said.

"I forgot my phone," Shay admitted.

Duncan shrugged. "I never learned how to read."

Max sighed. "I'll do it."

An awkward quiet descended upon the car. Despite what Max said, Shay couldn't help but think Rose was right.

"I think Shay and Duncan visiting the landing has something to do with him being possessed." Rose was the one who broke the silence. "His soul was extremely close to Finnias's, possibly intertwined. Getting Finnias yanked violently out of him over and over again , well, there's definitely something residual, maybe something worse. This is all speculation, but I imagine you keep being drawn back to the landing because you have…something of him in you still. It's trying to reconnect."

"That sounds bad," Gideon had stopped at a stop sign. The wheel creaked when he tightened his grip on it. "Is it bad? Is it like…a ghost infection? Will it eventually take over his mind?"

"It's not good, but it's not quite as dire as that," Rose said.

Duncan sighed. "That sounds like my luck, yeah. All right, I'm on board the find Finnias train. Choo choo. Gotta get his…whatever stuck back on him. I'm thinking a strainer and some wood glue should do the trick."

"That's not how it works," Rose told him.

"What, are you the…soul expert on this?" Duncan asked. Shay couldn't help but laugh. "That's the spirit, Shay Shay. We have more than a ghost of a chance."

"Stop," Max said.

"Hey, I have a chip of someone else's soul in me and I got thrown around by a scary ghost, you have to listen to my bad puns and like them," Duncan said.

"I am a soul expert," Rose said. "You need to be very careful. I don't trust how flippant you're being over this."

"Oh no, I'm freaking out," Duncan said. His voice shook and he tugged a hand through his hair. "This is how I freak out."

Gideon pulled up in front of Jo's. They got out of the car, and he pulled Duncan aside, speaking quietly. Max led her up the sidewalk.

"Let's let them talk," they said, quietly. "Shay—"

"I'm okay." She wasn't. She was as far from okay as it was possible to be, and she was terrified Max was about to ask her about something she didn't want to talk about. "We have a lead on Finnias. So. I'll get him back and…he can help, maybe. I think Rose might be right, because he was already missing things, and…and I did punch him out."

"You did what you had to do," Max said.

"Maybe." She toyed with the knitted end of her jacket sleeve. "Thanks for saving me back there. I don't think I thanked you."

"I don't think I did much," Max said. "But of course. Always."

She smiled. It felt strange. "Aww, Max. You're being awfully nice to me today."

"Well, you did get attacked by…several ghosts," Max said. "You deserve a little special treatment."

"I think I deserve special treatment for being adorable," Shay countered.

"I can't really argue with that."

Jo met them at the door. She'd pulled her hair back into a messy bun and she looked angry and tired for a moment, but her expression smoothed over. "Rose. Nice to see you again."

"Jocelyn." Rose nodded.

"I can't let you two go anywhere, can I?" Jo ushered them in. The tarot reading table was set up. A few bookshelves were pushed aside to give them space. She sat Shay down and pulled up a chair to sit next to her. Her fingers were hot against Shay's wrist as she checked it. She would have complained, but she didn't have the energy. "You're freezing, and this doesn't look good—"

"It looked worse before," Shay said. "Before the ghost disappeared. Did anyone else see that or was it another Shay special?"

"See what?" Max asked, which answered her question.

"Nothing," she said. She didn't need to worry them. She didn't want to think about the way her sleeve had rotted away or the dark spots on her skin.

"Between you and Duncan…" Jo sighed, bowing her head. Her glasses fell off and dangled from her neck. "This is my life now. This is it. I have some herbal mixture that will help, let's get it on these marks and get you into a really, really hot shower."

"Wait," Shay said. "I have news. I have a lead. The ghost we're looking for, he's out on the town."

"Great," Jo muttered. "How do we get him to lead us to Arlo, then?"

"Well, we used a spirit board, and I think we can find Finnias at the mirror in the Raven's Nest Café. Or at least a hint. Maybe. If Duncan is having…issues because of Finnias, finding him can only help, right? We need to follow up on it."

She was very certain of that. More sure than she had felt of anything.

It wasn't personal bias. It wasn't because she needed to see Finnias.

"It's almost ten—" Jo started to say.

"Which is a great time to check it out," Shay cut her off. Her voice was more thready the more she talked, but she needed Jo to listen. "Duncan can break us in. No one will be downtown this time of night."

"Shay has a point, but she's tired, and Duncan is…something," Max said as Duncan and Gideon stepped into the shop.

"Oh, are we talking about me?" Duncan asked. "Because I'm fine. Peachy, even. Peaches, plums, the whole fruit basket."

"Basket case, maybe," Shay muttered.

"I won't argue," Duncan said.

"Are you sure?" Gideon asked, putting a hand on his shoulder.

"That I'm fruity? Absolutely. Bananas? Maybe," Duncan said. "But I do feel fine, if that's what you're actually asking."

Jo put her glasses on and inspected him. "As far as I can tell you're okay. Rose, what do you think?"

"He seems fine to me," Rose said. "For now, but a lot of this is new territory. What I can tell you is my office is now extremely haunted. You still clear out ghosts, right? Can I contract your services?"

Jo made a face. "As much as I would like to help you, and believe me I am being completely sincere, Arlo is…indisposed at the moment, and the rest of my team is pretty new. I don't think I could remove a powerful ghost by myself. Max?"

Max sighed, a line deepening between their eyebrows. Shay was struck with the sudden urge to wipe it away. "I couldn't do anything. I don't think I'll be much help, and we should check those wards in Shay's room, because I don't know how good they are."

"But you made such pretty lights," Shay said.

"Shay—"

She shook her head. "I don't think it was your fault."

"She's right," Rose said. "It was a powerful ghost and we were under prepared."

Jo nodded. "You're new to a lot of this. No one expects you to be banishing strong spirits right away. And I might not be an expert, but those wards felt strong to me."

"I guess," Max conceded.

"And I couldn't do anything, either," Shay said. "I couldn't even get the sachet in him. I don't know if that's weird or not, but it feels weird."

"It should have done something." Jo frowned. "If that's the case, I doubt there's anything Max or anyone could do. But if it was strong and your other abilities weren't working…that might be all it was. I'm assuming he retreated to wherever he's keeping Arlo, which…isn't great, but there's a possibility of a lead there."

"But Finnias-"

"We'll find him as well," Jo said. "If all else fails, he was at least a semi-helpful ghost. I'm trying to cover as much ground as we can, that's all."

Shay nodded.

"I can check the wards, I'm not an expert on it, either, but I can at least give them a look," Rose offered.

"Oh, yeah, that'd be good," Max said. "I want it to be safe. Thanks."

"Yes, thank you, and I promise, once Arlo comes back we'll clear out your office," Jo said.

"Thank you," Rose said. "For now, I suppose it's closed. I was thinking of putting a pause to it for a while, anyway. Quite a few of my people quit with the ah…happenings. Around town. Now, are you going to go ahead with the insane plan to break into an old café to look at a mirror?"

"Wait, we're planning what now?" Duncan asked.

"I am not doing any more breaking and entering with you guys," Gideon said. "I'll drive the getaway car, though."

"You are a good driver, probably a role well suited to you." Duncan grinned. "I love this plan. Let's do it. Distractions are great. When are we doing it? I work tomorrow night. And the night after. Halloween, should be exciting."

"Tonight," Shay said. "Right now."

"Seriously?" Duncan stared at you. "Haven't you had enough today?"

Shay shrugged, not sure what she could say to make her point. There was an urgency burrowing underneath her skin. If she kept moving she didn't have to think too hard about anything. And if she didn't stop she couldn't be crushed under the weight.

If Finnias had answers, all the better.

Jo sighed and stood up. "Okay, we should put together a semi-decent plan. Shay, I wasn't joking about that hot shower. You're freezing cold, I'm not letting you go out like this."

"Maybe we shouldn't go at all?" Max suggested.

"We have to," Shay said. She couldn't put it all into words, it was too overwhelming.

"Okay," Max said. "I trust you. Let's figure out this plan."

"We can plan, you can shower and drink something hot." Jo stood up and helped Shay to her feet. "C'mon, let me get you the ointment."

Shay almost made it into the bathroom before Duncan stopped her.

"Hey, can we talk?" He seemed uncharacteristically nervous.

"Shoot," she said.

"Pew pew." He gave her finger guns. "Okay, but seriously, none of this is your fault. You know that, right? None of it. Not me, not Finnias, the tear, the ghosts, possession…nothing is your fault. You don't have to keep trying to fix everything."

"I know." She wasn't as confident as he was, but it wasn't something she wanted to talk about.

"Liar." He sighed and leaned against the wall. "Things are all crazy. I guess I hoped if we found dad he could help and…I dunno. Closure would be nice. Kind of weird I was hoping our dad was dead, but…"

"A little bit, but I get it," Shay said. "I kind of hoped he was, too."

If he was dead, nothing was his fault, it was all bad luck. Alive, everything was squarely on his shoulders again, and he'd dropped it, so they were left picking up the pieces.

"He wasn't a bad dad," Duncan said. "When he was around. But maybe I'm remembering something that wasn't real. I thought if he was dead, he didn't leave me. If he's alive…I wasn't enough to keep him around."

Shay's heart broke for her brother. "Dunc, no, don't ever think that. He's the asshole, not you. We were kids. He was the adult. And he left. That's on him."

"Yeah." Duncan clearly didn't believe her. "And the spirit charmer caused all of those problems. That's on her. She's the asshole. See? I can turn it around."

"Yes, yes, you're a master of wordplay." Shay rolled her eyes. "Can I take my shower now so Jo will let me leave?"

"Yeah, didn't want to say it, but you kinda smell." Duncan made a face. "I think it was from gloopy the biker man."

She thought about throwing the crystal cut jar of ointment at him, but settled for a rude gesture he laughed at.

Chapter 8: Dangerous Jaunting

"This sounds like a trap."

Shay looked up from Jo's tablet, where a list of everything she thought could go wrong, from "getting arrested" to "probably dying" had been typed out.

"You did say we need help," Shay said. "Everything I know I learned from him."

"How do we know that this is safe?" Jo asked. "We have no idea what told you to go back to the café. It could have been the spirit charmer. I know she hasn't been active since the tear, but that's normal. Ghosts go into dormant stages all the time, especially after a large show of force. We need to be on our toes. I wouldn't even count Finnias as a friend."

"I'm aware," Shay said, dryly. She knew Jo only agreed to find Finnias because she thought he could lead her to Arlo. She didn't understand what Finnias had done.

To be fair, Shay hadn't talked about it. She'd mentioned the landing, she'd told them he helped her, but that was the extent of it. She didn't know how to put the rest into words. The memory of the tear had blurred and frayed at the edges, leaving her only with the knowledge that Finnias had assisted her in closing it, and the feeling it was because she'd done something she wasn't supposed to.

"Unfortunately, I can't tell you who gave us that information." Rose's voice cut through Shay's thoughts. "My instinct says it wasn't Finnias, at the very least. I'm coming with you."

"You are?" Jo blinked, clearly surprised.

"Of the two of us, I'm more likely to know if it's a trap," Rose said. "Besides, you can put me on your payroll."

"Ah, about that—"

Rose smiled a bit. "I'm joking."

"Oh." Jo nodded. "Well. Good."

"We're not going to all fit in my car," Gideon said.

"I can drive, too," Max offered. "But I'm coming in."

"We don't have a plan," Jo reminded them.

Shay stood up. "Go to the café, Duncan picks the lock, I yell until the mirror ghost talks to me or I pull Finnias out or whatever, and we chalk it up as a resounding success."

"Or the mirror ghost doesn't talk to you, and we come home," Max said. "And I'll make waffles."

"With chocolate chips?" Shay asked.

Max rolled their eyes. "I'm not an animal, of course there will be chocolate chips."

"Resounding success either way, then," Shay said. "Think of it as a nighttime stroll. A jaunt, if you will."

"A dangerous jaunt," Max added.

"Or it's a trap and we die," Jo said. "Or fall into the influence of the spirit charmer. Or we get caught and get arrested."

"What if Finnias isn't there?" Duncan asked. He'd been awfully quiet, considering chocolate chip waffles were potentially on the table.

"I dunno, this is the only lead I have." Shay tried her best to not sound desperate, but she was. It had been a week and a half of talking into a completely unhaunted mirror. A week and a half of Jo trying a dozen divination methods a night, the bags under her eyes heavier and darker with each passing day.

Of being absolutely terrified.

She knew she couldn't keep living like that. She doubted anyone else could.

"You know it's a terrible plan," Jo said. "You might have the worst plans of anyone I've ever met, and I know Arlo. You haven't met Arlo, but trust me, that's saying something."

"Great, something fun and fresh to put on my resume," Shay said. Max laughed, at least.

"I think it's a great plan," Duncan said. "Are you not coming?"

"I think I should drive," Jo said. "And of course, I'm coming. If all else fails, I'll use the mirror to scry."

"That's the ticket," Duncan said. "Back up plans within back up plans. I love it. Let's get going, shall we?"

Shay ended up in Jo's sedan with Max and Rose. The car was ancient - apparently it belonged to the same grandmother who used to own the house. She'd left everything to Jo, no mention of parents or anything else. Shay wasn't sure if she should ask about Jo's family dynamics. If a good time existed, it wasn't that moment.

"So, this Finnias helped you close the tear?" Rose asked. "I was told most of the story, but not much about that part."

"It was just me and him," Shay said. "It's…complicated."

Max hadn't asked, and she hadn't volunteered. It was the longest she'd ever gone without telling them something. It was a weight she thought she could carry alone.

It was too heavy.

"I think…I think I did something I wasn't supposed to, but I can't remember." She stared out the window. Lights flashed by. The sky was thickly overcast, the clouds a dull orange of reflected light. It was cold, maybe it would snow. "I think I should have been able to close it alone, but I saw something, and…and I think he saved my life."

"Wait, you saw beyond the veil?" Rose asked.

"Shay, you don't have to talk about it," Max's voice was quieter than hers. "It's okay."

"No, I…I don't remember it very well," she admitted. The memory was hazy, at best. She remembered Finnias helping her close the tear much more clearly. "It…had this pull. I can't explain it. I mean later it was terrifying, but in the moment it was peaceful, I guess. Finnias saved my life and helped me close the tear, but he was stuck on the other side. I don't know what it means for him or…or anything. But if the mirror is a gateway we can probably get him out, right?"

Silence filled the car. Max took her hand. She was surprised at how warm their fingers were. She'd taken the hottest shower she could stand, but she was still cold. She wasn't sure she would ever warm up again.

"I'm glad he was there to save you, I guess the least we can do is return the favor," Max's voice was full of forced cheer. "And maybe figure some things out."

"Like why I can't punch any ghosts into oblivion?" Shay hoped someone else would bring it up, but it fell on her shoulders, in the end. "Because I still don't get it. With the other ghosts it just sort of happened, and these ones were actively threatening my life, so if it was an instinct thing then my instincts are terrible. What if I can't even do that anymore? What if—"

"Shay," Jo cut her off. "What you told us sounds really traumatic. Of course you're not going to bounce back. That's completely normal. No one expects you to."

Traumatic? She supposed she didn't remember it well, and she had lost Finnias, but she hadn't known him for long. He'd saved her life a handful of times, and she knew how he looked when he was alive, but it had still only been a few hours. It wasn't like she'd lost Max, or her brother.

But she'd been alone, except for him, and she'd let him go.

"Jo's right." Max squeezed her hand. "It was only a week ago. You need time. It's okay."

"A week and a half," she corrected.

"Still."

"But if I get us all killed because of trauma or whatever, it's kind of not okay." Shay knew that wasn't fair, to anyone, but it bubbled up and spilled over.

"It's not whatever," Max said. "And that's why you have us. We'll keep you safe. Okay? You don't have to do everything by yourself. You're not meant to. None of us are. You've looked out for me a lot. Let me do the same for you."

"Yeah, I know." She knew she hadn't been acting like it. "I think you look out for me a lot more."

"Agree to disagree."

"Fair." She squeezed their hand back.

"Just…don't keep things from me, okay?" Max dropped their voice so it was quiet enough it was feasible Jo and Rose couldn't hear them. "I can't help if I don't know what's wrong."

"I'll do my best."

"That's all I ask." Max smiled a bit.

They drove past the cafe. It was sadder than she expected in the poor light. The infamous raven was still stenciled on the side of the two-story brick building. Once there had been a nest on the roof, but it was long gone. To the elements or taken by the owners, she wasn't sure. The only thing left was a little tower jutting out of the top. There was a surprising lack of graffiti littering the buildings around it. Maybe people remembered it as fondly as she did.

Or they sensed the darkness lurking behind the metal coverings.

"I used to come here all the time," Jo said. "Before they closed, what, five years ago?"

"Give or take." Shay craned her neck to keep staring.

"It was a nice place," Rose agreed. "Our office used to be near here."

"Spiritual Connections has been open that long?" Max asked.

"You'd be surprised how popular that kind of thing is around here," Rose said. "Or, well, it used to be."

"Any ghosts, Shay?" Jo asked.

"Not that I see." Shay sat back down. "I think it's clear."

"Oddly clear," Jo murmured.

She was right, the area around the cafe was disturbingly free of any glows.

The world holding its breath.

"We'll park a few blocks away, just in case," Jo said. She pulled into the parking lot of a tiny 24-hour family grocer. Their sign was lit up and turning with a terrible grinding sound echoing off the building next to them.

Jo called Gideon to coordinate their positions or whatever dumb jargon they were trying out. Shay walked out to the sidewalk.

"Anything?" Max asked, quietly. They stepped up beside her.

"No," Shay said. The street was dark and empty. One of the streetlamps on the next block flickered. "For now."

"Here." Max handed her something. "I made it! With supervision. I hope it'll help, at least."

It was a little velvet sachet. Rocks clattered against each other inside of it when she took it. She looped it over her head. "Thanks, Max."

"Of course." Max grinned at her, their smile brilliant despite the poor light. "I did say I'd keep you safe."

"Aww you." She stepped closer to them. "You're the best. When did you guys even do this?"

"While you were in the shower," Max said. "I know I haven't sounded grateful, but I am really glad she's helping us out. Though we eat too many cookies. And muffins. And bread. Between her and Nana you'll have to start rolling me out the door."

"Reporting for rolling duty."

Max laughed. "You're in danger, too!"

"I have willpower like iron," Shay said. "My mind is a fortress."

"Is that why you had four cookies?"

"Yes. Four is exactly how many I meant to eat," Shay said. "A lesser person would have eaten five."

Max laughed again and it left Shay warm for the first time in days. Things almost felt normal. Even entering a heavily haunted, abandoned building.

Duncan and Gideon parked next to Jo. They got out of the car and met under the sign. Shay grinned and bore it, even though the grating was setting her on edge.

"I found a book," Duncan said.

"Wow, glad you went to school for ten years to be a librarian, really paid off," Shay said.

"Shove it, you." He waved his phone at her. "Ghostly Abilities and Their Wielders. I got it, I'm gonna read it, maybe it'll help. Probably won't hurt."

"I've never heard of it." Jo took his phone. "Ah. Hans Lyman."

"You bought a book to help us from a guy whose last name is literally Lie Man?" Shay asked.

"...Now I do sort of regret the seventeen dollars I spent on it," Duncan said.

Gideon coughed. "Seventeen dollars? For an ebook?"

"Hey, indie publishing is a rough industry," Duncan pointed at him. "I just paid for this guy's groceries for a week. And I lost many books in the fire. I'm in mourning. No one can judge my impulse buying in this time of grief."

"You're always impulse buying, though?" Max reminded him.

"Oh, yeah, that's the ADHD, but in this case it's mourning."

"Hans Lyman is an old pen name for Robert Lichfield," Rose explained. "You know that name, Gideon."

"Wait, the Robert Lichfield?" Gideon asked. "Oh man, he invented a bunch of our equipment. He's a rock star. In the world of paranormal sciences, anyway, so more of a big nerd, but holy crap! People say he knows when a place is haunted the moment he walks in, but he made equipment so he could prove it."

"Ha, Lichfield," Duncan said. No one else laughed. "You know, because he's in the field. Of studying dead things. It's fitting. And his pen name is Lyman? I want to meet this guy."

"If he knows a place is haunted, it's probably a legitimate book, right?" Max asked. "Because he has abilities? Most likely?"

"Oh yeah, good point." Duncan took his phone back from Jo. "See? I make great decisions. I'll let you read it later. Let's get going before the guy in the grocery store calls the cops."

"I'll go buy a soda or something," Gideon offered. "And stay with the cars. You guys be safe, all right?"

"I'm always safe, in fact, it's my middle name. Duncan Safe O'Brannon. It's not sexy, but I think I wear it with dignity." Duncan pulled him down and kissed him on the cheek. "You be safe, too."

"Always."

Shay made a lot of exaggerated gagging noises, and it was worth it, even if Duncan elbowed her.

They fell quiet, walking down the sidewalk. It was a cold night. The only light came from the streetlamps. Tiny pools in the dark.

They approached the cafe through the alley. The metal back door had the name stenciled on it, though the nest part had worn away, leaving only "The Raven".

"All right, step back and watch a master at work." Duncan stepped forward. He pushed the handle down to test it and the door cracked open with a loud creak.

"Wow, you've gotten better." Max grinned.

"Watch it, Maxaroni and Cheese."

Max sighed. "You've used that one before.

"Yeah, but it was in the pasta." Shay high fived Duncan. Max rolled their eyes and turned on their flashlight, pushing the door open the rest of the way. It groaned on its hinges. They led the way, holding a sachet in one hand.

Two long counters lined the wall with empty spots where appliances must have sat. "Hey, it doesn't look too bad. I bet we could reopen this place."

"You could make chai and I could sweep," Shay said.

Rose stepped in with them, head tilted to the side.

"There's something here," she said. "I can hear whispers."

It was colder inside the café than it was on the street, the warmth completely sucked out of the air. Shay shivered and wrapped her arms around herself. They passed the glass display case separating the front from the back and into the main body of the building.

If she really focused, she could hear the whispers. An undercurrent of static lifted the hair on the back of her neck.

It was as they'd left it a week ago — sad, empty, and dusty, their footprints still visible.

They had been there only a week and a half ago. Shay stepped into one of her own footprints. She was even wearing the same shoes. Some part of her must have changed, but it wasn't her small shoe size. Her foot fit perfectly in the print.

The mirror was still on the wall. The curling frame had a few new cobwebs. Its surface was dark.

Even though there were more living people there than before, it was emptier. Hollow.

A ghost was like an empty house.

"Something's definitely here," she said.

"Do you see anything?" Jo asked.

"Think I'm starting to get feelings," Shay said. "Or at least, understand them."

She walked towards it and was abruptly standing on the landing again. Duncan stepped down next to her.

"Okay that's not fair, I didn't even grab you this time," Duncan said.

Finnias still wasn't there.

"Finnias?" Duncan called, too loudly. Any moment the man would come up the stairs.

"We need to get out of here," Shay said.

"You got an express ticket out of ghost memory city?" Duncan asked. "You didn't exactly ask Jo or Rose about this."

"I thought you would! You're the adultier adult. I don't even have a driver's license."

Footsteps below them. She backed up towards the stairs. They probably led up to the hallway. She didn't know if they'd be able to climb them.

The window turned black.

Darkness spread from the stairs below. The rich brown of the woods faded to gray and color leeched from the carpet, holes fraying and spreading. The wallpaper peeled back and a crack ran through the plaster behind it. A tree grew through the window, its branches scraping the ceiling like claws.

"What did you do?" Her question was squeakier than she would have liked.

"Me? I didn't do anything!"

"You're the...medium person!"

"I'm a librarian!"

The man walked up the stairs.

He was hunched over, but taller than she remembered. His suit was torn and his hair was limp and white, falling over his face.

Except his face was gone. A blank hole, completely black.

Shay took a step back.

The man was in front of her. Fingers clutched at her shoulders, tight enough to bruise. She cried out and he slammed her back into the windowsill with a cracked,

"Get out." The voice didn't sound human. It was a dozen voices, blended into one, emanating from the hole where his face should have been. "Get out get out get out!"

The voice roared around her, a windstorm, a hurricane, a force of nature blasting the walls apart and shattering the floor beneath her feet.

She screamed and fell, landing back in the café.

Chapter 9: No Experience Necessary

Shay didn't want to move, even with dust already in her throat, forcing a cough.

"Holy crap." Max was already next to her, helping her sit up. She shivered so hard her teeth rattled. They yanked her into a hug. "You're freezing! What happened?"

"Are you okay?" Jo was kneeling, too, helping Duncan sit up. His eyes looked too bright, completely unfocused.

"I don't…I don't know." She shuddered, cold all the way to her bones. "We were on the landing again, but it was all wrong. Dunc?"

He didn't answer, staring at the wall.

"Donuts?" she tried again.

He blinked and shook himself when Jo touched his shoulder. "Present. Good. Great. Doing awesome."

"You're like ice." Jo wrapped an awkward arm around his shoulder, clearly expecting him to pull away, but he didn't move at all.

"Cause I'm so chill." He shrugged. "Chill with not being able to do anything, actually. I'm good. I think I'll stick to being a librarian forever. As nice and snuggly as this is, can we get off the floor? There are probably seven bajillion dust particles getting in my lungs right now."

"Right, sorry." Jo climbed to her feet and gave Duncan a hand up. Max did the same for Shay.

"What happened?" Rose's voice made Shay start. She'd completely forgotten she was there until she spoke. "Sorry, if you need a minute…"

"No, I'm good." Shay shoved her hands in her pockets, trying to warm them up, but her jacket felt like it had been left in a freezer.

She explained what happened, as best as she could. Duncan interjected a few times but seemed mostly content to let her do the talking. He must have been much more shaken than she initially thought. Max had a hand on her back. A twinge of phantom pain raced across her shoulder blades, even though physically she'd never left the cafe.

"Three times now." Jo rubbed her forehead. "And it's getting worse each time. Lovely. Rose, have you ever heard of anything like this?"

"No," Rose admitted. "There's astral projection, which I think is related to what's happening, but I've never experienced it myself. Not to this degree.

Jo nodded. "Okay. You two aren't allowed near each other anymore."

"Fine by me." Duncan took an exaggerated step away from her.

"Same to you, loser," she said, more out of a need for normalcy than anything else. "You stink of hair products, anyway."

"I smell like coconuts and awesomeness, goo girl."

"Okay yes you've viciously one-upped each other," Max said before she could open her mouth to retort. "There's the mirror. Let's…get in and get out, right?"

"Right." Shay curled her hands into fists to hide the tremor in her fingers and stepped up to the mirror. A skull floated where her head was, along with half a ribcage. "What, no theatrics today? I'm glad you're okay, though. I was getting worried."

Max's reflection didn't show up. They looked at her. "I don't see anything."

"Hello, Shay." The skeleton leaned against the frame of the mirror.

She knew exactly who was talking, even if she'd never heard her actual voice. She narrowed her eyes, her hands balling into fists. "Not Taylor."

Echoing laughter filled the room.

"Shay, don't listen to her," Jo said. "Let's go."

"Is that what you're calling me? That's cute." The spirit charmer laughed again. "Calm down. I'm not here to hurt you. Any of you, to be clear, though you're the only one that can hear me."

"Somehow I don't believe you." Shay ignored how her ears and cheeks felt hot, despite the chill. "What are you doing here? Last time wasn't enough for you? You want more?"

"Oh, so much more," the spirit charmer said. "But that's a discussion for another time For the moment, I have a proposition for you."

"Give Arlo and Finnias back and I'll think about listening to it," Shay said.

"That's the spirit, negotiating with you is going to be so much fun." The spirit charmer snapped her fingers. It sounded like twigs cracking. "Go back to where you lost Finnias. The door will be open for you. How's that for generosity? As for Arlo, your little witch friend will be able to find him the day after Halloween, guaranteed. There! Now you can listen to me."

"I don't think so," Shay said. "I won't until they're right next to me."

"Then don't find them, I don't care." She shrugged. "How about you listen to what I have to say, but we don't reach an agreement until Arlo is back, safe and sound. I'll even help. I think it sounds fair."

"Yeah? How do I know I can trust you?" Shay asked.

"You can't! Fun, right? Now, for me." The skull leaned in closer and the faintest image of a face surrounded it. Long, dark hair pulled away from a thin face with strong cheekbones. "I want you to join me."

"What?" Shay couldn't have been more surprised if the spirit had reached through the mirror and stabbed her. "You literally tried to kill me the last time you saw me?"

"Please, that was so last week." One bony hand waved off her concern. "Besides, look where it got me? You're special, Shay. I need necromancers of your caliber on my side."

"You need what now?" Shay stared at her.

The face couldn't change, but she sounded delighted. "Wait, you don't know? Your little witch friend didn't tell you? Ooh wait, I bet she doesn't know, either. That grandmother of hers would want her to stay far away from any necromancers, and one still drops into her lap! Incredible."

"I'm not…" she glanced at her friends, not sure if she should say it out loud. "I'm not…not that. I have abilities, I can't…I'm not."

"What a cute and sanitized little word. We deal with the dead, my dear, and we are very good at it," the spirit charmer said. "Call us whatever you want. Night Witches. Ravens. Necromancers. But we are what we are. You, in particular, have an amazing gift. You can make spirits solid. Imagine if you stopped spending so much time with these low-grade witches and really nurtured it. The things you could do!"

"I'm not—"

"Well, of course not, you're boring. Like Finnias." She sighed, her broken ribcage expanding dramatically. "He was a necromancer, too, you know. I suppose even with most of his memories gone that would remain."

"You knew him?" Shay asked.

"Probably better than he knew himself," she said. "If he's so important to you, join me. I'll tell you all about him. Help you find him. I'll even tell you how to use your gifts."

"You tried to wipe the town off the map," Shay said.

Something in her stance was indignant. "I did not. You little town was merely collateral in a much bigger scheme."

"Twenty-thousand people isn't collateral." Horror curdled in Shay's gut.

She shrugged. "Depends on who you ask."

"I'm asking you."

"If it helps, I'm doing my best to move in a new direction. Unfortunately, I need you. And your brother, I suppose. It would be safest if we all stuck together for what's coming."

"And what's coming that I can just ignore your last scheme?" It took all of Shay's willpower to not punch the mirror.

"When you decide to join me, and you will, you're going to find out," she said. "I'll give you a hint. The three of us aren't the only necromancers in Teton Falls, and it's about to get…crowded."

Shay's stomach dropped. "Wait—"

"Night after tomorrow! Happy Halloween, Shay, I'm sure it's going to be a very exciting one for you. You might want to stay in. The moment the sun is down the day after, I'll make sure Jocelyn will be able to find him. Ta!"

The mirror cleared up, Shay's reflection pale even in the dark cafe, one cheek smudged with dust and more hair hanging loose around her face than she had tied back.

"…That didn't sound good," Duncan said. "So… the spirit charmer is making a move?"

"What did she say?" Max asked.

"…Who's up for more breaking and entering?" Shay asked. The rest could wait. It would have to wait. She didn't know how to begin. "I mean, sort of, the door should be open?"

"Shay, what did she say?" Jo grabbed her shoulders and forced her to look at her.

"We can find Arlo the day after Halloween," Shay said. "So… since Halloween is tomorrow, soon. And Finnias is where we lost him. The governor's house. She said the door would be open for us."

"And?" Jo's grip tightened. It reminded her too much of the ghost with no face.

"She wants me to join her."

Jo let go and stepped away.

"No," Max's voice was hoarse. "Absolutely not."

"Why would she want that?" Rose asked. "No offense, but Jo explained things and said you stopped her plans last time."

"Maybe so I don't keep stopping her plans?" Shay couldn't bring herself to say the real reason. "Something about what was coming, and I don't know what it means but it sounds bad. And because I'm awesome. Obviously, I'm not going to do it, but I have the information. Let's save our friends and figure out what's next, I guess."

"Shay, are you sure?" Max asked. "Not about not joining her, that's obvious, but it's already been a lot tonight."

Shay shoved down everything she was feeling. She didn't have time. "The rest of you don't have to come. I'll do it myself, if I have to."

"Of course I'm with you," Max said, quietly. They were worried and scared, Shay could hear it, but they were still there. A little bit of the tightness in her chest eased.

"Can't let you waltz into danger by yourself, what kind of big brother do you think I am?" Duncan asked.

"The terrible kind." She smiled.

"Terrible and kind, yes, that is me, like a semi-benevolent god." Duncan nodded.

"Let's go get Finnias, and…wait until we can find Arlo," Shay said. "Halloween isn't going to be bad, is it?"

"Samhain," Jo said. "It's…a little like our new year. Traditionally, it was when the crops were harvested in preparation for winter. It's also when it's easiest to contact the dead."

"That sounds bad for me. I don't need it to be any easier," Shay said. She opened her mouth to say more, to tell Jo what she was, but there was too much. She couldn't even unpack it, so she closed it again.

They'd get Finnias first. There would be time after.

"It…could be," Jo said. "Ghosts crave connection, solidness, something that makes them feel alive. Unfortunately, you. Don't worry. We'll lock you up in your room with as many wards as we can. You should be fine, especially if…if Finnias can help. So. I'm in, too. It must be another trap, but that just means you'll need me."

"I'm out," Rose said. "Entering an abandoned café is one thing, the governor's house is another."

"That's fair, and seriously thank you for your help," Jo said. "Do you need one of us to walk you back to the Save Mart?"

"If you do, you should know I'm the handsomest and strongest." Duncan flexed one arm.

"Quick, someone grab a magnifying glass," Shay said.

"I think this will need a microscope," Max added.

"Ha," Rose said. "Max, will you walk me to the car?"

"Oh uh. Yeah. Okay." Max nodded. "I'll meet you guys in front of the house."

They left the cafe. Shay stopped at the mirror. It was still just her reflection in corroded silver.

"Shay! Are you coming!" Duncan yelled. "I'll lock you in!"

She hurried to the door.

Wind rattled down the sidewalk, leading them to the governor's house at the end of the street. It crouched on top of the hill, dark and imposing. Part of the wall was still broken, but the debris had been cleared away and a chain link fence covered the hole.

No light shone through the dark windows. Nothing sinister stirred in the shadows. Other than the wind it was completely quiet.

"This place feels dead," Jo said.

"Is that a joke or…?" Duncan asked. "Because I mean. It's haunted! Big surprise!"

"I don't see anything." Shay squinted, but no glows appeared in the dark windows.

"And I meant there's a… lack of energy here," Jo explained. "It's completely vacant. No ghosts, no nothing. We should be feeling something, believe me, but there's absolutely nothing."

"Because of the tear?" Shay asked.

"I don't know, these are uncharted waters," Jo said.

Duncan nodded. "Here there be monsters."

They stood there, staring up at the house, for a few minutes. Nothing glowed in the windows or on the street.

Shay recognized the spot. She'd saved Finnias there, when a horribly strong wind had pulled him from Duncan. She'd kept him from becoming part of the conglomerate, only to lose him not even an hour later.

Max jogged up a few minutes later. "Okay, Rose and Gideon are safe, and we can head on in. How are we doing that?"

"Hm." Duncan considered the fence, ignoring the warning signs about trespassing and federal offenses. "Give me a boost and I could make it over. Shay might have some trouble but maybe she can scale up it. Like a squirrel."

"Shut up," Shay said.

Duncan grinned at her. "Didn't have enough acorns today?"

"Go ahead, give me an acorn, see where it ends up."

The gate swung open and a man in a security uniform stepped out. They all jumped back, probably looking comically surprised.

"Miss Shay?" he asked.

"Yeah?" She agreed without thinking it might be a bad idea.

"This way, please." He stepped back and gave her a shallow bow, one arm extended towards the gate. "You've been expected."

Chapter 10: Room With A View

The security guard led them to the house and opened the door for them, face completely blank.

"Sorry." Shay didn't know what else to say. If the guard heard her, he gave absolutely no indication, holding the door open for her.

The last time Shay had been in the governor's house, it had been lit up in blue and green.

No ghostly light led them into the depths of the house. Jo kept her flashlight carefully trained on the wood floor. They walked down a hallway that was rendered familiar and alien all at once.

Shay could practically feel the fingers on her neck, marching her past walls lined with cold light.

"You okay?" Max asked, quietly.

She willed herself not to jump. There was no drawl to Max's words, no malice at all. It was just them, nothing else.

"Yup," she managed to say, after too long of a pause.

She half expected the poltergeist to come barreling down the hallway. For everyone to turn on her, their eyes catching the light,

But nothing happened. It was dark, and quiet, and no one was even looking at her.

"Are you sure?" Max touched her shoulder and she stepped to the side, completely by instinct.

She couldn't look at them. She didn't want to see the hurt in their eyes, and she didn't want to have to prove to herself that they weren't possessed. She couldn't.

"So, what did you and Rose talk about?" Duncan deftly changed the subject.

"Oh, um. Nothing really." Max didn't sound upset, at least. "She asked about my show. Wanted to know if I was continuing it."

"Oh yeah!" Shay was eager to launch herself onto the new topic, talking past the fear trying to strangle her. "You should. I liked your show."

"You booed the name in the last episode." Max sounded more amused than angry, at least.

"It was friendly booing," Shay said. "Out of love. Affectionate disapproval."

"That's not a thing."

"Sure it is!" she insisted. "You could start a new series. 'My Journey to Becoming an Awesome Witch'. That would be cool."

Max snorted. "Is that what I'm doing?"

"It is," Shay said. She kept talking, like if she stopped the silence would fill her lungs. "Or you could still do ghosts. Just. Without me. Probably. Unless you want it to get real exciting real fast. Or you could do urban exploration. Perfect opportunity, right now. Governor's house."

"Pretty sure we're doing the entering bit of breaking and entering," Max reminded her. "Probably shouldn't post that online."

"Only cowards don't record their crimes for the approval of strangers."

Max actually laughed at that.

Jo shushed them. "We're here."

They were standing outside the door.

Shay didn't want to look in. Didn't want to take a single step over the threshold. Her hands shook and she folded her arms tightly in an attempt to hide it.

She still ached from that night, like the cold from the void had wormed its way inside of her and refused to let go. She didn't remember the tear, not really, shaped by the room around it.

It took everything she had to look inside.

The study seemed smaller than she remembered.

The door was covered by yellow bars of police tape. The desk was gone. The shelf that had fallen hadn't been replaced, just a gap of painted drywall.

Just a quiet, empty room.

She ducked under the police tape before she lost her nerve. No one else followed her. Maybe they wanted to give her space.

Or they were waiting to see what she would do.

She knew she had to be standing where the tear had been. It wasn't any colder than the rest of the house, but she shivered, anyway. The air felt strange. Charged and electric, in a way the rest of the house had just felt empty and stale.

Nothing happened.

"So, um." She held out her arms and spun in a circle. "What do I do?"

"I don't know." Jo finally followed Shay into the room.

"We could hold a seance," Max said. "I mean, none of us are a medium, but we should be able to do something. Duncan could get possessed again."

"How about we don't do that but say we tried," Duncan suggested. "We don't have any candles, anyway."

"Yes, we do." Max slid off their backpack and pulled out a package of thin, white candles.

Duncan clapped, a little sarcastically. "I stand corrected."

Jo considered the room, walking around it and frowning. "I don't think a seance is the answer, but it's a good thought. If Rose was here we could certainly try, but I think Duncan and Shay have to take this journey on their own."

"What?" Duncan asked.

"No," Max said at the same time. "I made a promise."

"I know," Jo said. "We'll do everything we can to keep that promise, but…I can't think of any other way. Something keeps pulling them to Finnias's landing, I think they need to finish their journey."

"But—" Max started to say.

"Max, it's okay." Shay put a hand on their arm. Nothing happened. She could even see their face, only the barest glint of light in their eyes.

Everything was fine.

They weren't possessed.

She wasn't alone.

"I don't think it's okay," Duncan said. "I don't want to. Not really my idea of a good time so far, and I'm sure the journey ends with lots of screaming."

"Don't be a big baby," Shay told him. He spluttered at her, but she ignored him. She needed to keep moving. If she stopped and thought about it, really considered if she was okay with it, she knew she'd leave the room without even trying. "This is where the tear is. Was. I think this is where we need to start."

"You sure?" Duncan was clearly stalling.

"I'm sure, get your stupid butt over here."

Duncan didn't argue with her, stepping closer.

And they were on the landing. It looked normal, or as normal as it could. Mist poured in from the stairs above, sunlight streamed from an empty window, and the murmur of a crowd rose from the bottom floor. The smell of lemon and polish assaulted her nose.

The fog rolled back, revealing the stairs leading up one by one, until it was completely burned away. They led up to another landing, exactly like the one they were standing on. Footsteps sounded below them. Slow and steady.

That left them one direction to flee in.

"Let's go," she whispered.

Duncan nodded and followed her up.

The stairs went up for a long time, switching back and forth between landings identical to the first one - the wallpaper with golden diamonds, the carpet, even the window. She couldn't be certain they were really moving at all. Despite their haste, and the stitch forming in her side, the footsteps were always the same steady tempo to the overlapping music of muffled conversation.

They didn't waste energy on words. Shay's breath burned in her throat, barely grazing her starving lungs.

She could have cried with relief when they climbed up not to a landing, but to a hallway, clear and as brightly lit as the landing. White plaster walls stretched on for so long she couldn't make out the end, studded with dark, wooden doors. Glass covered sconces were set between each one, flames bright and cheerful, brighter than she thought they should have been, casting no shadows on the floor or walls.

"Finally," Duncan gasped out. "What's behind door number one?"

The knob didn't move at all under his hand.

The footsteps drew closer.

"C'mon." Shay tried the next one. It might as well have been carved from the same wood as the door.

"You take that side," Duncan told her, quietly. "Hurry."

Every door was locked.

She kept trying, each one, pursued by the measured beat of footsteps. She wouldn't think they were moving forward at all, but there was an occasional table graced with a beautiful vase and an arch of orchid or lily flowers. She didn't dare turn around, couldn't imagine trying to see behind them, though surely Archibald could see them. The hallway had no turns.

The farther they went, the dustier and plainer the vases were. The flowers wilted.

Until they were glass jars full of brackish water and black stems.

It was darker, the candles were nubs of wax, flames open to the wind. The covers were broken or missing entirely. Deep shadows pooled beneath them. She could see her breath.

She didn't know what made her pause, or what made her look back.

A solid, black shadow stood in the middle of the hallway. Everything they'd passed — the beautiful vases, the flowers — was gone. All that remained behind it was a shattered and broken floor, the walls torn apart, the ceiling open to a gaping void of a night sky.

She yanked on the next handle. It turned under her hand and she scrambled into the next room, Duncan right behind her. She slammed the door and it locked with a click before she even touched the mechanism.

It was bright.

The golden light of a late afternoon spread in honeyed stripes across the plush carpet and rose patterned wallpaper. It was the sitting room — thickly stuffed and patterned couches around a table with a basket of fruit in the middle. Glass French doors were open into a bedroom. The far wall was made of tall, arched windows.

Finnias stood in front of them.

Shay's heart lurched in her chest and she stopped walking, but Duncan grabbed her arm and pulled her through the doors, closing them with a snap. Finnias turned at the sound, confusion plain on his face. He wasn't wearing the vest she was used to, just a button-down white shirt, open at the collar. His hair was much more rumpled than it was as a ghost, falling softly over his forehead.

The room around them was soft at the edges, dreamlike and airy. Finnias was in sharp clarity, from the light glinting off of his hair to every fold in his sleeves. Outside, the same sun gilded the tops of old-fashioned buildings in an unfamiliar city, the streets already lost to the dim blue of twilight.

"How did you get in here?" Finnias picked up a large book from the table next to him and held it threateningly in front of him.

"…Please tell me that's Finnias," Duncan said.

"That's him," Shay said. There was no recognition on his face

"How do you know that name?" he sounded more angry than confused, no recognition on his face.

"Great." Shay hadn't really thought about what would happen when they actually found Finnias. She'd been so focused on getting to that point, she'd never considered what came after. Or that he'd even remember her. He'd had memory problems already. "Hi. You don't remember me, obviously. I'm Shay. You helped me close a big tear in reality and I'm here to get you back."

"I have no idea what you're talking about." But something flashed in his face, something like a realization. "What tear? In the veil?"

"I know this is a lot to take in, but we're kind of on a time limit," Duncan said. "Yup, tear in the veil. You helped close it. You're a real hero and all that, but we need you back in the game."

"I—" He shook his head and put long fingers to his temple. "I don't… there's something there. I know you. But I don't know you. And I…I was here. For a reason. Wasn't I?"

He looked at her like she might hold the answers.

"I was waiting for someone," he continued. "I was waiting…who was I waiting for? Was it you? It was important. Please. I know it was important."

The confusion on his face, the desperate hope in his voice, stabbed at her with every word.

"Finnias—"

Cold pressed against her back.

The first room darkened. Holes widened the ceiling. The table tipped drunkenly when a leg rotted away before her eyes. Spoiled fruit rolled across the floor. The couches were moth eaten, misshapen lumps on either side, black with mold. The carpet wore down to nothing.

The black silhouette slid through the broken doorway.

Shay squeaked and yanked Duncan farther into the room.

Darkness spread across the walls. Wallpaper faded and curled under the onslaught. Cracks spiderwebbed dark and deep in the plaster. The windows cracked, glass falling to the floor like the first drops of rain.

The figure was clearer now. It was the man in the suit, but he was horribly twisted. His arms were too long, the skin gray. His curly blond hair was gone, leaving a smooth plate behind, covered in thick, black veins spreading from his empty face. The vest and dress shirt were oddly pristine, but his pants ended in tatters above long, clawed feet.

"Stay behind me." Shay stepped in front of Duncan, holding up her fists. There was no strength in her, no conviction. The only thing was fear, trying to lock up her voice and freeze up her joints.

"Yeah, okay." Duncan's tone was not helping.

Even if she was at full strength, she wasn't sure it would have made a difference. They were in a memory, not a real place, and Finnias didn't know her at all.

The ghost didn't move. One moment he was in the doorway, the next right in front of her.

She screamed and punched him as hard as she could. Her hand sunk into the ghost, up to her wrist. It was icy cold. He grabbed her arm and pulled her closer, wrapping her up in a horrible, deathly embrace. The chill was so intense her thoughts slowed to a crawl.

"Let go of her, creep!" Duncan yanked her back and she stumbled into Finnias. The room fell apart around them. Pieces of the roof caved in. One wall fell away entirely, letting in a cold, sharp blast of wind. There was no late afternoon on the other side, just the screaming darkness. Window frames crumbled. The bed sagged in the middle, the creamy comforter going dark. Mildew spread across what was left of the carpet.

It took everything she had, but she yanked herself away from the ghost, coming free with a splattering sound. She stumbled back as Duncan grabbed her and pulled. She looped her arm with his and got a hold of Finnias's wrist.

This was a memory.

They were high above an old city lost in shadow.

The window was already gone, the glass glittering gold on the carpet. She stepped onto the sill. It sagged under her weight, but it didn't need to hold her.

"What are you—" Duncan started as she launched herself from the ledge.

They fell, all tangled together. She opened her mouth to scream but the wind ripped her voice away, howling in her ears. The windows in the buildings around them gleamed gold and orange, winking brightly. The blue shadowed street rose up to meet them and she twisted around.

Darkness spread across an orange sky, the clouds bruised to a dark purple. The moon shattered across the sky in a new constellation.

She closed her eyes.

Chapter 11: Rememberancer

Shay landed in deep, wet snow. She sat up and yanked her hair out of her face. Finnias and Duncan were on either side of her. Duncan spluttered through a mouth full of snow.

They'd landed in a large, circular clearing surrounded by scraggly aspen trees, their bare branches black cracks in the pale gray of the sky. She staggered to her feet. The snow came up to her knees and quickly soaked through her jeans.

"Are you crazy?" Duncan got to his feet, brushing snow off his jacket. "That was insane! What were you thinking!"

"Mostly that the city wasn't real, but that ghost is, and we had to get away from it." Shay shivered, the cold hitting her. "You're welcome."

Finnias shoved wet hair back from his forehead, but it flopped back into his eyes. "How did—we jumped out a window, how are we here?"

Duncan made a face. "You wanna take this one or should I?"

"You can," she said.

"Wow."

She shrugged. "You shouldn't have asked if you didn't want to."

"Wait." Finnias looked around the field. "I know this place."

"Great," Shay said. "Any idea how we get out of here?"

"I… I don't know. It's a bad place," he said. "But the hill. The house is over the hill."

There was a ridge on the other side of the field, rising above the trees. A thin wisp of blue was just barely visible above it.

"I guess we're going that way," Duncan said. "Especially since our friend followed us."

"What?" Shay glanced behind her. The trees were dark, their bark rolling off in thick clumps, the snow melting. "Oh, c'mon! I jumped out a window!"

They hurried through the snow, as best as they could. The cold air burned Shay's lungs and her boots were not waterproof. They hit the trees on the other side and had to push through a tangle of undergrowth, thorns and twigs catching at their clothes and hair.

By the time they reached the top of the ridge Shay was ready to collapse. She was hot in her coat, but her hands and feet were numb.

It wasn't a house.

It was a mansion of dark wood and stone with a sprawling lawn behind it. Thick stands of evergreen surrounded them. Something about it was familiar, but she couldn't place it.

Behind them the snow melted away to bare, dark earth in a perfect circle, the grass on the edges dead and gray.

The trees on the side closest to them drooped, the few yellow leaves clinging to them darkening to brown and black.

They half slid down the hill. Halfway down and they were suddenly walking through the front door of the house. Shay felt queasy from the sudden shift. She supposed this was how ghosts moved, and for all that he looked alive, Finnias was a ghost.

"Okay, I'm getting whiplash," Duncan said. "I hate this."

The entryway was beautiful. Wooden floors and wood paneling. A thick Persian rug stretched in front of a sweeping staircase. Finnias walked towards the stairs and Shay had to fight the urge to take off her shoes before she followed him. Their footsteps echoed off the ceiling. It smelled like lemon and polish, like someone had recently scrubbed the floors clean and they were dripping dirty snow all over them.

Despite the freshly polished look and the light glittering from the chandelier, they were completely alone. No murmur of conversation deeper in the house, no footsteps above them.

"Well, I'm pretty sure I've seen this movie, and I didn't like how it ended," Duncan said. "Alone in a mansion in the woods, being chased by a monster…guess that makes you the final girl."

"No, it's Finnias," she said. She thought something moved, out of the corner of her eye, but when she looked it was just an archway into what appeared to be a small library. "Did you guys see-"

"This is Holt Manor," Duncan cut her off.

"The murder mansion?" Even as she said it, she recognized the entryway and the staircase.

"I mean, I saw the stupid picture, what, six hours ago? Yeah, it's Holt Manor," he said.

It felt like days should have passed since Gideon told them his theories on who Finnias was and how he died.

Finnias walked past her and up the stairs. Shay hurried to follow him.

A hallway stretched out on either side of them, but the stairs continued up to a landing before they twisted around.

She recognized the wallpaper - detailed and covered in little golden diamonds. As Finnias climbed the stairs, a familiar gray vest creeped over his shoulders, his hair swept back from his forehead. He looked exactly like he had the last time she'd seen him at the landing.

"Finnias-

"This place…" he slowly climbed up to the landing. Sun shone through the window. He put a hand to his chest. "This is where I died."

"Yeah." Shay didn't think there was any point in hiding it. She wished she had something else to say, but the words died before they could be formed.

"Shay." Finnias recognized her for the first time, it was in his eyes. "Duncan. I—"

The doors slammed open. Sunlight faltered. Cracks made their way across the window. The banister ripped away from the wall with a screech, the rusty fasteners pinging on the staircase as the carpet rotted away. Shay backed up to the wall, but the window shattered like a gunshot. She crouched down instinctively, holding her arms over her head. Below, the chandelier crashed to the floor, its arms oxidized.

"How do we get back?" Duncan yelled over the cacophony. There was nothing on the other side of the door but darkness, the wind screaming through the house was cold and smelled like iron.

Shay caught movement again, above them, and looked up the stairs. She swore it had been normal a moment ago, but now every part of the wall was lined with mirrors in all sizes and shapes, crammed together into a reflective mosaic. Something clicked across the floor above them, but she couldn't see what it was. She didn't think she wanted to.

"Where are you?" Finnias asked.

"The governor's house," Duncan said. "Physically, I mean. Probably. This is feeling pretty real."

"There." Shay pointed. She knew the mirror, knew its shape and the curl of its frame. She'd been pulled through it.

Duncan didn't question it, just grabbed her arm and dragged her to the mirror, hauling Finnias along with them. They stepped through the mirror just as the wallpaper curled away and the frame darkened.

Shay stumbled and ended up sprawled on the study floor. Duncan stayed on his feet and she seriously considered kicking him in the ankle.

"Oh my god." Max was helping her out before she could even process they were back in the present. They hugged her, a little too tightly for her poor, abused ribs. "Oh my god. Sorry. Are you okay? You're freezing. And bleeding! And...wet?"

"It's less gross than you probably think it is?" Shay said.

"Did you get him?" Jo asked. She crossed the room and to Shay's surprise pulled her into a hug. "...You are wet."

"I was in the snow," she said. "I...I don't know. Duncan?"

"Finnias." He corrected her, adjusting the sleeve of Duncan's jacket. "It was the only way."

"Oh, thank god." The tightness she'd been carrying around in her chest loosened and she sagged against Max, who barely caught her shoulders to keep her from ending up on the floor again. "I did not want to do that again."

"Unfortunately, if I leave Duncan..." Finnias sighed, shoving Duncan's hair back. "I told you once I'm not like other ghosts. I don't think that's true, not when I'm...out there. I was repeating the events that lead to my death, over and over and over again. You broke the cycle, but it will start again if I leave Duncan."

She wanted to sit back on the floor again. "Can you...shuffle control around?"

"I may have a solution," Jo said. "But it would be temporary and should wait until we get home. Where we should go, right now, before something worse happens. Gideon has been calling me every five min—there he is again. Yes. We have them. We're heading back."

"Wait, how long were we gone?" Shay asked.

"About two hours," Max said. "You were just…gone. You took at least two decades off my life with you. I'm going to go gray at twenty-one at this rate."

"You'd look good in gray, very distinguished." Shay didn't know what else to say. Two hours was a lot longer than their trip through the hallway and in the snow must have been.

And they'd been there. The scratches on her face and hands were still there. She was soaking wet, and a puddle was gathering beneath her feet. Wherever they'd been, it had been real.

And she'd jumped out a window.

She took a moment to breathe, swallowing down bile and trying desperately to not think of the roar of the wind as it rushed past her ears, the street in its blue shadow coming closer and closer, the room behind them falling into ruin. Small figures jumping from a tower, just like the card Jo had pulled for her, once.

"Shay?"

"I'm okay." She didn't know if that was true.

But they were fine. All three of them.

Mostly.

"Are you sure?" Max tucked a loose strand of hair behind her ear. "Shay?"

"I'm okay." She nodded. Her heart hammered against her ribcage. "Really, I am, it was a lot. But we did it! We got Finnias back. So. I'm going to sleep for two whole days. And then we'll have Arlo back, and things will get better. We'll kick some ghost butt. Pew pew don't cross the streams style."

"Okay." Max smiled, though their eyes were still concerned. "Sounds like a plan. Except I don't think we'll be developing proton packs anytime soon."

"Lame." She could breathe, at least. That was all she needed to do.

They made it out of the house. The security guard nodded to Shay and she returned the gesture.

Gideon and Rose were waiting for them at the curb.

"I drove your car," Rose said. "He was getting worried and…frankly, I was, too."

"I was freaking out," Gideon admitted. He pulled Finnias into a hug before anyone could stop him. "You scared the crap out of me."

"I assume Duncan scared the crap out of you, not me," Finnias said, not returning the embrace.

"Oh, it's you." Gideon stepped back. "I mean, yay, it's you, you're back."

"We need to leave," Jo said. "Thank you for bringing the cars."

Shay spent the trip back telling Jo what happened, in fits and starts. She felt like she was always explaining something or another to her, but she knew everyone needed to be in the loop. She left out a few details, like jumping out of a window.

Shay was only tangentially aware of the drive home and was practically asleep on her feet by the time they were up the steps and in the shop.

It had been a long day.

"Finnias, you can either be in a mirror or a jar, which would you prefer?" Jo asked.

"I beg your pardon?" Finnias rose one eyebrow.

"Duncan has a work meeting tomorrow, I think he'd like to be in the driver's seat," Jo said. "And I need to talk to him. So. Mirror or jar? It's up to you."

"Mirror," he said. "I suppose it's better than being trapped…well. It's better."

Jo put her scrying mirror on the table. Shay recognized it from her many attempts to find Arlo in the weeks before. She took a small purple bottle from behind the counter and dabbed flowery smelling oil around the simple, silver frame. She drew a swirling design across the surface.

The mirror glowed a soft violet. Duncan's eyes glowed, too. He relaxed and Finnias flowed out of him like a thick mist, engulfing the mirror. The light faded into a soft blue.

"You just…yanked him into a mirror. Okay." Duncan blinked, heavily, and Gideon put an arm around his shoulders. "Oh hi. You're warm. Did you know that?"

"I'll make sure to put it on my list of skills," Gideon said, squeezing him.

"You and Shay should get to bed," Jo said. "But first, Rose and I think I've figured out your abilities, and you need to be careful."

"Yeah? Am I a super medium?" Duncan asked.

"There's no such thing," Rose said, quietly.

"It's memory," Jo explained. "You can relive a ghost's memories. It's all that makes sense to me. I could be wrong, but...where ghosts are largely memories, I suppose that makes sense."

"I'll let you borrow my book," Duncan said. "So, I... remember stuff? I'm a rememberancer?"

Shay flinched. It was too close to the truth. She still hadn't told him, but now didn't feel like the time, either.

"No," Max said.

"Pretty sure I'm a rememberancer." Duncan grinned. "And since Shay has ghost touch, that makes her...the ho in ghost. But the h is silent. So she's just an o. Who's a donut, now?"

"I'll punch you again, and this time I won't be so nice about it," Shay warned him, but she was glad he sounded normal.

"Ooh, so scary."

She needed to tell him. Exactly what they were, what their abilities were. If it was her, she'd want to know.

"So, are you...okay?" Shay couldn't say it, the words wouldn't come. "Not...possessed for sure?"

"Pretty sure I'm me, but ask me a thing that only I would know," Duncan said.

She grinned, she always had a question ready. "How did you end up in the hospital in March of-"

"You're very cruel, bringing that back up." Duncan held up his arm where there was a faint scar across the inside of his forearm. "Okay, this looks bad, but it was a box cutter accident. Was trying to slash those little packing bubbles. I was very tired and...well. Not my finest moment."

"And that's how I found out that I'm your emergency contact," Shay said.

"Who else would it be?" Duncan looked at her. "I guess it could have been Max."

Max shook their head. "No thank you."

"See?"

"Please be more careful." Gideon gave him a little squeeze.

"That's my middle name."

Gideon laughed. "I thought it was safe."

"I have two middle names, actually," he said. "Duncan Safe Careful O'Brannon. They're practically synonymous but I guess the point really needed to be driven home."

Gideon and Max both snickered.

"He actually does have two middle names," Shay said. "But they're-"

"Nope! Not talking about that!" Duncan put a hand towards her face and she just barely ducked out of the way. "Let's focus on more important things! Like am I okay? Am I all me and Finnias all him? Is that a thing? Please tell me I'm all me. I really want to be able to sleep tonight."

"Let's talk," Rose said. "I can probably tell from there."

Duncan nodded. "Being the soul expert and all. Great. Lemme say goodnight to Gid, first."

They all said their goodnights. Max offered to help Jo get the shop in order. They grabbed Shay's hand before she could leave the room. "Do you want me to stay?"

"You have work in the morning," Shay reminded them.

"So do you." They shrugged. "I brought clothes. I can stay."

Hours before, she might have said no. But she just wanted to feel safe, even if it was an illusion. "Yeah. I'd like that. Can…I talk to Finnias while he's in the mirror?"

"…I'm not sure," Jo admitted. "You're free to try."

"Great." She took the mirror with her up to the room, changing into her pajamas even though she really wanted to ignore that she was still damp and immediately try. She cradled the mirror gently. It felt heavy and old, just like everything else in the house. The oil on the surface was still glowing. She wondered if it was that way for anyone else, or if they just saw a greasy mirror.

"Hey, Finnias," she said. "I don't know if you can hear me."

The glow remained steady. There was no answer. The mirror just reflected her exhausted face.

"Well, if you can, and even if you can't…I'm sorry," she said. "And…I'm really glad you're back."

CHAPTER 12: HALLOWEEN

A soft scratching, somewhere far away.

Shay turned to find the source, and a faceless ghost reached for her. She jerked away.

And banged her shoulder on the floor hard enough to wake up.

"Ow! Ow ow ow stupid original wooden floors stupid Victorian piece of—" She took a minute to untangle herself. Most of the blanket had been pulled off the bed with her.

Sunlight flowed across the floor, gleaming off the wood. It was Halloween.

The day before had been one of the busiest she ever had in the shop. Jo promised her Halloween itself would be worse.

People were afraid. Shay could understand, but it didn't mean she enjoyed helping them find the perfect candle.

Max was already gone. They'd left her a little note with a bad doodle of themself and a heart. 'See you after work! Have a great day!' They'd shown up right after work the day before and helped Jo dye her hair a fresh dark purple.

Jo wanted to give Finnias the day before he possessed Duncan. Something about finding his footing. Shay didn't think time really mattered to a ghost, but she had no choice but to agree and continue to try talking to the mirror. So far it hadn't yielded any results. She was sort of hoping he couldn't hear her, because she was probably starting to sound insane, like someone who kept texting despite the lack of replies.

But she wanted answers. She didn't know if he had them, but she had to make sure that the spirit charmer wasn't lying before she talked to Duncan. Or anyone else.

Jo was already at the kitchen table, typing away on her tablet. She was completely ready for the day, in jeans and a sweater, her hair pulled back. Shay was still in flannel pajama bottoms and an ugly library t-shirt she'd stolen from Duncan's stash.

"Do you ever sleep?" Shay slumped across from her.

"On the rare occasion I do, I have nightmares," Jo said. "How about you?"

"You, y'know." Shay waved one hand. Jo had probably heard her fall out of bed. The old house was many things. Soundproof was not one of them. "I like your hair."

"Thanks." Jo brushed a strand behind her ear. The color really did suit her.

"So. Busy day?

"Very busy," Jo said.

Shay sighed and draped herself over the table. "What happened to me hiding in my room?"

"You can hide in the shop," Jo said. "Max and I refreshed the wards, it should be perfectly safe."

Shay groaned. "Did you really have to do that?"

"I have to drive out to meet a client but I'll be back before the afternoon." Jo ignored her whining. "Don't forget to wear the costume I got you."

"I have to wear a costume?" Shay made a face. "Wait, what costume did you get me? Sexy witch? Sexy nun? Sexy pumpkin?"

"Sexy Mailman." Jo grinned. "No, not really, it's cat ears and a tail. I thought it would be cute, since I'll be a witch…it's corny, isn't it."

"Aww no, that is cute." Shay was just relieved she didn't have to wear something too ridiculous. "Glad that's all it entails. Let's start the meowvalous day. Everything has to be purrfect."

"I should have known." Jo groaned.

"Don't be catty, Jo. You named your magic book shop Spellbound." Shay grinned at her.

Jo sighed. "You have a point."

"But seriously, I totally got this. Lavender for ghosts, garlic for vampires, silver for werewolves—"

"Wormwood," Jo corrected her.

"Say what now?"

"It's wormwood for werewolves," Jo said.

Shay paused for a moment. "Wait, are you telling me werewolves are real?"

"I'm not not telling you that." Jo smiled and picked up her coffee cup.

"That's not funny," Shay told her. "Not even a little bit."

Duncan walked in. He looked tired, Shay was pretty sure he hadn't been sleeping at all. "What's not funny?"

"Werewolves are maybe real," Shay said.

"Awoo." Duncan wiggled his fingers at her. "Good morning, Jo. Butthead. Oh, thank God, coffee."

"You're welcome," Jo said. "I can't always promise to be a kind and benevolent god."

"Hey, as long as there's coffee." Duncan poured himself a mug and held it in his hands. "So, tonight after work I can…Finnias it up? Rose said our little session last night didn't fix our little problem, which is highly annoying and I'd like a refund."

"It might be because he was just trapped in his own memories," Jo said. "We'll find out more tonight, I'm sure."

"Great, because I started reading that book, and Hansy boy is…dense," Duncan said. "Lots of words that don't mean anything at all. And I enjoy research! I read dry academic papers for leisure! So unfortunately, Shay is right and Finny boy is probably going to be our best bet."

"Which one is unfortunately?" Shay asked.

Duncan ignored her. "Are you guys coming to the library thing or…?"

"Oh the P.E.I.R.S. thing!" Shay gave Jo her absolute best puppy eyes. "Can we? It's a movie. And I'm in it! Kind of."

"Technically it's a stitched together video of evidence of ghosts," Duncan said. "And not a particularly good one, from what I understand. But hey, might be a good time. We're going to have a costume contest, too. Be glad I can't enter, I would win."

"Uh huh." Shay had no idea what Duncan's costume was, but knowing him, he'd bought it the night before off the rack. "But seriously, I think you and Max could keep me safe, and we'd come home right after."

"We'll see how things are looking when it gets closer," Jo said. "When does it start?"

"At eight. There's going to be donuts but with candy spiders on them," Duncan said.

"You don't look like you have any candy spiders on you," Shay said.

Duncan fake laughed. "Wow, Shay, you're hilarious. Anyway, come if you want apple cider and old-fashioned Halloween games."

Jo nodded. "We'll be here until about nine, so if things are calm…"

"Yes," Shay said. Duncan always put together great fantastic events for the library, especially for Halloween, but she'd never been able to attend. Max talked incessantly about the murder mystery party he'd thrown the year before.

"No hard feelings if you can't, it's not my finest work, and Vic's going to be there so Gideon already bounced," Duncan said. "But, y'know, if he bounced permanently I wouldn't blame him. It's a low gravity moon type situation here."

"Only because he's over the moon for you," Shay said.

"Aww you can be sweet, Shay Shay," Duncan said. "Did he say anything?"

"Maybe," Shay said. "Maybe not. What's it worth to you, Donuts?"

"I think I have some cash somewhere…"

"You, eat food before you go." Jo used her mug to point at Duncan, then to Shay. "And you, go get ready, we're opening soon."

"I'll be at 100% cat-pacity before you know it."

Busy didn't really fully explain how the day went. The store was packed from the moment Shay opened the store to when she finally closed for a quick dinner and set up for Halloween events. Jo helped when she could, but she was in and out of the shop taking care of other things.

Shay leaned against the doorway. "Oh my god. That was awful. The worst day ever."

"So bad you've stopped making cat puns," Jo said.

"Mewver." Shay put a hand to her heart, pretending to be offended. In addition to the cat ears and tail, she had a black turtleneck and Jo had drawn a triangle nose and whiskers on her face. There had been gloves, but she couldn't work the register well enough with them on. "Now we prepare for kidlets. Right?"

"Don't worry, your entire job is passing out candy." Jo patted her shoulder.

"Oh, thank god," Shay said. "I mean, my pawsome costume is probably better at helping the kids. But what about the other thing? The big event. I mean. I work here, so…"

Jo's eyebrows rose. "How's your cartomancy?"

"I know what that is," Shay said. "And that's about it."

"Then I think that's going to be all me. Help me set it up."

They got out the table Jo used for group readings, draping it with a cloth embroidered with moons and stars, matching the hem of Jo's witch dress. Shay hadn't dressed up once in college, no one else really had, so she had to admit it was a little fun.

Dusk settled outside, the lights coming on up and down the street. Max parked in the back and came in through the kitchen entrance. They were dressed as a cowhand, complete with the hat.

"Meowdy, pawdner." Shay tipped their hat for them.

"That's sheriff to you." They made their badge flash in the light. There was glitter on it that Shay was pretty sure was not from the original costume. "Watch it or I'll put you in the clink."

"Somehow I don't believe you," she said. "But nice costume. I'm meowed. It's the cat's pajamas."

"Yeah, that's enough of that."

"Are you pawsitive? I have meowr."

Max ignored her. "Jo, you look great."

"Thank you." She smiled. "And thank you for agreeing to help. I'm not good with kids. At all."

"No problem." Max smiled. "I'm glad to help, and I love kids. They're weird and fun."

"You're weird and fun," Shay told them. "C'mon, Jo made fifty million rice krispie treats with chocolate and she said we could have the ones that don't meet her standards."

It was a quiet night, spiritually. No mist hugged the ground, no glow came from the street.

The physical world was more hectic. Lots of kids with buckets and pillowcases begging for candy. Max complimented each costume. Shay let more people into the shop than she thought was allowed under fire code, but none of them stayed long. The readings were all short, more to pique the curiosity of their guests and get them coming in for more.

Shay's phone rang and she checked it, but she didn't recognize the number. She silenced it and didn't think anything of it. It was either spam or someone finally replying to one of the thousand job applications she'd put in over the months she'd been staying with Duncan.

Until they left a voice mail.

She frowned and stepped into the kitchen to listen to it.

"Hi, um." A young woman's voice crackled though the speaker. "Shay O'Brannon? This is Kylee Miles. I um. I work at the library? Your brother has you as his emergency contact. You need to call me back."

Her stomach dropped.

She dialed the number back immediately, but a three toned beep sounded and a woman's voice came through. "We're sorry. The number you have reached is no longer in service. Please check the number and dial again."

She tried again. The same message. She tried Duncan's cell after that.

"This is Duncan!"

"Duncan, I—"

"And I am not here right now! Aha leave a message!"

"Ugh!" She yelled as the phone started directing her on how to leave a message. Once it finally beeped she was livid. "You stupid jerk! Call me! Right now!"

She hung up and called the direct line to the library.

The same three toned beep. The same message.

She texted him asking what was wrong. It was delivered, but not read.

"Dunc, c'mon." She hissed, stabbing at the screen with one fingertip in an attempt to convey her sense of urgency. The line at the library was still down. So was the number Kylee called from. Duncan wasn't answering his phone.

It was supposed to be okay now. She'd saved Finnias. She would refuse the spirit charmer. They'd find Arlo.

She should have known it wouldn't be that easy. Of course the spirit charmer would go after people she cared about.

"Is everything okay?" Jo stepped into the kitchen. "...Shay?"

"Here." She played the message back for her. "And I couldn't call back, or call any of the library numbers. Duncan isn't answering."

"...Okay. Let's call Gideon," Jo said. "Maybe he's heard something."

"Right." She dialed Gideon, trying to stay calm, but her fingers were shaking. Jo took the phone from her.

"Hi, Gideon, it's Jo," she said after a moment. "Have you talked to Duncan at all? I see. We had an...interesting message from the library and I wanted to make sure...no, no I'm sure it's fine. I'm going to head over there just to put our minds at ease. Thank you."

She handed the phone back to Shay. "He hasn't heard anything. I'll head over right now, you two can handle the shop until close, right? Nine o'clock. Another half an hour. Please."

"Jo, I…" she wanted to scream. Jo was asking her to keep the shop open for a few curious people and a bunch of sticky kids who could have gotten candy in their own neighborhoods instead of gawking at the decorations that had been up since the beginning of October.

But it was Jo's place of business. It was important to her. Even if Shay wanted to smash her phone on the floor and tell her it wasn't fair. "…Okay."

"I know, I'm sorry." Jo put her hands on her shoulders. "It's going to be okay. All right? I'll call you as soon as I know what's going on."

Shay nodded. "Yeah. I know. I trust you."

She headed back into the shop where Max was telling a kid in a Captain America costume they looked awesome. They glanced at Shay, but didn't say anything until the kid scampered back to their parents on the sidewalk.

"What's happening?" they asked.

"Got a weird voice mail," Shay said. "Jo's looking into it."

"What kind of weird voice mail?" Max frowned.

Shay couldn't play the voice mail again. "Something about Duncan and me being his emergency contact."

"Is he okay?" Max put a hand on her shoulder.

"I don't know, he's not answering." Frustration leaked into Shay's voice. She cleared her throat. "But Jo asked me to hold down the fort so here I am. Pinning it down. Keeping it held. How are things here?"

Max still looked concerned. "Okay. Plenty of candy and treats left. Some of these kids have been kind of weird."

"Werewolf weird?"

"What? No," Max said. "I don't know. They're off. But I deal with the same kids every day so maybe I'm just good with those kids."

"Kids love you. It's Halloween, they're hyped up on sugar," Shay said. "But, y'know, it's kind of a weird year, with the ghosts and…everything else. Maybe they're just scared. Halloween is going to be wild from now on."

"You being a believer is still kind of weird," Max said.

She laughed, even if it was strained. "You'll be happy to know I think Mothman is a barred owl.

"Aww c'mon, that's one of the fun ones."

"Owls are fun."

"They're really not."

The half hour dragged on. She kept checking her phone, slowly wearing down the battery and not doing much else.

Five minutes before they closed Jo sent a text message. 'Come to the library. Now.'

The nervous energy had sent her fingers tapping on the screen made her pulse rocket in her temples and for a moment it was all she could hear. She let Jo know they were on their way.

She looked at Max. "Any trick or treaters out there?"

"No, looks clear," they said. "Why?"

"We have to go to the library."

Chapter 13: Authentic Pirate Garb™

Shay tried to call Jo, but all she got was a generic voice mail message. She hung up and flopped back against Max's car seat

"Nothing?" Max asked.

She wanted to say something biting and sarcastic, but she knew it wouldn't be helpful and swallowed it down. Max didn't deserve it. "No. Maybe we should call Gideon? Or Rose?"

"If you think it'll help," Max said.

"If they could help Jo probably already texted them," Shay sighed.

"Hey, there's no ambulance, no big crowd, whatever it is, it's probably not very serious." Max put a hand on hers. Their fingers were cold. She'd been so focused on herself, she hadn't thought about how anxious Max must have been, but they were still there.

"You're right, sorry." She leaned back into the seat and breathed, making sure to keep a hold of the strap of her bag. "Maybe it's nothing. Maybe Duncan...cut himself with a box cutter again. Or a bookshelf fell on him and he's shaken up. Okay, they're bolted to the floor, that's not likely but...you know, he needed four stitches. For the box cutter. And I was eight hours away. What did he think I was going to do?"

"Drive back in your imaginary car and tell him he's an idiot," Max said.

She found herself laughing, despite herself. "That sounds like me. I guess I could have called you to tell him he's an idiot"

"Next time," they said.

"Yeah." She pulled the bag into her lap.

"What's in the bag?"

"Finnias's room," she said. "Which is what I'm calling the mirror. I figured...better safe than sorry."

She'd wrapped it in two towels before putting it in Duncan's padded laptop bag. She hoped it would be enough. She didn't know what would happen to him if the mirror cracked.

"That's a good idea," Max agreed. They pulled into the library's parking lot. It was a big, solid building of rusty red brick and reflective windows. The upper levels were dark, but yellow lights seeped through the gaps of the blinds on the ground floor.

"Thanks. For being here." She reached over and flicked the brim of their hat. "But if you do have a revolver or something, now's the time to tell me."

"Sadly, I am a peaceful sheriff, no guns for me." Max patted her hand.

"How do you plan to throw anyone in the clink without a gun?"

"I'm a witch cowhand, obviously."

She breathed in, then out. "Okay. I'm calm. Do I look calm?"

"As a cucumber."

"Thanks, you too." She forced a smile.

They walked down into the entrance. A bunch of kids were leaving and they squeezed around them.

Inside it was almost disturbingly normal. A big screen set up above the circulation desk had the investigation projected onto it. Vic was sitting in front of a group of teenagers, telling them about the history of the building. He didn't notice them.

Duncan walked into the room a moment later and Shay could have cried. He waved a plastic sword at them and swaggered up in a cheap pirate costume. The parrot attached to his shoulder swayed drunkenly. "Welcome to the Librarrrrry. I didn't expect you guys for a while, glad Jo let you out of your carrier."

"What the heck, Donuts?" She glared at him. "Bad taste is not a medical emergency. Not even a little bit. Where's Jo? Did she want me to see this and mock you? Consider yourself mocked."

"Says the person with the laziest costume here. At least Max has a cool hat. And what are you talking about?"

Duncan asked. "I haven't even seen Jo. I was giving a haunted tour. Do you want one? They're only five bucks and it goes to a super good cause. My job! I was going to man the projector but I broke it so I guess they feared my lack of technological prowess more than my sense of humor."

"There you are," Jo walked over. Her dress looked weird when paired with her jacket. "They sent me after the tour, but I think I got turned around…what are you two doing here?"

"You texted me," Shay held up her phone.

"I did not." Jo dug around her enormous tote bag for a moment and frowned. "My phone…"

"Okay, is someone going to explain, or do I have to extrapolate based on context clues?" Duncan asked.

"Your coworker called and said there was a medical emergency," Max explained. "But we couldn't get a hold of you or anyone, so Jo came, and she told us to head over, soooo we did. And now we're here. Aaaand this is bad, huh?"

"My super authentic and completely accurate pirate garb does not have any pockets, which I know I find it odd, too, but maybe they hadn't been invented yet, but I digress this is why my phone is in my locker," Duncan said.

"Your stupid costume is why we're here?" Shay asked. "I hate it even more than I already did."

Duncan grinned. "Oh, I see, this aggression towards my totally amazing and definitely not bought at the last minute from the clearance rack costume is misplaced because you were worried about me. Aww Shay Shay, I wuv you, too. And, you must have called the wrong number, because our phones are working just—"

He leaned over the counter and picked up the phone with a flourish. His expression fell. "Not fine. Not at all, actually. Hm. Okay, I'll call that weird. Who called you, exactly?"

"One of the blond ones?" Shay had been so concerned she'd forgotten the name entirely.

"There are so many blond ones, you'll have to be more specific." He clicked the hook a few times, holding the receiver loosely in one hand.

"Kylee Miles," Jo siad.

"Oh, yeah, she's blonde, but went off to college," Duncan said. "So I don't know why she'd be calling you about—"

A burst of static emitted from the phone, followed by a loud shriek. Duncan slammed the receiver down and took a step back.

The lights went out.

People screamed, more out of surprise than actual fear. The projector shut down and a scene of Duncan moving through the theater seats, eyes eerie in the night vision, played on the open laptop next to it.

"Woah, everyone stay calm!" Vic yelled over the crowd. "Probably the breaker! Nothing to worry about!"

"Library patrons! Please head to the main exit in an orderly fashion!" Duncan didn't so much yell as project his voice. "You can see the exit sign from here. Nothing to worry about, but this is not part of our scheduled Halloween festivities!"

People filed out, some faster than others. Duncan grabbed two flashlights from behind the desk.

"Jo, you're an honorary librarian now." He handed her one and clicked on his own. "Max, get Shay out of here."

"I'm not going anywhere," Shay said.

"I gotta make sure no one got back in the stacks, and we had a tour group upstairs," Duncan said. "This is my job, Shay."

"I know, I'm not stopping you," Shay said. "But I'm going."

She wasn't letting him out of her sight. Not after he'd been kidnapped once already. And definitely not after she'd almost gotten him killed in Finnias's memory loop.

"No, you're not," Duncan said. "If this is a ghost thing, you'll be in trouble, and I'll have a split focus."

She hated that he was right. "But—"

"Shay, we should go," Max said.

Tears stung her eyes but she refused to cry. "Right. Okay. Be careful. Yes, yes, I know, your middle names."

"Careful safe," he said. "Or was it safe careful? Either way, I got it covered."

Vic joined them before Duncan and Jo could leave. He still had the man bun and thick rimmed glasses, but it had only been a week and a half. "Hey, what's going on? Do you guys need help?"

"Nah, just a power thing." Duncan gave him a vague handwave. "You should head out. With Shay and Max here.

Shay shot him a venomous look, but he didn't see it

"Oh, hey, guys!" Vic grinned at them. "Been a bit, glad you found this wily guy here. Bit of a scare, am I right? Kind of like right now. I'll get you out, safe and sound."

"Right," Shay said. She slipped the bag off her shoulder and held it out to Duncan. "Here."

"What's this?" He grabbed the handle. "What do you have in here, bricks?"

"Um, it's Finnias's," she said, trying to be vague. Duncan's eyes widened. "Just in case, right?"

"That…was a good idea," Jo said. "But don't worry, I'll take care of him."

Duncan spluttered a half-denial and they headed out into the atrium.

"Let's go," Max said. "It doesn't feel great in here."

"Yeah, kinda heavy," Vic agreed. Shay hoped he didn't wait with them until Duncan and Jo came out. He was a nice enough guy, but she was already on edge, and she didn't want to spend more time with anyone who didn't know the full gravity of the situation than she had to. "Follow me, kids. Well, cat and cowboy."

"Cowhand," Max said.

"Or just sheriff," Shay added.

The first floor of the library was empty. Their steps rang hollowly on the atrium floor. Vic pushed on the front door. Nothing happened. He frowned and tried again.

The door didn't budge.

"Maybe it's a pull?" Max suggested.

"No, it won't open." Vic stepped back and put his hands on his hips, glaring at the door.

"Okay." Shay tried to squash down her rising panic. There wasn't any mist. The only sound was the water from the koi pond in the atrium. "I'm not seeing anything, but you had a bad feeling and you're good at feelings and…we're fine, right?"

"Woah, calm down there, kitten," Vic said. Shay honestly could have punched him. She considered it. "Let's all chill out for a moment, okay? Only a wonky door. I'm sure Jo and Duncan will be back, and they'll have another way out."

"I have some stuff." Max held up their bag. "If all else fails. Do you have one of your bad plans?"

"First, I'm offended. Second, maybe. There's a side exit." She tried to remember the library's floor plan. She had come here often enough to get out of the apartment and use the marginally faster wifi. "Over there, other side of the children's section."

"See? There you go." Vic smiled. It wasn't comforting, the red exit light made his face cadaverous. "Let's head that way."

"The uh. Children's section isn't the best," Max said. "Any other exits?"

"The basement," Shay said. "There's a loading dock? But I don't know exactly where or how to open it. And the basement is super creepy.

She'd only been down there once or twice, but it had been more than enough

"Side exit it is." Max pulled out their own flashlight and handed it to her.

The children's section was a square of space surrounded by dark shelves. The spaces between deep in shadow, even with the light. She turned and shrieked, jumping away from a bear. Not a bear, a horrible statue looming over the tiny poofy seats for little kids.

"What! What happened?" Vic swung his own light around wildly.

"Oh my god." She could feel her pulse in her fingers. "Oh my god Honey Bear almost killed me."

The flashlight gleamed off of the ancient, solidified hot glue that was supposed to be honey dripping from the bear's sharp claws and glinted off of the tiny, soulless eyes. The statue had been festooned with glow in the dark cobwebs and plastic spider rings.

"Oh," Vic did not sound impressed.

"To be fair, Honey Bear is scary, even in the daytime," Max said.

A long, low moan echoed from the depths of the building. Cold air rushed over them, sending their hair fluttering. It smelled like an open grave.

"What was that?" she swung her flashlight around.

"It's the building settling," Vic said. "Let's go."

She was frozen to the spot. It was cold, much colder than it should have been. "I don't—"

Mist poured between the stacks, violent in its suddenness. It swirled around them. Max pulled out a sachet and poured a ring of salt around them. It pushed back the mist. "It's not fancy, but it works. Let's wait here until Duncan and Jo get back."

"I hate to ask this now, but what's the library haunted with?" she asked.

"Um, supposedly the children's section was built over an old cowhand cemetery," Max said. "Along with a woman and her baby. Um. I think there's been reports of crying and sightings of tall, dark shadows."

"And, once or twice, full apparitions in cowboy outfits," Vic said. "Not too weird for this area, but they disappear. We've been wanting to do an investigation here forever, but they wouldn't let us. Something about a deal with that guy who bought the new wing."

Dark shadows moved between the shelves. A book slid out and fell to the floor with a dull thud. Followed by another. Shay squeaked and stepped closer to Max. Her skin crawled, goosebumps covering her arms.

"Holy crap." Vic was filming, of all things. Shay supposed she couldn't blame him. "Are you guys seeing this?"

Books fell to the floor, tipping out of the shelves. A cart upended, scattering picture books. They inched across the carpet towards their circle, pages fluttering.

"Shay?" Max looked at her.

She squinted. "Just shadows, so far, nothing concrete. Max-"

"How are you not seeing anything?" Vic didn't even spare her a glance. "This is intense! You guys aren't doing this with fishing line, are you?"

"No!" Shay and Max said at the same time. The books converged in all directions, some tumbling end over end, others sliding across the carpet. Max pulled a candle out of their bag and tried desperately to light it, the lighter clicking and sparking.

"C'mon," they murmured. "Oh, c'mon, if this was going to work any time let it be now, please—"

The flash light flickered and died as the first book slid into the circle.

Chapter 19: Brilliant

The air froze.

Mist swirled up into a tall, thin figure. A skeleton. For a moment she thought of a pinstripe suit and a top hat, but the thing filled out, flesh forming on the bones into something that looked like a half-formed person. It lunged for Shay. She stumbled over a pile of books and onto a low table, banging her hip against the edge and landing flat on her back.

A hand with sharp finger bones jutting from the translucent flesh reached for her. She squeaked and rolled under the table. Another hand grabbed her ankle and yanked her out, despite her scream and attempt to catch her fingers on the short carpet. It loomed over her, holes for eyes and an uneven tear for a mouth that left its jawbone and teeth visible.

Max yelled and took a swipe at it. Their unlit candle passed harmlessly through it.

The face leered down at her. Shay focused everything she had into punching it, as hard as she could.

No spark. No flame. Her knuckles slid off of the ghost's cheekbone, leaving her knuckles coated in blue residue, so cold it burned. The ghost jerked away, long enough she could scramble to her feet. She wiped her hand on her jeans, but the cold lingered.

"Shay! Get over here!"

When had she gotten so far away from Max? More figures rose from the mist, their limbs spindly and long, joints bent the wrong way. They'd filled the space between them, making the ten or so feet as impassible as an ocean.

"Max!" She started forward, but they all turned to look at her at once.

"I almost have it!" They were still fumbling with the lighter. "C'mon, c'mon…"

Vic swung his phone around. "I've never seen anything like this! Shay, try to communicate!"

"I don't think they want to talk!" Shay barely ducked under a swing. She shook her hands, willing anything to happen. "C'mon, please work. Please!"

Nothing. Her fingers had gone numb from the cold and dark blue ghost mark blooming across her knuckles.

"Look out!" Max yelled.

She looked up just as a long, crooked limb swung at her. She barely ducked under it. Another swipe knocked her into one of the kiddie poofs and right over it, landing on the carpet again. Sharp fingernails scraped at her jacket and she rolled onto her hands and knees crawling back to the shelves. She grabbed a low shelf that was devoid of books and used it to haul herself to her feet.

An arm made of shadow slid around her middle, pinning her to the shelf, so fast the air exploded from her lungs. She couldn't breathe. A long hand with too many fingers filled her vision, each ending in wicked points. A great roar filled her ears.

Vic yelled something but the words didn't make sense.

Max lit the candle, a tiny spot of orange in a sea of blues. The light flared, brighter than any votive candle ever should have. The flame billowed up to the ceiling and scorched the tiles. The same burst of light hit the ghosts and they screamed, horrifically as one, shifting to shadows and vanishing all together.

The temperature rocketed back up to normal library cold. The air hit Shay's lungs and she started coughing, sliding to the floor.

"...What was that?" Vic was halfway towards her. He turned to Max, who fumbled with the candle before getting it into a tiny metal lantern. They put it on the table and hurried to her side, helping her back to her feet. Something had knocked their hat off, leaving it dangling at their back by a string around their neck.

"Are you okay?"

"Holy crap, Max," she said when her voice finally worked again. "That was brilliant."

"Just…a little thing Jo showed me. I didn't expect it to work. Wait, was that a pun?" Max's face fell. "That was a pun."

"Now you're illuminated," Shay said.

"Wow, Shay. Just wow."

"I think you mean meow."

"Sure." They fixed her cat ears, which she had completely forgotten she was wearing, and took her hands and inspected them, running a thumb over her knuckles. "Ouch, this looks bad."

The mark was such a dark blue it was almost black.

"Honestly, my hip feels worse," she said. She could feel the bruise forming there. Her hand was just numb. "Stupid books. Stupid table."

Vic clicked his tongue. "That looks like frostbite. We should get you to the hospital, and quick."

"It's not, it's bruises. And from my makeup," Shay lied. She couldn't be certain, but she could feel the heat from Max's hands, so it must have been a ghost mark. She hoped.

"Still think we should at least get you into the clinic, I'll give you a ride," he offered.

"I'm fine, thanks. ...Are you okay?" She supposed she could at least be polite, even if she really didn't want to.

"I'm great!" Vic said. "Got some amazing footage. I can't believe they attacked you, Shay. That was an incredibly rare encounter, I've never seen a spirit get so riled up. Was there a reason? Did you do something?"

"Messed with an ouija board," she said.

"In a cemetery," Max added.

"Oh yeah, that'd do it." Vic nodded. "You know, I know a great medium that could probably help you out."

"I'll keep that in mind," Shay said.

"Y'know, Vic, I think you should head to the entrance and make sure everyone gets out," Max said. "Direct them to the side door. We'd better let Jo and Duncan know the front door is...stuck."

"Oh, yeah, that's great idea!" Vic nodded, his bun bobbing drunkenly. "You guys going to be okay? She's looking a little rough."

"She will be fine." Shay wasn't so sure, but what choice did she have? The night was far worse than she'd expected, and if she got to the side door and it didn't open, everyone else would be trapped inside. Better to have Jo along, who could probably at least get the door open.

Vic asked again if they would be okay, most likely out of some sense of obligation, but there were a few people in the atrium. They left him to direct them to the side door, heading up the stairs next to the koi pond.

"I hope it doesn't freeze," Shay said. "Poor fishies."

"Yeah," Max agreed.

She elbowed them, gently. "That was seriously amazing back there. How did you do that?"

"All I did was use a spell Jo taught me for emergencies." Max shrugged. "I think they were particularly susceptible to light, so I mostly got lucky, but maybe I am a witch, after all."

"You're definitely a witch," she said. "Best one ever. Calling it now."

"Sure. Honestly, I was terrified, I'm just glad it worked," Max said. They reached the second floor. Max held up their lantern. It didn't provide nearly enough light, but Shay's flashlight was dead and her phone battery was sucked dry. "I'm still terrified, actually. My anxiety has gotten to the point where I'm only vaguely feeling things? My resting heart rate is a panic attack. But hey, it'll keep me on my toes. Probably."

"I've got your back," Shay said. "For what it's worth. I don't get why that punch didn't do anything. I was lighting ghosts up back…last week. Then. Maybe Duncan's stupid dense book has answers."

Or maybe there were no answers, and she was just stuck being grabbed by ghosts without being able to do anything about it.

"I hope so," Max said.

"Besides, we'll find Arlo tomorrow, Jo thinks he's going to be a big help, so…tomorrow. Just have to…survive all of this first."

She gestured to indicate the entire library. As if in response, another cold, low moan rippled through the building. It sounded like it was coming from the basement, and she didn't want to think too hard about that. She had only been down there a few times, mostly for book sales, and even in the middle of the day and full of people it was dark and cold.

"Shay um…" Max turned to her. She could make out their face but couldn't read their expression. "Hey, I know this isn't a great time, but um. Can I ask you something?"

"No time like the present, because it's a gift," Shay said. Her insides tilted to the left, unsteady and scared. Something had shifted, ever since the governor's house. She'd been trying to carry on like normal, more or less successfully, but she was scared. She was keeping things from Max, which already felt strange, but there was the possession, and everything else. She knew it was causing a rift and she didn't know how to stop it. "So…what's up?"

"Are we okay?" Max asked. Her stomach plummeted. It was definitely the question she'd been afraid of. "Things have been. I dunno. Kinda off? Are you mad at me?"

"What?" Shay had not expected the second part of the question. "Of course I'm not mad at you. Why would I be?"

"Just…" They fidgeted with the lantern. "You um. If you weren't with me, you probably wouldn't have gotten…all of this, and none of this would have happened. So. If you were mad at me, I would understand. I also understand if this is not the time or the place or—"

"Max, no," she said. "Have you been…thinking that this whole time?"

They nodded.

She was a crappy friend. She'd been so caught up in everything about her, she hadn't really actually stopped to consider how Max was feeling. They were her best friend, the person she cared about more than anything, and she'd just taken for granted that they were there. "Oh geez. Okay. I don't blame you at all. You're the only thing keeping me somewhat sane in all of this craziness. It's not your fault."

"Then…is something else wrong?" Max asked.

"I mean, not…not because of you," she said. "There are so many things wrong, but none of them are you."

Max took her hand. She hadn't realized she was clenching her fist so hard that her nails were digging into her palm until their touch forced her to relax. "You know you can talk to me, right?"

"I know! I know I just…I'm so scared," Shay admitted. "All the time. Because everything is so different now, and I just want things to be normal, and I'm scared they won't be. And your show and…and…"

She couldn't talk about them being possessed. She just couldn't. That wasn't their fault, and it wasn't fair to put it on them.

"And I'm a necromancer."

That hadn't been what she meant to say, but it came out, anyway.

"…Oh." Max blinked, like it wasn't a big deal. "Okay. Yeah. I mean, dead things, you make them solid. Yeah, that tracks."

She pressed her lips together and inhaled, slowly, trying to keep calm. "I've been freaking out about it and it's just…okay yeah?"

"Why are you freaking out about it?" Max must have seen something on her face because they backtracked quickly. "I mean, you have every right to, I'm just trying to understand you're reasoning so we can work through it together."

"Nice save."

"Thanks, I try."

She looked down at their hands. Max wasn't a big person, she knew that, objectively, but their hand still engulfed hers. "I guess. I dunno. It sounds…evil? It's what the spirit charmer called me, and I know she's full of crap, but if she's one too, then…"

"Shay, you're not evil." Max let go of her to put their hand on her shoulder. "I think we've both been worried about things that we didn't need to be worried about."

"Yeah?" She forced herself to smile.

"I know." Max leaned down a bit. Their eyes glittered with the candlelight. For the first time in a while, she didn't automatically search for a glint of something else. It was Max, only them, and she knew they'd never hurt her. "It's just a name, and you're about the furthest from evil I know. So you can see ghosts now, so what? You're still my best friend. I still think the world of you."

"You could be biased against my evilness," she joked.

"Oh, definitely," they said. "But I'm also right."

Shay let her head drop onto their shoulder, just for a second. She hadn't realized how badly she needed the conversation to happen, even if the timing wasn't ideal. For the first time in days she felt completely safe, even if it was just for a moment, and a complete illusion. "You are. Always. Thanks, Max. We good?"

"We are awesome." Max pulled her into a one armed hug. "We should go find your brother before Vic tries to find us."

"Ugh."

Max laughed, and it sounded easier than it had all week. The difference was so obvious to her, she couldn't understand how she hadn't noticed before.

"You know how I said you could join P.E.I.R.S.? Well, I changed my mind. You can't now. He's awful," Shay said, just to get them to laugh again. "Completely unlikable when he's not behind a camera. And he has a man bun. I wasn't going to hold it against him but now I am. Plus, the glasses? And what is Vic short for, anyway. Victor? Terrible."

"I love how petty you are." Max grinned. "Well. I don't see any lights, I think-"

A shape loomed out of the darkness. Shay shrieked and tried to punch it.

Max grabbed her shoulder and pulled her back before she did. "Woah! You scared us!"

It was a person. She'd come close to punching a normal person. A teenage boy, even. A girl clung to his arm, looking more scared of her than the library.

"Sorry!" The boy held up his free hand. "Dude, is that a lantern?"

"Yes." Max didn't elaborate. "Head downstairs, we're making sure everyone gets out."

"Right." The boy nodded.

"We just wanted some time alone," the girl said.

"It's fine, head on down," Max said. Once they were gone, Shay realized Max was trying hard not to laugh. She elbowed them, gently. "Sorry! Sorry it's funny. The noise you made. Their faces. That was incredible."

"We are in a dangerous situation right now," Shay reminded them.

"Like when that owl went for my face?"

She sighed. "You are never going to let it go, are you?"

"The heat death of the universe will come first," Max said.

Shay had to admit, it was kind of funny. "Okay, fine, you get to pull out the 'owl came for my eyes' card whenever you want. Now, as romantic as this horrifically haunted building is, we have to go find my brother. And my boss. See? Less romantic all the time. If only Gideon was here. We could have it be the trifecta of not sexy."

"And here I was about to pull out my really serious moves," Max said. "I don't think they're on this floor. Hopefully third floor is the charm?"

"Wow, so smooth, I'm in awe," Shay deadpanned, and they laughed. "Hopefully."

Mist curled down the steps, so dense on the top floor it was glowing. "...Or maybe hopefully not."

Chapter 15: Blanket Statement

"Shay, slow down!"

Shay couldn't slow down. She took the stairs two at a time.

The third floor was the reference level and outdated computer lab. A bank of clunky old monitors took up the area around the stairs. The stacks stretched back from there. She reached the top and had to stop. The outside lights poured giant rectangles of dim light across the ground, but only enough to make out the shapes of the computers, their silhouette made strange with Halloween decorations.

An eerie silence filled the air.

"It feels extremely bad up here," Max caught up to her. "Heavy and oppressive. What are you seeing?"

"Just mist," Shay reported, but the mist itself glowed in a way that made it hard for her to see anything else. "Not much else."

A sound, high and piercing. For a second, she thought it was a cat. Duncan's cat Becky made a similar noise when she was hungry.

Then she realized exactly what it was.

"Is that a baby?" she asked. "Please don't tell me that's a baby."

The crying rose and fell in volume, more despondent with each passing second.

"It sounds like a baby," Max said. "And if I'm hearing it, too…What on earth is it doing here?"

"I don't know, but we'd better go find it."

"What if it's a ghost baby?" Max asked.

"What if it isn't?" she countered.

It didn't sound ghostly. Even if there was the slightest chance it was a real baby, she had to find it.

Max nodded. "You're right, but we need to be careful."

"That's Duncan's middle name," she said.

"And yours is 'runs right into danger without thinking'?" Max suggested.

She frowned. "Bit of a mouthful, isn't it? Amazing it fit on my birth certificate. I'm shortening it to danger."

"I thought you might."

Their conversation stalled, but the crying continued.

They walked past the computer bank and deeper into the stacks, following the noise. The cries were so loud and hard there were great hiccuping gasps. Shay had little experience with babies, being the youngest, but what little maternal instinct she had drove her forward.

If it was a ghost, she didn't want to see it.

But she kept moving forward, mist swirling around her ankles. She expected to run into someone every time they reached the end of a shelf, but it was all long, empty rows, stretching out around them, barely visible in the mist and the stuttering light of the candle.

"Give me a second." Max put an arm in front of her to stop her. She thought, for a moment, they were going to tell her they needed to ignore the crying and get going. "We need a new candle, this one is going fast."

"Oh. I mean, yeah, okay."

Max swung their bag off and dug through it.

The crying was louder than ever, it had to be at the end of the shelf, right near the back wall. She would take a peek and scoot back over to Max.

She peered around the corner.

A white blanket was bundled under the window. The clouds moved enough that moonlight spilled into the room, shining on the material. A small shape moved under it. The crying turned quiet and thready.

She knew she should wait for Max, but she stepped forward anyway. The tiny fists and feet shifted the blanket.

It was a baby, but she couldn't tell if it was a living one.

Terror welled up in her, yet she stepped even closer, drawn in with absolutely no thought to how dangerous it was.

She crouched down. Her hand hesitated over the blanket. What would she find under the blanket? A living baby? A ghost? Something horrible and rotten?

The blanket caved in on itself and the crying stopped.

"Oh, thank god," she breathed. "Ghost baby. Definitely a ghost baby."

Cold air loomed behind her and the window went dark. A dragging noise filled the aisle behind her and she turned, slowly.

A woman stood behind her. She was a pale green that darkened towards her waist, her old-fashioned skirts vanishing into the mist. Her head was bowed, hair tangled over her shoulders.

Shay took a step back.

The ghost's head jerked up. Her eyes literally blazed with fire, her mouth a gaping hole. She reached for Shay with bony hands.

A spray of salt cut her in half and she vanished, revealing Max behind her. The blankets faded into the mist.

"Eugh, salt," Shay brushed the salt from her jacket. At least it had taken the brunt of the blow. "Thanks for the save."

"Next time, wait for me," Max said. "And I'm bringing matches. Or finding out how to light candles with my mind or something. Witches can do that. Probably. Ghost baby?"

"Ghost baby. Kind of," Shay said. The dragging sound flowed from the next aisle over. "And there's our cue, let's go."

"Right." Max nodded. They turned and stumbled, grabbing the shelf for support. Shay jerked forward, intent on helping them, but they were already straightening up. "Sorry, I think I might have overdone it a little. Maybe I don't want to be magic, after all."

"It's okay, take a minute." Shay tried to force down her panic. She'd been relying on Max too much. She took a step back and shook her hands again, willing anything to happen. "C'mon, please work."

The ghost swirled into existence at the end of the aisle.

"C'mon, c'mon." Despite her pleas, nothing changed. If she still had the ability, it wasn't working anymore.

The ghost moved in odd jumps and jerks, one moment she was at the end, the next she was halfway down, getting closer far too quickly. Max grabbed a sachet. She snatched it from their hand.

It had worked before.

She got ready to punch the ghost, but the aisle was empty.

She was behind Shay, grabbing her wrist. Shay tried to wrench her hand free but the grip was iron hard and much colder.

The ghost wrapped her other hand around her throat. Thin, delicate bones lightly touched her skin. A half rotted cheek pressed into hers, dull green hair spilling over her shoulder. She could still breathe, the sickly sweet stench of decay filling her lungs, making her dizzy.

"Shay!" Max grabbed another sachet but the ghost yanked her around so she was staring straight at them. They were more scared than she'd ever seen them.

"Don't worry, little hero, I won't hurt her," the ghost's voice was the whispering hiss of something slithering over dead leaves.

"Shay?" Max took a step forward. "What's she saying?"

"It's the spirit charmer." The voice was unfamiliar, but the cadences were the same. "I thinks she wants to talk."

"You got it." She sounded delighted. The fingers around her neck shifted and fluttered. "This ghost wants to hold onto you, Shay. Take everything you have and then some, steal your warmth and life and magic. She wants to feel something so badly, if only for a moment. And there's very little you can do to stop her. But with me, well…you're still alive, aren't you?"

"I'll punch this ghost out of existence—"

"But you would have already if it was working, wouldn't you have?" the spirit charmer laughed. It sounded like something was dying in her throat. "Face it, you don't know how this works. You're an untrained baby necromancer stumbling through haunted buildings, stirring up ghosts as you go."

"You're doing this," Shay said.

"I'm not!" She sounded delighted. "Oh, I'm not. All of these ghosts? This is your fault! Fantastic, isn't it? I don't even have to do anything. If you weren't hiding behind wards all the time, you'd be dead, but even they aren't strong enough to keep you safe, are they? You eat away at them without even meaning to. You have no idea how to control any of it. But I do. I've bested far better than you could ever hope to be. With me, you can learn how to use your abilities. I can keep you safe from ghosts.

Safer than this one can, look at them, they're already so tired and it's all your fault."

Bony fingers slid down her cheek, leaving thin trials of ice cold. She shuddered.

"What will you do when you're all alone? Do you want to find out?" the ghost's voice became a throaty whisper, thick and deep. "Or do you want to stop playing this silly game and join me? What will it be, Shay?"

She looked at Max. They had a candle in hand, their face determined, but the light made them look pale.

Tired.

It gave her the strength to say what she needed to. "I have until tomorrow, don't I?"

"I suppose you do," the ghost sighed. "Unless you get killed by the thing in the basement. You can ask Jo, she's nearby, but you know what she's going to say, right? If I'm right, and I am, the only way out is through the basement. Unless I help you."

"Did you orchestrate this whole thing to show me how helpless I am?" Shay asked.

She snorted. "No, don't flatter yourself. I didn't even call you here."

"Liar."

"I didn't! Someone else did the heavy lifting for me. Whether to test you or get you out of the way, well, we're going to find out." The spirit charmer sounded delighted. "Still, is it working? Are you realizing that you need me?"

"Tomorrow," Shay reminded her.

"Fine, if you insist. Just get through this, all right? But, I will give you a hint, because I'm so very generous. You are going in the right direction with that sachet. Might even save your life. Have fun, kids. Or don't. Toodles!"

The grip on her wrist loosened, enough she could yank her hand away, turned, and punched the ghost.

Her fist sunk into its abdomen and the ghost tried to back away, but Shay grabbed her hair and yanked her forward. Blue and green flames swirled over the ghost and she disappeared with a shriek so loud it shook a few books off of the shelves.

Shay dropped to her knees and Max followed her, grabbing her hands. Theirs weren't much warmer.

"Still got it," she said.

"Still got it," Max agreed.

This was her fault.

"I'm sorry."

"Shay, you never have to be sorry with me," Max shifted so her hands were held against their chest in and they pulled her closer, rubbing her back a little. Their heartbeat was the only thing keeping hers from trying to break through her ribcage. "I'm just a little tired. I'd do it again."

"It's my fault," her voice cracked. "All of these ghosts are stirred up because of me."

"You don't know that," Max said.

"It makes sense, though," she whispered. "And your wards aren't failing because of you. It's because of me. I…I don't know what to do. Maybe I should just join her."

"Nope." Max took a step back. "Shay, look at me."

She did. The candle was still lit, the lantern on the floor, just enough illumination she could tell they were scared and exhausted, but they were still with her. They weren't leaving.

"If that's what you want to do, then I won't stop you," Max said. "I'll come with you, even. But if you don't want to…we figure it out, okay?"

She nodded, calming down in degrees. "Sorry I kept stuff from you. Don't think I said that."

Max shook their head. "You don't have to tell me everything."

"I like telling you everything," Shay said. She always had.

"Still." Max was smiling, at least. A real smile. "Did she actually say anything useful or was it all mean gibberish?"

Shay barked out a laugh at that. "Wow. Sorry. That was…well, she said Jo was nearby."

"Then let's start there, and work on everything else."

A scream, way too close. It didn't sound human.

Shay pulled away from Max and got shakily to her feet, running towards the source of the scream. She reached the end of the row as light poured around a few shelves down.

She made it to the aisle and Jo threw salt at her. "Ow! Hey! It's me!"

Shay?" Jo stared at her.

"Ha, serves you right," Duncan said. His parrot was missing, leaving a ragged hole in his jacket. "I mean…what are you doing here? You guys look awful. Why didn't you go outside?"

Jo's lantern was brighter. Max was a little ashy and her hands were both dark blue. Her knuckles weren't any better, the mark so deep it was concerning

"We couldn't leave," Shay said. "I have it on…some admittedly pretty terrible authority we'll have to go to the basement."

"You guys didn't bring Vic, right?" Duncan peered behind them. "Or kill him?"

"Please, do I look like I want to be haunted by him?" Shay asked. "…I have an idea. Let me see the mirror."

"Why?" Duncan held the bag possessively. "What do you want with him? He's delicate."

"You're so dumb," Shay told him. "If he's so delicate let him possess you."

"I'm also delicate," Duncan said. "Precious cargo."

"If he can take enough energy from me he can see if there's any other way out of the library," Shay explained. It had to be something she could do. If she was going to be a necromancer, she might as well use those abilities to their fullest extent. "Or give us some insight. Or something. My…stuff isn't working, and Max is tired, and…I don't know what else to do."

He hadn't responded when she'd talked to him before, but that was behind wards. Maybe here, in a charged area, it would be different.

She had to try.

Max put their hands on her shoulders and she took a breath. Panicking wouldn't help, even if it was clawing through her chest and she wanted to scream until it went away.

"It's not a bad idea," Jo said. "But I don't know if he'll be able to."

"Please, let me try," Shay held out her hand. "Please."

"Fine." Duncan handed over the bag. "And don't be dumb. You're already pretty tired, don't let him drain you."

"I won't," she said. She had no idea if this was going to work, but she knew with absolute certainty she did not want to go to the basement. She opened the bag and pulled out the mirror.

Chapter 16: Rotten

The mirror glowed, faintly. Shay held it up and it showed her a small room. It wasn't the landing, or the room they'd originally found him in. It was older, the bed threadbare and the plain wallpaper peeling into curls. If Finnias was there, she couldn't see him, but at least she could see something besides her reflection.

"Mirror mirror in my hand?" she tried. "Who's the fairest in the land?"

"Really?" Duncan asked.

"You're right, silly question," Shay said. "It's obviously Max."

Max put a hand to their heart. "I will use this power only for good."

"That's a lie," Jo said. Max shrugged and nodded. "Please focus. Maybe Duncan should hold the mirror."

"Won't he just possess me?" Duncan asked.

"He might, but since you spent twenty minutes on the ground in a fetal position because the ghosts were so sad, I think it might be an improvement," Jo said.

Duncan's face darkened a few shades. "Okay. Yeah. I told you I'm delicate. This rememberancer stuff is hard. And a joke. My memory is crap, but I can see ghost memories?"

"Isn't that just the way," Shay said.

"Right? Anyway, no judgment or I will cry."

"Again," Max whispered, probably only loud enough for her to hear.

"No one was judging you." Shay struggled to keep a straight face when she handed him the mirror. "It does sound hard."

"It is, thank you." Duncan looked into the mirror. "Hey, Finn? You wanna uh. Join us?"

The mirror brightened.

Two white figures loomed behind Duncan. The same spirits Max had banished down in the children's section. They'd rebounded much quicker than she'd expected.

"Watch out!" Shay yelled. He was already sinking to his knees, long fingered hands reaching for him. One grabbed Shay's arm and she tried to shake it off. The cold sank through her jacket.

"They're so cold," Duncan murmured. "They're so—"

His eyes glowed, briefly. He stood up and swiped the mirror at the nearest apparition. It reared back. The next wasn't so lucky, hitting the surface of the mirror and being yanked into it with a shriek.

The other ghost vanished.

"Hey Finnias, thanks for the save." Shay rubbed her arm. The cold lingered like a stain.

"It's not a problem. Sorry about your mirror." He held it out to Jo. "I'm not sharing space with…whatever that was."

"Thanks," Jo didn't sound grateful. "Put it in the bag."

Shay grabbed the sleeve of the horrible pirate coat, ignoring the way the cheap polyester made her entire body want to recoil away. "Are you…okay?"

There was so much more she wanted to say, but apologies and explanations remained locked behind her teeth.

"Hm?" He looked up from setting the mirror back into the bundle of towels she'd made for it. "As well as I can be. I heard you, in the mirror. Unfortunately, your plan isn't going to work. I can't leave Duncan, not without…returning to where I was."

At least he'd been able to hear her.

"The landing," Shay said.

Finnias nodded. "But I can keep Duncan safe. I'm sorry, that's the best I can do."

"Good enough," Shay said. It wasn't the time for her to talk about everything she wanted to. "The spirit charmer says the only way out is through the basement. We couldn't get through the front doors, and I didn't want to get the side door stuck before anyone else got out…you guys could probably get out without me? But I don't know."

"No," Max said.

"Absolutely not," Jo added.

"Well, good, because I didn't want to be stuck in here by myself," Shay admitted. "Anyway, I don't think Duncan would be too happy with us breaking windows—"

"He's not," Finnias confirmed. How would it be, not having control of her own body, riding along while someone else took charge? She'd tried to ask Duncan, once, but he'd brushed her off with a terrible joke.

"To be fair, they're double paned and pretty tough, I think we'd have a hard time if we tried," Max said. "Do you have any idea what could be down there?"

"No," Finnias said. "Duncan says it's always cold. Always dark. Even during the library sales events. There's a strange smell, he doesn't know if it's regular basement mustiness. That's the only information I have. Jo would have better luck."

"I mean, you're not wrong." Jo nodded. "I'll try, but I can't guarantee anything. I suppose we shouldn't trust her, anyway. I'll check, as best as I can. Watch my back and stay quiet, hopefully this doesn't attract any of our…little friends."

"Got it." Max nodded.

Jo sat cross legged on the ground and pulled two candles out of her bag, putting them on either side of her and lighting them with a long match. She pulled out a vintage compact mirror, the silver casing adorned with flower details and gems, flashing bright colors. She opened it and held it loosely in her hands, closing her eyes and letting out of breath. A white circle of light drew itself in the carpet around her, barely visible.

She stared into the mirror.

Several minutes passed by and nothing happened. The candle flames were steady. Shay and Max sat down, leaning against each other. She wanted to ask if they were feeling better, but Jo needed quiet.

She wanted to talk to Finnias, too, but he was pacing, glancing down the aisle next to them.

"Something's coming," he said, softly, after what could have been hours but must have been only a few minutes. Shay had shifted at least five times and was currently half laying on the floor, propped up on Max's leg, discovering just how infrequently the bottom shelves were dusted.

"I'm close." Jo didn't look up from the mirror.

The candles guttered dangerously low. It had never been warm, but the temperature dropped so low her breath was visible.

"We have to go," Finnias said. "Now."

"I almost have it," Jo snapped. Finnias moved towards her and was forced to take a step back when the circle around her sparked.

Shay climbed to her feet and helped Max to theirs. There were footsteps down the aisle, getting closer. They were slow and deliberate, followed by a dragging sound.

Finnias glanced around the shelf and jerked back, pressing himself up against the books.

"What is it?" Shay moved down the aisle, but Finnias grabbed her arm before she could see. "Finn—"

"I don't know how it's here," he said, his voice plaintive. "I'm…I'm sorry. I think it followed me."

"What?" Max's voice squeaked. "What followed you?"

Rust bloomed across the metal of the shelf, the paint peeling and flaking, falling like snow. The books moldered, their covers curling, pages slipping between the cracks and littering the floor, brittle and yellow. The carpet beneath them unraveled to nothing, holes spreading over weathering and cracking floorboards.

"...Oh." Shay backed up a few steps.

"I got it." Jo snapped the mirror shut. "I found a way out, we have to—oh dear."

Long, clawed fingers curled around the edge of the shelf. It buckled towards them. Jo passed her hand over her candles and the flames went out. She got to her feet and grabbed her lantern, swinging it at the ghost.

The candle dwindled to nothing but a pile of wax. The frame of the lantern rusted, the glass covered in grime, cracking and snapping before the whole thing fell off the handle.

The faceless ghost from Finnias's memories peered around the shelf.

It was the gray stretched out shape from the tower room. The suit hung off of him in tatters, the limbs too long to be contained, the joints turned wrong. He took a step forward.

They were backed into a corner, a single dark window behind them.

Jo grabbed one of the candles and the wick burst back to life. She swung it like a sword, light and sparks crackling in a crescent that hit him in the chest. He stared down at it and Jo thrust the candle again. He grabbed it, the wax cracking.

Shay hit him with her shoulder, and he staggered against the half-broken shelf.

Finnias grabbed Jo's arm and yanked her out of the aisle.

Shay ran as fast as she could. The cold, the aching in her bones and her exhaustion were all washed away by a shot of terror-filled adrenaline. The shelves crumbled and warped around her, books falling from the shelves and thundering against the floor, keeping time with her footsteps.

She reached the computers. Their screens cracked and popped.

The emergency stairs were just ahead when Jo stumbled and fell. Finnias crouched next to her.

"Jo, get up—"

"I'm up." She coughed, breathed too deeply and coughed again. "I'm up, I swear."

Shay turned to face the ghost, holding up her fists, but nothing happened.

"C'mon!" Her eyes stung. Her friends were in danger, and she couldn't do anything. She could only stand helplessly while a horrific ghost bore down on them.

Not even a spark.

Finnias yanked her back by her hood as the ghost slammed a hand down right where she'd been, the carpet unraveling.

"Finnias."

The ghost's horrifying twistedness melted away, until it was a tall blond man with a neat mustache, wearing a vest and a carefully pressed shirt and pants, a suit jacket slung casually over his arm.

He didn't look like a ghost, not even out of the memory. He could have been a living, breathing person and she wouldn't have been able to tell the difference.

The rot and damage repaired itself instantly.

"That's quite the form you've chosen to take," he said. Shay backed up right into Max. He was the ghost that had possessed her friend, who had dragged her off to the spirit charmer. "Possession? Have you fallen so low?"

"You were possessing someone not very long ago," Finnias reminded him. His voice was cold, and he'd arranged Duncan's face into a mask of politeness normally reserved for their mom. "I'm afraid I don't know your name."

"That wasn't my idea," the ghost said. He was so clear, his voice so loud. It shouldn't have been possible. It hadn't even happened with the mirrors powering up every ghost in the area.

"I'm afraid I don't know your name."

"Well, I don't want to be rude. My name is Archibald." The ghost smiled. It made Shay's stomach curl with revulsion. "We were friends. Very good friends. We could be again."

He held out his hand to Finnias.

Finnias stared at it, like Archibald had offered him a dead spider. "What do you want from me?"

"To get you out of that body, for one," Archibald said. "For another, to show you…how much more you can have. You could be like me. There are two witches here, more than enough."

"Why do you need witches?" Shay's voice cracked. She glanced back at Jo and Max. Jo was still sitting on the floor, only held up by Max's arm around her shoulders.

"Oh, you're still here?" Archibald looked down his nose at her. "Well, little necromancer, I think you know exactly why I need them. After all, power like this…it must come from somewhere."

His voice deepened on the last sentence, becoming layered, his eyes becoming widening dark pits, black veins spreading across his face, mouth open wider than should have been possible.

A moment and he was back to normal.

Shay's stomach dropped for more than one reason.

"What do you say, Finnias?"

"No." He shook his head. "You need to leave."

"Or what?" Archibald laughed. "Even if your little friend could do anything to stop me, I'm far too powerful for her. And the witches nearly died keeping me back for a moment, their magic won't work again. What could you possibly do against me? There's nothing you can do to stop me. You might as well join me now or be absorbed. I suppose if you're going to be so rude, I don't mind either way."

"I think I have a better idea." Max threw a sachet at the ghost. It landed short of him. He laughed.

He stopped laughing when salt formed a circle around him. He pressed against an invisible barrier, green sparks flying from where he touched it.

"Oh, you're a clever little witch, aren't you?" He bared his teeth. "You're strong. They'll come for you, sooner than you think. You're going to wish Finnias had chosen me."

"I think we're good," Max told him.

Archibald pressed a hand through, heedless of the green fire flaring up his sleeve.

"Okay time to go." Shay pulled Jo to her feet. "You good?"

"Yeah." Jo stood up but she swayed on her feet and Max had to get an arm around her shoulders.

They hobbled to the stairs. Max put down a line of salt. "For how much good it'll do."

"If he's being powered by A…by a witch, our magic won't work against him," Jo said. Shay knew she almost said Arlo. It made her sick. "Did he call you a necromancer?"

Shay winced. "I guess we do have a word?"

"Oh." Jo blinked at her. "Can you do anything about him?"

Shay wished she could give up any necromancer abilities she might have to keep them safe.

"Apparently not." Shay led them to the emergency stairs. Finnias and Max helped Jo. "Sorry, I don't have a handle on this."

"All I have is a handle." Jo held up her lantern handle.

"What happened, anyway?" Shay asked. "You…fell over."

"Magic is energy," Jo explained. "I used too much. Luckily, Max is a quick learner. You picked up the salt thing fast."

"Direction and energy," Max said. They stumbled and Finnias barely kept them all upright. "I'm okay, just tired.

When I'm less tired, please show me how to do that candle thing. I knew it was a thing."

"Sure," Jo agreed. "How did he find us? Isn't he the one from Finnias's memories?"

"When I moved from the mirror to Duncan I believe he was drawn here," Finnias explained. "We can't do that again unless it's back at your shop. Even then, I don't know how well your wards will hold."

"Not at all," Jo admitted. "And I'm not risking Shay's room."

Shay felt a little warmer. "You're okay with the…necromancer thing?"

"I'm okay with you," Jo said. "We'll figure it out, whatever it means. And I'll figure out how to keep you safe, Finnias, once we get out of here."

"But why is he drawn to Finnias?" Max asked. "Because they were friends?"

"I don't believe so," Finnias said. "I have no memory of him, and ghosts are deeply tied to memories."

"Is it because he killed you?" Shay asked. It wasn't going to be a subject she could broach delicately, and she'd never been subtle.

"I…" Finnias hesitated, putting a hand to his chest. "…Yes, I believe you're right."

Chapter 17: Rootie Tootie McShooties

Shay led the way downstairs.

Unlike the steps visitors used, the back stairs were must more utilitarian. Gray concrete, edged with yellow, and a metal handrail leading all the way down to the basement. She'd been back there a few times - the lights always flickered, and it was colder than it should have been, even in the height of summer.

The emergency lights either never kicked on or the power was drained too completely. With only Max's lantern for light, it was slow going. Jo was leaning heavily on Max and they weren't doing much better. Finnias was in the best shape of all of them, but he'd gone completely silent.

Shay couldn't blame him.

"I guess now we know what the spirit charmer meant," Jo said when they were taking a breather on the first floor. "Archibald must have Arlo. Somehow. I didn't know ghosts could do something like that."

"They shouldn't be able to," Finnias said. "Shay, even if your powers were working, I don't know if this is something you could fight. Archibald has…transcended into something much worse than a siphon."

"Yeah, that isn't helping," Shay said. She was queasy with the thought. Archibald was two stories above them, and nothing was keeping him there.

Even if they made it outside, nothing would protect them at the house. Not even the wards would help. He could walk through her wall and kill her in her sleep. There was nothing she could do to stop him.

"Do you think Arlo is okay?" Max asked.

"I have to believe he is," Jo said. "

"He has to be alive, or Archibald's party trick wouldn't work," Finnias said. Jo gave him a tight smile. "I can't vouch for what condition he's in, but…he's alive. And we'll find him.

"Thank you," Jo said. "I appreciate it."

Finnias nodded.

"Do we try the side door or head straight to the basement?" Shay asked. "Please tell me we can go through the side door."

Jo shook her head. "That's what took me so long, there are so many ghosts by the side door it might as well be under water. "

"Awesome, love that for me," Shay said. "So…the basement."

"Which presents another problem," Jo said. "We are all tired and completely unequipped to go head on with anything strong enough to have a presence. And whatever is in the basement is much worse than that."

"How much worse?" Shay asked.

"I didn't have time to get a good read on it, only that the door down there is the only one that will allow us through," Jo explained. "But whatever it is, it's old, and it's alert for the first time in a long time."

"Great, sounds fun," Shay said.

"It most certainly will not be fun," Jo said, clearly done with her sarcasm. "It will be ready to feed, and…that can never be good."

"Could it be a cowhand ghost from the old graveyard?" Max asked. "Maybe all of them coming together, some sort of cluster haunting, that could read as a powerful ghost, right?"

"You're not wrong," Jo said. "But I wouldn't count on it."

"I don't want to fight a bunch of cowboy ghosts," Shay said.

"You could demoralize them by calling their guns rootie tootie mcshooties," Max offered.

Shay nodded. "I do like demoralizing."

Finnias tilted his head to the side, eyes closed. "Duncan warns us to be careful. He'd planned to have an event in the basement, but lately there's a pressure down there, something that makes it hard for him to breathe."

"If we're careful and quick, and head straight to the doors, I know we can make it out without getting hurt." Jo bundled up her hair at the back of her head and zipped up her jacket. "We just need to not draw their attention. Max, just in case it is a cluster haunting, it'd be best if you left our hat here."

"And my awesome sheriff's badge." They unpinned it from their vest and tucked it in their pocket.

Shay zipped up her coat and her hand hit the bell of her cat costume. "At least you didn't try to fight a ghost with whiskers on your face."

"And you're not dressed like… whatever this is." Finnias waved his arms. Underneath the coat he was wearing a billowy white pirate shirt. "I highly doubt this is how anyone has ever dressed."

A cold wind blew past them. The entire building sighed.

"Maybe I should lead it away," Shay said. "Until you can get the doors open and I'll run like hell. It's going to come after me, anyway."

"No," Max said. "That is not happening."

"Jo can barely walk, you're exhausted, and Finnias is having an internal conflict," Shay said. "Get everyone to the doors and yell for me. I can make it. If anyone is going to keep a ghost focused, it's me."

"I'm fine," Jo insisted.

"Sure." Shay didn't believe her for a moment. "I'm still faster than you. I just took out that ghost upstairs with a sachet, I can do it again. At least slow it down. Right?"

Jo hesitated, but finally nodded. "It's not…okay, it's not a good plan. You don't get any good plan points for this."

"That's fine, I wouldn't want to edit my resume again," she said.

"But it's not the worst idea," Jo admitted. "I hate it. I don't want to use you as bait."

"I'm the tastiest bait," she said. "It's okay, Jo. I offered. I can do it."

She knew it had the potential to go badly, but it was the right thing to do. Maybe the only thing to do. It still made her feel like she'd swallowed powdered glass.

"No," Max repeated. They stood up and led her out of the door and into the atrium. The water was still moving. She glanced up the stairs, but it was too dark to make out anything. "Shay, you don't have to do this."

"Yeah, I do." She took a deep breath and let it out. "I'm fast in small bursts and the basement isn't big. I'll be okay. I can shove a sachet in the ghost and run like hell."

The idea sounded worse the more she talked about it. "Shay-"

"I have a great arm." Shay gave them a friendly punch in the shoulder to show if off.

They made a face and rubbed the spot. "Okay, fine you do have a good arm. Shay, I'm scared."

"Don't be, you have the easy part." Shay said with confidence she didn't feel. "I'll be the one running around with a murder ghost on my butt."

"I never want to hear that sentence from you or anyone else ever again," Max said. "Is this because you still think this is your fault?"

"No." Shay realized it wasn't entirely honest. It was her fault, at least in part. She knew some of it had to be Halloween, but a lot of it must have been caused by her. "Maybe a little, but I think this is our best bet."

Max squinted at her for a moment before sighing. "Okay. I trust you, I know you wouldn't do this if you didn't think it was the right thing."

"I don't know what you're talking about." She flipped her ponytail off of her shoulder. "I'm always this self-sacrificing. I'm the least selfish person on the planet."

"And you're so humble about it, too." Max smiled a little bit. "I'm going to check for flashlights at the desk, there are probably more. Stay here this time."

"...Okay, yeah, that's a fair thing to say." She nodded.

Max found another flashlight to arm themself with. They met up with Finnias and Jo in the emergency stairwell.

The temperature plummeted further, like stepping into a freezer.

"Hey, wait, before we go any farther, can we open the door with the power out?" Shay asked. "It's a loading bay thing, right?"

"There's a side door, I have the key." Finnias jingled Duncan's lanyard. "It's right next to the large loading doors. Do you remember where they are?"

She tried to make a map of the basement in her head, but she had a terrible sense of direction. "More or less."

"That is not comforting," Finnias told her.

"I got it, don't worry."

They headed down the stairs. She already thought it was cold, but it was worse the farther down the stairs they walked. The door had ice crystals glistening around it. Her lips cracked.

Max shone the flashlight on the building map. "We're here, and this is where the door is."

Maps were all well and good, but mostly it was a garbled web of lines to her. The door was easy to spot, at least. It was across the basement from the stairs, marked with a star.

"Shay, are you sure about this?" Max asked her.

"Stop asking me that. I got this." She did not remotely feel like she had anything. "Run away and then punch. Run some more. I can definitely do that."

"That's the spirit," Finnias said. He sighed and rubbed the side of his head. "That was Duncan.

"Tell him thanks." Shay elbowed Finnias, but made sure it was gentle. She could jab Duncan harder when he'd be the one feeling it. If she made it out. She needed to go, before thoughts like that overwhelmed her and froze her to the floor. "All right, open the door, let's do this."

The door stuck at first, but the ice broke and it swung in. Beyond, it was so dark the glow from Max's flashlight didn't even show the books on the other side.

"Here." They handed her the lantern. "It can only help."

The candle was barely burning, but it would be enough light she probably wouldn't run into a shelf.

All she could do was trust them.

"Thanks," she said. "You know what the sign is?"

"I didn't think we agreed on that—"

"Hoot like an owl." She slipped into the room.

The cold was intense, but it was nothing to the smell. The overwhelming scent of damp, wet earth wormed into her lungs. She stepped into the stacks, barely avoiding a pile of books marked with a sticky note she couldn't read.

The silence was complete, pressing against her ears. Her pulse thundered in her temples. The door behind her opened again, followed by the hushed sounds of her friends moving across the room.

Otherwise, silence dominated the space. No ghostly glows. Not even mist.

Maybe Jo had been wrong. Maybe it was simply freezing cold in the basement.

Jo hadn't been wrong, yet.

A scrape, in the next aisle over, proved her very wrong. She stepped away from it, but there was only so much room. She hadn't really taken the rows and rows of shelves into account when she made her plan. Even if she knew where the door was at the moment, it wouldn't take much to get turned around in the maze of the basement.

A violent gust of wind threatened to yank her down the aisle, pulling the lantern from her numb fingers. She staggered blindly between the shelves, tripping over a stack of books and hitting the floor painfully on her hands and knees.

She could see the lantern, just ahead, lying on its side, the candle glow feebler than ever, but still bright compared to the dark around her. She crawled towards it, slipping on the books she'd knocked over, occasionally her fingers brushing against the very cold concrete floor.

She had almost reached the lantern when her hand sank into something cold and damp. She squeaked and shook her hand, afraid she'd touched something really foul.

Her fingers were covered in something gritty, and she tried to wipe it away. It smelled like dirt. She hoped it was.

She reached for the lantern again and something grabbed her wrist.

CHAPTER 18: FAVOR

Shay yanked her hand back and scrambled away from the lantern. She kept her eyes trained on the flickering flame, the tiny pool of light surrounding it.

Something large passed in front of it.

She backed up more, clumsily moving over books, but instead of cement her fingers encountered something with much more give.

Dirt.

Cold and so damp it was nearly mud, covering her hands and jeans. She clumsily pulled herself up, her feet sliding on the books spread across the damp earth. She took a step and her ankle tried to twist under her, and she only saved herself by grabbing the shelf, knocking more books loose.

Running wouldn't be as easy as she thought.

She took the sachet out of her pocket. She would just have to hope that getting a sachet inside whatever was in the aisle with her would do the trick, give her the time she needed to run. Her heart pounded so hard she could feel it in her fingers. The quiet so complete she could hear the blood rushing through her temples. Her breath was a loud and uneven rasp, and she desperately tried to breathe quietly, to keep herself calm, but the fear was a poison, freezing in her veins everywhere it spread.

A rattle of breath that wasn't hers, right next to her ear, cold air spreading across her neck. She jerked away and nearly fell again. The earth had pulled her in, and she was up to her ankles in dirt. She yanked one foot free, but as she did her best to get the leverage for the second foot, a cold hand touched her cheek.

She swung her fist forward. Nothing but air.

"C'mon you dirt clod," she whispered, more to hear something than to actually threaten the ghost. Her voice was too small, too shaky, and it only made her feel very small and alone.

The shelf behind her shook and slammed into her shoulder blades, knocking her forward again. The books were gone and all that was left was mud, pulling her in up to her elbows. She yanked her hands free, barely keeping a hold of the sachet. She struggled to get free, crawling across the floor just as the lantern was pulled into the earth and snuffed out.

The dark was so total and complete it pressed down on her. She could have been in a cave, miles below the surface, and she wouldn't have been able to tell the difference. It would have had the same all-encompassing dark and the stench of raw earth.

Something grabbed her arm and yanked her down. She tried to scream, but a hand clamped around her mouth, cutting off the sound. Her mouth filled with dirt, sour and heavy on her tongue.

She couldn't breathe.

Her struggling felt futile, her motions weak against damp soil that engulfed more of her every moment. Her lungs burned. Bright spots flashed in her vision. Her fingers loosened their grip on the sachet. She didn't know where it went.

If Max had given the signal, if everyone was out, she didn't think that she could possibly know. She was going to die only a few yards away from them, and they had no idea.

That thought gave her one last burst of strength. She didn't want to die there, covered in mud. She tried to make a noise, but she doubted it was one anyone would hear.

If someone was there. If someone could just help her. She'd even take the spirit charmer's dubious assistance.

She just wanted to live.

Her lungs were on fire, but the only thing she could inhale was dirt. Just as she was intent on doing that, the crushing weight vanished.

She coughed, spitting up mud and dirt, breathing in as much as she dared, but when the air hit her throat it made her cough all over again. Her tongue felt gritty. She wiped at her mouth but her hands were still encrusted.

It was still dark. If the lantern was above ground again, it had been put out. She spat at more dirt and climbed to her feet, slowly. The cat ears slid off and she jumped when they hit the ground. She tried to wipe her hands on her jeans, but they were filthy, too. Even the stupid cat bell around her neck was full of earth. She yanked it off and shoved it in her pocket as she limped down the aisle, feeling every single bruise she'd gathered through the night. Her wrist hurt. She wished she had the brace, still in her room.

She kicked the lantern on accident. It skidded across the cement. She felt the end of the aisle and looked for the door. Either she couldn't see it from where she was standing, or Max hadn't gotten it open yet. She didn't like the implications, either way. The dirt could come back at any moment and pull her back down. She wasn't even sure why it had relented in the first place.

The skittering sound again, but this time she hadn't kicked anything.

She hurried forward, ignoring the scratching sound as best she could. She needed to get to the door, and quickly. She'd lost the sachet, and if ground turned to sinking mud again, she wasn't sure she'd be able to pull herself out.

Something blue darted past her, moving on her right. When she turned to look it had already disappeared between the shelves.

She went the other way, feeling along until she made her way down another aisle. She ran right into a library cart. It rolled away from her with a screech of wheels.

It hit the shelf and stopped. She groped along until she found it again, holding onto the handle.

It felt like little paws scurried across her hand and she pushed the cart away from her, snatching her hand back and shaking it like it would rid of her of the sensation.

Something clung to her jacket.

She did a little dance to try to shake it off. It fell to the floor, too heavily to be her imagination. She gingerly put out one foot, but the concrete was bare.

A whisper, low and rasping, close enough it tickled at her neck. When she swapped at it, nothing was there.

More whispers, all around her, things moving through the books and in the shelves.

They moved through the books, claws clicking across the floor as they scurried across the cement. She tried to keep her breath even, but it came out too quickly. She couldn't get any air. Cold hit the back of her throat. She coughed again, despite herself.

A hundred tiny eyes looked out from the dark, all around her, glinting with their own light. Something crawled across her shoe. Something else through the shelf close to her head.

Rats.

She didn't know how she knew, but she was very certain they were rats. Hundreds of them. She took a step forward, and the eyes followed her.

She kept walking, slowly, to the end of the aisle. Max and the others must have made it out already, she just needed to get herself oriented and leave the basement to the probably ghost rats.

Something leaped out at her and she hit the opposite shelf trying to dodge away from it.

It was heavy, the weight pulling her arm down. She shook it and the light bobbed furiously. The silhouette of a large rat clung to her sleeve. It dropped to the ground, but the others swarmed on her, crawling over her shoulders, tangling in her hair, little claws pricking through her jeans and scrabbling on her jacket. She screamed again and tried to shake them off. A few fell but they were quickly replaced.

"Quiet." It was a myriad of different voices, failing to blend into one. Whiskers tickled her ear and she slapped down on the spot. Immediately it was on her other side. "We said quiet."

She froze to the spot, her hand still up on her shoulder. She couldn't move except to let out a shuddering breath. Horror lodged in her throat. It took her too long to find her voice.

"Get off of me," she said. She was shaking so badly she barely understood her own words.

"Not yet." A tail wrapped loosely around her neck, scratching across the fabric of her turtleneck. She whimpered. "Oh, it's been so long since we had one that could see and feel. So long since we were called. And yet you fear us."

"I didn't call you," she whispered. She wanted to say something about how she would have remembered. Something witty, a deflection, but all she could do was stand there, shaking like a leaf in a hurricane.

"You did call," they said slowly, voice low. "And we have come, and we have saved your life, Shay O'Brannon."

It knew her name.

"Working for the spirit charmer?" Her heart was going to crack her ribs.

A loud, collective hissing swirled around her. She wanted to put her hands to her ears. She wanted to scream again. Anything.

She still couldn't move.

The tail around her neck tightened to the point she could barely breathe. It relaxed after a moment, still heavy against her collar bone, like a horrible necklace.

"No," they said, when the sounds died down. "We do not work with that one."

"What are you?"

Laughter, from every side, but not the canned hilarity of a sitcom. It was shrieks and screams, hysterical and breathy, deep and hearty. Battering against her like a storm.

"You called us, and yet you do not know us?" the voices in her ear murmured. "We are a mischief, Shay O'Brannon. The many. The multitude. We have many names, and many faces, but you may call us what the one before did. We are the rat king."

She shuddered. This wasn't a ghost, it wasn't even something like Archibald. It was much, much worse. "The one before?"

"The one like you," they said. "So very long ago. We made a bargain with the one before, and we would like to bargain again."

"I don't want to bargain with you." She knew it couldn't possibly be a smart thing to say, but it slipped out of her, anyway.

They laughed, but it was quiet this time, a smattering of titters and chuckles. "You do not have a choice, Shay O'Brannon. You called us, and we have saved you. You can surrender to us, or you can provide us with a favor. We suggest the latter, if you value your life as much as it seems."

"What kind of favor?" she closed her eyes. She didn't want to see. She didn't want to know.

"You do not have the luxury of bargaining with us," the voice hissed. The presence on her shoulder was heavier than ever, little sharp teeth scraping her ear. She'd heard once that rats could chew through copper. She didn't want to find out if it was true. "We will not tell you. Not until the time is right will we lay it out before you."

"Wh-what if I don't want to?" Shay whispered.

Another laugh, pressing in on her as surely as the darkness. "If you refuse, now or later, then you surrender to us. We will make sure there is nothing left of you. That is fair, is it not?"

Her face was wet with tears slipping between her eyelashes. "I—"

"Your friend is calling for you," the rat king said. They licked her cheek and she jerked away, finally able to move, but she didn't dare try to run. She'd never make it out, no matter how fast she was. "You could accept our offer. Or you could die. An easy choice, either way. It does not matter to us which you choose."

"A favor," she said. Her voice sounded like she had been screaming for days, hoarse and breathy.

"Good. Then we shall light the way. Until we meet again, Shay O'Brannon." The rats whispered, soft as the wind. The weight hanging on her shoulders and coat disappeared. Her arms dropped to her sides.

Mist poured out from beneath her feet, weaving through the stacks to the other side of the room. She hadn't even been going the right way.

She ran for it, stumbling a few. Her lungs burned and her throat was tight, but she kept going. She couldn't bring herself to glance back. She knocked over a stack of books and left it there. Glittering eyes followed her every movement, a threat and a promise.

The exit was a square of orange light. She dashed through it, leaving the rat king behind.

Chapter 19: Questions

Shay tripped over the door sill.

Max grabbed her arm, saving her from eating concrete. "Woah! Are you okay? Why are you…is this dirt?"

She looked down. In the light from the streetlamps she could see the dirt covering her jacket and shirt, caked onto her jeans and forming dark crescents under her fingernails. Her knuckles were still dark with ghost mark under the grime.

"Oh." She would have ended up on the ground if Max wasn't holding her up. Her mouth was still gritty. She spat to the side. It was dark on the bleached-out sidewalk.

"What happened?" Max tried to brush the dirt off of her shoulders in vain. "I yelled for you, I was about to go back in-"

"We all were," Finnias clarified.

"I…" she couldn't say it. Could barely even comprehend what had happened. She hadn't been able to do anything against whatever the dirt ghost had been, and then… "I need to sit down."

No one asked her anything else the entire ride home. Max drove Duncan's car and she sat in the front seat on a towel, staring at the dashboard.

She left her jacket and boots at the door, but she still trailed dirt into the house on her way up to change and take a shower. She'd forgotten she had a nose and whiskers drawn on her face until she looked in the mirror. Her face was smeared with mud, but she could still see the faint dark marks of the makeup. She rubbed at it, but her hands were too dirty to make a difference.

The only part of her that wasn't covered in dirt was the sachet Max had given her, looping it over her head. Inside the rocks were blackened, like they'd been stuck in a fire. One was cracked down the center. She shuddered and threw it away.

She took the hottest shower she could stand, trying to scrub away the physical dirt and the feeling of rat claws on her skin. A blur of dark sediment swirled down the drain. Her skin was red by the time the water started to go cold. She still didn't feel entirely clean, swabbing out her ears and cleaning under her nails didn't help as much as she'd hoped.

She stared in the mirror longer than she meant to. She half expected a skeletal face to loom out at her, but it was just her, alone in the bathroom, her wet hair raked into a clump over her shoulder. There wasn't any dirt, not that she could see. Just her face, pink from scrubbing and the heat of the water where it wasn't marked blue from ghosts, though the marks were already fading.

The rat king said she called them. That someone had done so before, long ago. The knowledge didn't help her at all, except knowing that she wasn't the first. Whoever had bargained with the rat king before was probably long dead.

She tried to smile. Her reflection didn't seem to want to comply.

She walked down to the living room and was immediately bundled up on the couch by Max, a mug of hot chai pressed into her hands.

"Thanks." She sounded awful.

Max sat next to her, as close as they could, trying to chase off the deep chill that the shower hadn't quite been able to touch. "Better?"

She nodded, taking a sip.

"Can you…tell us what happened?" Jo asked. "If you're not up to it…"

"No, I should probably tell you." She leaned against Max. "Have you…it had a lot of names and a lot of voices, but it was all just…rats. Like a thousand rats, crawling all over everything and me and…It was called the…the mischief? But it wanted me to call it the rat king."

Becky hopped up and curled up in her lap. She scratched the cat between the ears and was met with a rumbling purr. It helped, a little bit.

"I've never heard of that," Jo admitted.

"Was it rats?" Max asked. "Then why all the dirt…?"

"Unrelated ghost." She didn't want to talk about it. "Almost got me, didn't really see it, but the rat king…saved me? And asked for a favor?"

She took a sip of her chai. Talking about it was harder than she thought. Not because the memory was faded and soft, like the tear. It was too real, harsh in her mind against the soft glow of lamps in the overcrowded living room.

"You promised it a favor?" Jo was the first one to talk.

"That or die, and decided to not die," she said. Max's grip tightened a little too much, but she didn't say anything. "So…now I owe a favor to an eldritch library basement horror. Or something. Is this ringing any bells at all?"

"I've heard of it before." Max dug out their phone and began searching. "Let's see…a group of rats is called a mischief? And a rat king is when they're entwined by their tails…was it…?"

She put a hand to her neck, the phantom sensation of the heavy tail still fresh. "I don't know. I couldn't see."

"Oh." Max looked back at their phone, but if their search gave any more answers, they didn't say.

"It said I called it," Shay said, quietly. "That someone like me called it before. Another necromancer, I guess. A long time ago. So…at least there's…I don't know. There were others? There have to be more than just us and the spirit charmer, right? She said there were more, I don't know."

"Did you call it?" Jo asked.

Shay shook her head. "I don't think so. Not consciously. I was just so scared, and I thought I was going to die, and…is it bad?"

"I don't know," Jo admitted. "I'm sorry, that's not helpful, but I don't know what it was. The first ghost must have been what I scryed for. The second thing…I have no idea. It was probably old, whatever it was. There's more out there than I could know."

"Werewolves?" Shay tried again.

Jo smiled, faintly. She was paler than normal, her robe looser than it used to be on her shoulders. "While I have never encountered one, I wouldn't rule it out. Let's focus on the present. You're okay, and we have a lead for Arlo. He has a pretty big network. He might be able to find something out."

"Right." Shay nodded. It wasn't what she wanted to hear, really, but at least Jo wasn't telling her to pack her things. She sighed and looked at Finnias. She'd found him to help answer questions, she was going to try to get any information she could, while he was still present. He was struggling to not be engulfed by an overstuffed armchair. "Well. While we wait for that to clear up, I have some questions for you."

"I guessed that you might." Finnias picked up a doily that had fallen into his lap with a look of distaste, draping it far enough over the arm of the chair that it fluttered to the floor.

"You seem to know more about this necromancer thing than anyone else in this room," she said. The word still tasted strange on her tongue. "So…why isn't it working. Why can't I… do anything?"

"Shay, I don't know," Finnias said. "I'm sorry. I don't have all the answers, I know I must have been like you, once, but it's not something I actively remember."

"So, if I ask you more specific questions, you might be able to tell me something?" Shay asked.

"Potentially," he said. "I can't guarantee anything. And I'd prefer to…not have an audience, if you don't mind."

"Come on, Max, let's go talk in the shop," Jo offered.

Shay really didn't want Max to go. It felt like they were back to normal, for the first time in a while. And they were warm. But they nodded and got up to follow Jo out of the room, closing the door behind them.

"Ask away," Finnias said. "Just don't expect anything."

"Right." It was strange, to be talking to Finnias while he was wearing Duncan's face. Which made absolutely no sense, most of their interactions had been this way. But she never pictured Duncan when she thought of him, just how he was. "So…is anyone who can see ghosts a necromancer, or…?"

"Some people are naturally more sensitive and attuned to the spiritual world," Finnias sounded like he was reading a Wikipedia article. As if it was information he had access to, but didn't consciously know. "So no, not everyone who can see or sense ghosts is a necromancer. And there are many people with interesting abilities that we wouldn't consider necromancers, even if ghosts fall in line with that."

"Like what?" Shay asked.

"A medium," Finnias answered. "Scrying, like Jo. There are some people who are so far removed from their necromancer ancestor that they just have some trace of ability."

"How many abilities are there?" Shay had been curious about that. Her own were so far removed from

Duncan's and the spirit charmer's. She had no idea what Finnias had been capable of in life, it could have been similar to hers, or something completely different.

"I…I'm not sure," he admitted. "I know you have the potential to be powerful. So does Duncan. But I can't tell you how to make things work."

She sighed. "Well. I know more now."

"I'm sorry, Shay. I wish I could help you."

"I'm sorry, too," she said. "Not for. You not knowing. Well, I am sorry you don't have your memories, but mostly I'm sorry I left you in the void. I think it was my fault, and-"

"Shay, no," Finnias cut her off. "It's not your fault. You have nothing to be sorry for. And don't worry, I heard you. In the mirror."

"Oh, that's embarrassing." Shay laughed, but it came out choked, and she was terrified for a moment she was going to cry. "Can we not repeat anything I said ever?"

Finnias actually smiled about that, a little smile that was out of place on Duncan's face. "I can do that."

"Do you…want to be here? I didn't really take that into account."

"It's better than many alternatives," he said. "Unfortunately, possessing even your brother is…tiring. I think I'll have to retreat, for the moment. I'm sorry I'm not more help."

"I'm just really glad you're here." She was surprised to find she meant it. The answers she wanted weren't there, still out of reach, but at least Finnias was safe. At least she hadn't left him to rot somewhere awful. "Wait, do you know about the rat king?"

Duncan blinked, hard. "He's uh. Taking a back seat. So…gonna take that as a no."

"It's not his fault we put so many expectations on him," Shay said.

"So…I'm a necromancer?" Duncan frowned. "I was joking with the remembrancer stuff, but I was right?"

"Yeah," Shay said. "I…I wanted to tell you, earlier, but I didn't know if it was true, but—"

"Three people saying it, well, a person? And some ghosts? Do we think the spirit charmer is also a ghost?" Duncan frowned. "Anyway, third time is the charm, I guess."

"Yeah," Shay agreed.

"We need a plan, for tomorrow," Duncan said. "Better get everyone in here. We need to get Arlo back. Because, y'know, he's a guy and a person and whatever, but mostly I need to get this dead Victorian dude out of my head before I go back to work on Monday."

"So glad to see you have your priorities in order," Shay said.

They brought Max and Jo back in for planning, but very little planning was getting done. They were all too tired, and Jo said they had a few other people she could call. Then they were silent, the clock on the mantle ticking away minutes of time. Shay knew she should go to bed. Her chai was gone and she felt heavy with exhaustion, but she didn't want to go upstairs.

"What about your book?" Jo asked, suddenly, startling her out of being half asleep.

"Oh yeah, I don't know, it's…I left my stupid phone at work so we don't even have the dumb book," Duncan said. "Uuuuugh Shay can I borrow your phone? You're logged into my stuff, right? And I should call Gideon."

"It's dead," she said.

"Why is it always dead?" Duncan asked.

"I don't know, Donuts, maybe because it's a million years old and I have ghosts," she said. "Just ghosts all the time."

"Mine's missing," Jo said. "Use the landline. His contact info is on the front desk tablet."

"Perfect, thank you." Duncan got to his feet. "Can you come log me in."

"Sure." Jo accepted his hand up.

It was an obvious ploy to give her and Max some alone time, but Shay wasn't complaining. The clock on the mantle ticked away the moments.

"Shay—" Max started.

"I don't want to talk about it," Shay said, quickly. If she thought about it little claws pricked her skin, even after the shower. "I never, ever want to talk about it again."

"Okay, that's fine." Max held up their hands. "I was going to ask how you're feeling. After…your talk with Finnias. Not the other thing. Nope."

"Oh. Well. I'm glad he's okay. That's what really matters." She pulled her knees up to her chest. It didn't help the hollow feeling slowly carving its way in there. "But no real answers, huh? Just. How do I make this work? It worked before, if It doesn't again…"

She curled her hand into a fist. It just looked small.

"It'll work." Max put a hand over hers. "We're going to figure it out, Shay."

"Maybe."

"It will, I-"

"I have an idea, it's kind of stupid, though." Duncan walked back into the room, using the tablet. Maybe he really just didn't know how to unlock it and Shay had overestimated him. "Or not stupid. Why try and read the book when we can just call Hans Lyman himself?"

"You mean Robert Lichfield?" Jo followed him in.

"It's an old Facebook page for his German persona," Duncan explained. "I'm assuming it's for his publisher. I'll give them a call tomorrow."

Jo nodded. "It's not a bad idea, especially if it works. …Wait, did we leave Vic at the library?"

"I'm sure he got out," Shay said.

"If he didn't, he's happy about it," Max said.

She gasped. "Max, that was so mean. I'm shocked. And proud."

"I follow him, I'll check." Max had a small smile on their face, but it faded a moment later. "Oh. Oh no."

"What?" Jo walked over to see what was making Max's face turn ashy again.

They turned their phone so everyone could see a video labeled "raw footage of ghosts at the Teton Falls Public Library!" just in time to watch Shay, with a very discreet black box over her face, get knocked into a table.

"…Ow." She rubbed her hip. It still hurt, but it had blended with all the aches and pains she'd accumulated. "I think I got a bruise."

The ghosts flashed in and out of frame, not as formed as she remembered, bits of mist and smoke, the occasional face. It was more than strange, seeing herself get yanked around by something barely visible "Does it always look that bad when I get tossed around like a bean bag?"

"Yes," Jo and Max said together.

"Oh. Well."

"This isn't great, is it." Max exited out of the video after giving it a thumbs down.

Jo bit the inside of her lip and slid her glasses on top of her head to rub the bridge of her nose. "I…don't know. I don't know. I'm sorry. I'm too tired to deal with it. How many views does it have?"

"Ummm a lot," Max said. "Like way more than…well, most people think it's fake, if it helps."

"I'm going to bed," Jo said. "I will deal with it in the morning. And with…everything else. Are you going to be okay, Shay? …That was a stupid question. Do you need something to help you sleep?"

"What, melatonin?" Shay asked. "That always just makes me feel more awake. Do you have whiskey? I'll take the whiskey."

"You don't drink," Max reminded her.

"I might start."

"I have a sleep tonic," Jo said.

"Is it whiskey?" she joked, weakly.

Jo smiled, anyway. "No, but it will help you sleep and protect your dreams. You're one of the bravest people I've ever met, but I don't think it would be a bad idea."

She hesitated. Bravery wasn't a word she would use to describe herself. Especially not in the moment. She was trying to act normal, but any time there was a lull in the conversation, a pause in the moment, she was frozen in the basement again, teeth against her ear.

"Yeah," she said. "I'd like that."

Chapter 20: Lichfield

Shay woke up to sunlight streaming through her window. Jo hadn't had the chance to put up new curtains.

The light speared through the half-bare branches of the tree out front, already winter weak and soft.

It was November.

She'd had no dreams at all. Jo's tonic had tasted awful, but it worked exactly as advertised.

"Morning," Max said when she rolled over. They were already sitting up against the headboard, messing with their phone. They put it down when she sat up. "Well, afternoon. Jo said to let you rest."

"Morning." She yawned and her jaw cracked. "Wow. I don't know if I slept or if I died for…holy crap thirteen hours?"

It was well past four. The sun would be setting soon enough.

"You needed it," Max said. They moved like they were reaching for her, but their hand landed on the pillow next to her. "Yesterday was a lot."

"Hey." She put her hand over theirs. "I'm okay."

Things in the early afternoon light were better. Less like her thoughts were grating together.

The rat king would be back, for their favor. Her hands shook.

"Yeah?" Max didn't look convinced.

"Yeah. I'm tough. Tough as nails." Shay patted their knee. "The kind that keep growing after you die—"

"Which is a myth."

"—And the iron or whatever metal kind. Also, very hungry. Wow."

The hearty smell of bread filled the kitchen. Jo and Duncan were at the table. He was messing around with the shop's tablet.

"Good afternoon." Jo glared at a mirror laid out in front of her. She had a few bottles off to the side.

"Oh hey, you're not dead," Duncan said. "I was about to come and check your pulse. I made bread."

"I would have noticed," Max muttered.

"You?" Shay's eyebrows rose.

"Excuse you, I make great bread. I'm a fantastic baker." He held up a piece. It was slathered in butter and jam. "Now that you've risen, you should crumb loaf around with us. What, too much?"

"Way too much," Max said.

"The bread is good, at least," Jo said. "Duncan, tell Finnias he ruined a perfectly good scrying mirror. I only have so many of these."

"He apologizes for saving your life," Duncan said. He held up his hands when Jo turned her glare to him. "That was verbatim. Don't kill the messenger. Not like it would hurt him. I say you should just buy in bulk from the dollar store. Or there's probably some warehouse making cheap replicas if you're that dedicated to your aesthetic or whatever."

"I am that dedicated," Jo said. "I live in a Victorian house. I have a sideboard."

She indicated the cabinet.

"Fair point," Duncan conceded. "Oh, bee tee dubs, Shay Shay, I have something for you."

He handed her a post-it note with a phone number scrawled on it.

"Yay, thanks," she said. "I've always wanted one of these."

"It's the number for Hans Lyman, dummy," he explained. "The number on Facebook was for his publisher, like I predicted, but they got me the actual number. Had to do a lot of sweet talking. Who wasted eight years, it was only eight by the way, in library school now? Huh? Not me."

"He asked and they gave it to him," Jo corrected him.

Duncan spluttered and took his turn to glare at her. "Why must you undermine me?"

Jo just smiled sweetly at him.

"Rude," he said. "Anyway, eat some food and give him a call."

"Why do I have to do it?" Shay asked.

"Because my phone anxiety only lets me make exactly one non-work call per day," Duncan said. "And because, as mentioned before, I have a squatter in my head who loves to argue and I don't really want to sound completely insane to the guy who might be able to help us. Most importantly, I'm your big brother and I say so."

"You suck," Shay told him. His expression didn't change at all. "Fine, fine, I'll call him.

"I could do it," Max offered.

"We could both do it?" Shay suggested. "Speaker phone?"

"There you go, Shay can ask questions and Max can write down the relevant answers." Duncan snapped his fingers and pointed at them. "Teamwork makes the dream work."

"It would be better to get it done soon," Jo said. "Remember, at sunset I can find Arlo. I'm calling a few friends in. We all need to be ready to go."

"Right." Shay grabbed a slice of bread. She felt like she hadn't had any time at all to recover, but rest would have to wait.

After eating something Shay and Max moved to Jo's office, a tiny closet of a room next to hers, mostly taken up by a roll top desk and a comfortable office chair, which Max stole. She found a pad of paper and a fountain pen in one of the desk cubbies.

"Wow, nice pen," Max uncapped it and inspected it. "Okay, what are you going to say?"

"I dunno, I guess just…spout utter nonsense at him and hope he doesn't hang up?" Shay looked down at her phone. Someone had charged it for her, but the battery was already draining completely on its own. It must have been Duncan, since her lock screen was some anime guy she'd never seen in her life, sticking his tongue out at her. She'd probably not remember to change it for a few weeks.

"Better idea, we don't do that," Max suggested.

"Wow, just calling my idea bad, no hesitation." Shay sat on the floor. A rug covered most of the hardwood, but the edge was a little uncomfortable. "Well, I guess I'll ask about the abilities, then get more specific?"

"Maybe I should write down a list."

"Too late, calling him." She dialed the number.

It rang a few times before a man with a rough voice answered. "What."

"Uh." Everything she'd planned to say abandoned her completely. "Is this Hans Lyman?"

"Who the hell is asking?"

Shay really wanted to hang up the phone. Max tapped the notebook, and she looked up to see "ask about the book" scribbled on the page. "Uh, so, I've been reading your book. Um. The one about abilities and ghosts? And I had questions?"

The man was silent for a moment. "Yes, fine. Hans Lyman is one of my pen names."

"And Robert Lichfield," she said.

"Yeah," he said. "You did your homework, at least. Why are you asking about my book? I didn't even know they were still selling it. It's not light reading."

Shay wished she'd allowed Max to write some questions down before she called, but she foolishly thought retail had prepared her to talk on the phone. Max wasn't writing down notes fast enough, so she decided to just get to the center of it. "I have abilities. So, um. As you said it's not light reading and I figured it was better to ask you directly, if I could."

Max scribbled "what about" and drew what was probably supposed to be a donut. She shrugged, not sure how to play charades to let them know she thought it was better to leave him out of it, if she could. Duncan had a career and an entire social life in Teton Falls. She was not going to mess that up for him if she could help it.

Lyman, or Lichfield, was quiet for long enough Max leaned over to check he hadn't hung up. They wrote some question marks down and then gestured for her to say something.

"Hello?"

"What?"

"Um, I think I have-"

"You think you have abilities," he repeated. "Necromancers are rare these days. Are you sure?"

She winced. There was the word she'd been waiting for.

"I have ghost touch and yeah, I'm pretty sure about it," she said. Max gestured for her to keep going and she seriously considered smacking their leg. "It's…a lot? And I don't know what I'm doing, and I'm a little…a lot scared."

"I can't help you," Lichfield said.

"Wait, please—" She couldn't just let him hang up. She'd fought so hard to get answers.

"I wrote something I shouldn't have as a pretentious undergrad," he said. "I can't help you."

"Just a few questions, that's all," Shay said, quickly.

He sighed, loudly. "Fine. Ghost touch, huh? Pretty raw deal. How long?"

"Week and a half?" She counted the days on her fingers. "No, two weeks."

"Shit." Something clattered in the background, and she wasn't sure if he was swearing at her or at himself for dropping something. "How...? You didn't...you sound young. You're just a kid, aren't you."

"I'm twenty-one," Shay said.

"Yeah, you're a kid," Lichfield said. "Shit. God dammit. Look, stay out of haunted places. Maybe find a priest or something to make sure your house is safe."

"I live with a witch?"

"Good enough." Lichfield sighed. "You're in Idaho, right? Area code was from there. Please say it's not Teton Falls."

That didn't sound great.

"I can't," she said.

Lichfield muttered a lot of words Shay wouldn't have repeated in any sort of company. "Kid, get out of there. As soon as you can. That valley is cursed, and it's just going to get worse, mark my words."

Max jerked, the nib scraping across the paper.

"I can't," she repeated. She didn't care for this conversation at all. "I live here."

And she was pretty sure moving out of town would count as surrendering to the rat king. They'd promised nothing would be left of her, and she believed them.

"Of course you're one of those types," Lichfield muttered.

"What type-"

"Wanna be hero types," Lichfield said. Shay opened her mouth to deny it, but he kept talking. "Or just plain stupid."

That one she was willing to accept. "Maybe."

"You at least know how to defend yourself?"

"Yes," she said, automatically. Max nudged her with their foot and she smacked their shin. "No. I mean, no. I did. I think. But…"

"Use your words, kid."

"Right, yeah." Shay ducked her head, even though Lichfield couldn't see her ears turning red. "About a week and a half ago, ish, I was able to…punch a ghost apart? But it stopped working, and I don't know why."

"Well, you keeping that heart on you all the time?" Lichfield asked.

Shay shared a confused look with Max. "That what now?"

"The heart," Lichfield repeated. "You didn't just get abilities out of nowhere, I know how it works. I'm not going to turn you in, I don't know if you got it on accident or what, but maybe put it away for a while. It won't completely stop it, but it'll help. You probably just burned yourself out."

"I don't…" She had no idea what he was talking about, and she wasn't sure how to explain that actually, his expertise on the subject was wrong. She needed help, not getting him angry. "Burned myself out?"

"Two weeks and you punched a ghost apart…how many times?"

"Two?" she wasn't sure how many the enormous conglomerate counted as, if she'd just broken it apart. "One was big."

Max gave her an incredibly exasperated look. They'd written "ask about heart?" on their notebook and circled it, tapping the pen against it.

"So, you're a new baby necromancer, just barely got your abilities, and you knocked two ghosts out right out the gate," Lichfield said. "You don't have a candle left to burn, is what I'm saying. You need recovery, and something that keeps you anchored. A person you trust."

"Got that covered." She glanced at Max. "How long do I have to rest?"

"You in a hurry to get yourself killed?" Lichfield asked.

"Bad stuff is happening," she explained as succinctly as she could. "I'm in a hurry to do the opposite."

"I don't know," he said. "I know people who can banish ghosts with their bare hands. They don't usually last very long. You're playing with fire, literally. How many ghosts have you encountered since?"

"…Give me a second." She counted on her fingers.

"Jesus Christ, kid."

"Do I count encounters with the same ghost as different ones or…?"

"Christ," Lichfield repeated. "You're really are going to get yourself killed. I give you two months, tops, unless you rein it in. I don't know what good tossing the heart at this point will do for you, but you need to do something. That's an incredibly dangerous ability."

Paper ripped. She glanced at Max. They stared at the notepad, lips pressed tightly together.

Two months. It wasn't a long time.

It was an infinitely small amount of time. Sixty days.

At the most.

She swallowed, trying to force down the panic in her throat so she could ask him what he meant, exactly. But the words didn't come. She didn't want to know.

If Lichfield noticed the sound, he didn't say anything. "Okay, you know what? I'm traveling right now. I could swing through there. Meet up in Doveton or something. A populated place. Bring whoever you like. I think I'll be more help in person."

"Really?" She wasn't if she wanted to meet Lichfield, but anything had to be better than what she was trying.

"Yeah, give me a few days," he said. "I can at least show you how to properly use that thing. What was your name, again?"

"Shay," she said.

No response. She checked the phone, but only brought up the lock screen.

"He hung up?" Max tapped the phone.

"Guess so." She tried dialing. It immediately went to voicemail. "Hey uh, Shay again. Text the details to this number, I guess? Thanks."

She hung up and stared at the phone again.

"…That…did not go very well, did it." She placed the phone on the desk and stared at it.

"No." Max took their phone back. They weren't looking at her.

"I keep trying to figure things out and people just keep…not helping." She was on the verge of crying, again. Out of frustration or fear, she couldn't say. "What am I supposed to do with take a nap and make a friend?"

"Shay-"

"Obviously you're my anchor point," Shay said. "If you don't mind, but…"

"Of course I don't mind." Max shoved the chair back so they could sit on the floor with her, their knee touching hers. "But…but two months? Tops?"

"Yeah, right." She hadn't forgotten it, but she didn't want to think about it. "Look, he's probably blowing smoke or…or something. Trying to get me to buy something. Another seventeen dollar ebook or one of those things Gideon was talking about. The ghost hunting equipment. Or…or something. What was he even talking about? What heart? Of course my heart's always with me. Right here. Pumping away. Doing heart stuff."

But it made her think of Finnias, with a hole in his chest where his heart should have been.

Duncan thought it was a metaphor. She was pretty sure he was wrong

"But you don't know that—"

"And that was without an…an anchor person, or witches," Shay said. "And I have both of those. Right? So, I'll be okay. And hey, maybe he'll text."

She checked.

No new notifications.

"I can't…What if I can't protect you?" Max asked. "We don't even know how this anchor thing works."

"We'll figure it out," Shay said. "You're smart and I'm a stupid hero type."

"That's not funny," Max scolded her. "What if we can't? What if Jo can't, either?"

She shrugged. "We'll find Arlo, and—"

"And what, Shay?"

She hesitated. Finnias hadn't had any answers for her, and everything Lichfield said led to more questions. Despite the jokes she'd cracked, she was pretty sure that he'd been talking about something entirely different than what she was actually dealing with.

"I don't know," she admitted. "But he's like…a super witch. And he can hear ghosts, Jo said that, once. He has to know something."

"Lots of witches can hear ghosts with practice, Shay, it doesn't mean he's a necromancer," Max said. "He probably isn't. I don't know if he can help you. We keep running from one person to another, but no one knows anything."

"We'll figure it out."

"You keep saying that, and I have to keep asking, what if we don't?" Max asked.

"Well, with that attitude—"

"Shay, I'm scared!" Max's voice cracked. "I'm scared for you, stop. Just…stop. We need to tell Jo, you can't help with…with Arlo. Or any of it."

Shay froze. Max always supported her, no matter what she did. They'd never told her she couldn't do something, not seriously. "What?"

"I'm going to go talk to her." They climbed to their feet and walked out the door.

She didn't even try to stop them.

Her lock screen anime man looked up at her, mockingly.

When her phone finally dinged, it was just an email from her school, clear across the state, letting her know about a movie night.

Chapter 21: Employee Knife Benefits

Shay leaned against her headboard.

Jo sent Shay to her room when she found out what little they'd learned. Like she was grounded. She knew it was for her own safety, but it still stung.

With a sigh she thumped her head against the wall. "Ow."

"Careful there, don't give yourself a concussion." Max stepped into the room and used their foot to close the door behind them. They were holding a large basket. "You've been put on sachet making duty."

"I do love to be included." She scooted over so Max could sit next to her. "We're going to get so much chunky sea salt in my sheets. Make them real crunchy."

Max smiled. "Lots of lavender, too."

"Looks like little bugs," she said. "So that's going to be an exciting few months before I change my sheets."

"I will change your sheets when we get back," Max corrected her. "Please don't tell me you actually go that long."

"Fine, I won't tell you." She grinned at them.

"Shay, please, I sleep in this bed sometimes."

"Oh, I don't, you're fine." At least she hadn't since moving to Jo's, which had been all of a week ago, but Max didn't need to know that.

She'd been living on the fourth floor and the laundry was in the basement. She was justified.

The conversation fizzled out. Shay put together sachets and Max carved sigils into white pillar candles. The sun slid closer to the horizon, bathing her room in soft orange.

"I like your knife." She had to break the silence, after a while. It was too heavy.

"Oh, thanks." They held it up. It was a small pocketknife with an abalone handle, catching the light in a myriad of colors. "Jo gave it to me. Said it was good for stuff like this."

"When do I get mine?" she asked.

Max almost smiled. "I don't think she plans on giving you one."

"What? I work here," Shay said. "I should get a cool knife. It's not like she's paying me. I mean, free room and board, and what a room it is. And what a board it is. Plus, free warding. But those student loans are looming. They're on the horizon. Getting a little nervous about those."

"Didn't you say you wouldn't pay them because you're lawless and flawless?" Max asked.

"Also, didn't graduate," Shay said. "But unfortunately, my flawlessness will not save me when the debt collectors come to hunt me down for sport. So, I need a knife."

"You can make ghosts solid, and you need a knife?" Max grinned at her.

"You're right, new plan, I'll lead them into a haunted building and offer them to the ghosts," Shay said. "Should work. Great plan. And hey, if it backfires and I die horribly, I still won't have to pay them back. Win win."

Max's knife slipped and they said a word they rarely used.

"Are you okay?" She sat up, reaching for their hand.

They pulled away. "Just a little cut."

She snatched a tissue from her bedside table and passed it to them. They pressed it against their thumb. Red bloomed across the white.

"I'll go get the first aid kit," she offered, clambering off of the bed. Max didn't stop her from leaving the room, but the first aid kit was in the bathroom next door, so she wasn't going far, anyway. Guilt gnawed at her guts, but she ignored it.

The cut was small, it had already stopped bleeding when she moved the tissue. She put more antibiotic ointment on than it needed, being careful to stay gentle. "Do you want a plain band-aid or a rainbow unicorn on?"

"Do you even know me?" Max asked. She was already ripping a rainbow unicorn bandage open open. She wrapped it securely around their thumb, kissed her finger and tapped it against it. "Thanks."

"You good to keep carving or—"

"I don't…I mean, yes, I just…" they sighed, grabbing the next candle and stabbing at the wax. "You know, you could have died."

"When, exactly?" she asked.

"You needing clarification is proving my point," Max said. "You…you don't…and you're joking about it like it's not a big deal. But it is a big deal. It's a huge deal."

"I'm a big girl," she said. "I can fight my own battles. Mostly."

"No, you can't, and you don't have to, but you keep acting—" they took a breath, clearly trying to calm down. She couldn't get her fingers to move to put more lavender in the sachet she was holding. It had been a long time since Max was really angry with her.

"I'm scared, Shay." Their voice was small. "I'm terrified, all the time for you. And after what Lichfield said…I can't just…I'm sorry, okay? I'm sorry I told Jo. I'm not sorry for doing it, but I'm sorry it upset you. But I can't sit by and let you get yourself killed, you know that, right?"

"Max—" she didn't know what to say. Anger she could deal with. Whatever this was, she was out of her depth.

"When you went to college, it was awful," they said. "I missed you all the time."

"I missed you, too," she said, not sure how it was relating to the conversation at hand.

"The thing is, if you're…gone, I could lose you, for real. No phone calls, no texts…I can't handle it, Shay." They put the candle down. "I can't."

They hugged her, tightly, their face pressed against her collar bone.

Their shoulders shook.

She hugged them back, heedless of the sachet still scrunched up in her hand. She ran her fingers through their hair. There was a tightness in her chest, painful and awful. How would she feel if someone had told her Max had two months, tops? There was no way she would have been able to shrug it off.

The thought alone made it hard to breathe.

"I'm sorry," she said. "For saying that, it was mean. Insensitive? Bad. You're right. I'll stay here tonight."

Max let out a shuddering breath. "Thank you."

"I have a lot of tv to catch up on, you know," she said, striving for nonchalant and falling short of it. "So much. All of the really bad ones you won't watch with me."

"A tv show that bad doesn't exist."

"I might even learn how to crochet since I won't be distracted."

"Do you even have a hook?" Max's voice was watery.

"You need a hook?"

They laughed. It was choked and soft, but she would take it. "I'm sure Jo has a bunch somewhere."

"I could add to her doily collection," Shay said. Max laughed again. She leaned her head against theirs. "Hey, I promise, I'm going to be okay. I'll dredge up every self-preservation instinct I have. I'll be safe and sound right here in my room."

"Okay." They finally pulled away and she wished they hadn't, she already missed the warmth. They sniffed and rubbed their eyes. "Sorry."

"You don't have to be," she said. "I get it. And...sorry."

"I know."

The sun set completely, the blue shadows of evening filling every space. Max turned on her lamp to chase them away.

"Jo will be figuring out where Arlo is any second, we should get these done." Shay didn't say what she was thinking. That she hated being left out. That she could be useful, in at least spotting the ghosts, and then could stay safe wherever she was needed.

Not this time. She could handle being left out, if it was for Max.

Once the candles and sachets were finished she followed them down to the kitchen. Jo was at the table with a man she'd never met before.

Max stopped in the doorway. "Dr. Ahmad?"

"Hi, Max. It's just Rahim, tonight," he said.

Rahim was a handsome man in his thirties. He was tall and thin, wrapped in a sweater and jeans, with warm brown skin and thick glasses frames. His hair was dark and curly, shaved on the sides, and his close-cropped beard was sprinkled with gray.

He was holding a full-on doctor's attaché.

"Wait, aren't you a vet?" Shay asked. "The handsome young man doctor?"

"Wow, Shay, you can't just throw Nana under the bus like that," Max said.

Rahim laughed. "Don't worry, Max, she calls me that to my face. It's good to see you. And nice to meet the infamous Shay."

"Whatever they said about me isn't true," she said, quickly.

He smiled. "Too bad, it was all good."

"What are you doing here?" Max asked.

"I need all hands on deck for this," Jo said. "I don't know what we're up against, but it's not going to be easy. Rahim has a unique ability that might be able to help, and I called Rose. And Gideon."

"Wait, you know about this ghost stuff?" Max looked absolutely flabbergasted. "I babbled about my stupid little ghost show to you-"

"It wasn't stupid." Rahim patted their shoulder. "And some. Mostly, I know how to tie a suture, no matter the species."

"And set a bone, don't forget that," Jo said.

Rahim laughed. "How can I forget?"

"Do we want to know or…?" Shay looked at Max, who shrugged, still looking like their entire world had turned upside down. "So, you're a vet, but you…what, practice illegal human medicine on the side?"

"I went to med school, it's not illegal if I have a license," Rahim said.

"Do you?"

Rahim shrugged. "If I need to pop a joint back into place, are you really going to care?"

Shay thought about it for a moment. "Probably not?"

"Shay won't be coming tonight," Jo corrected him. Shay shrugged when Rahim looked at her with one eyebrow raised. "She's holding down the fort."

"That's me," she said. "Holder of forts. Keeper of houses.

That sounded better than saying she was being forced to stay home for her safety. Probably.

"Always good to have someone back at base," Rahim said.

"Yup." She nodded. She was pretty sure it was better to have someone at base who could actually drive, if need be, but she didn't say that part.

It didn't take long for Gideon and Duncan to show up and they moved to the shop for the final plan. Jo said she'd already briefed Rose over the phone and she'd be there soon. Shay wanted to escape upstairs, but she didn't want to seem like a bad team player, either. Introductions were made and everyone stood in a circle like they were about to break apart for hide and seek.

"So, what's the plan?" Gideon asked. "I'm not exactly, I mean intent and all that but I don't think that's super applicable so00…What do you need me for, again? Driving?"

"Backup, mostly," Duncan patted his shoulder. "Probably holding a candle and standing around. Same job as me! It's going to be exciting. You should be excited."

"…Yeah okay you weren't lying about being Duncan right now," Gideon said.

"Finnias is still here, unfortunately, up in my head." Duncan shrugged. "But we have come to an agreement that he gets to provide a running commentary and I get to listen to it. It's a one-sided compromise. Hopefully we can take down Archie and he'll be free to do…I dunno. Finnias things."

"Great, if you're both done, we can discuss my actual plan," Jo said. "We are going to go in, trap Archibald, and force him to give Arlo up. I'm hoping for an exorcism, but I think our best bet is getting Rahim to keep him calm and off guard. We'll be in two teams. Rahim, Max, and I will go after the ghost, and the rest of you will be looking for Arlo. I'm sorry I don't have an exact location, and I know the place is big, but I don't believe he'll be too difficult to find. And Shay-"

"Is holding down the fort," Shay repeated.

"Good," Jo said. "Stay in your room as much as you can, it's the only room I believe is fully and completely warded. Keep your phone charged, but if the shop phone rings, you need to answer it."

"Why don't we have a cordless phone?" Shay asked. The shop phone was a corded monstrosity, older than Jo.

"Aesthetic," Jo said.

"We use a tablet for a register," Shay reminded her.

Jo sighed. "It has an old fashioned case? But okay, fine, it was free and it worked and…I don't know, I'll get one. I promise. Tomorrow."

"Where are you guys going?" Shay asked. Duncan narrowed his eyes at her and she held up her hands. "Totally innocent question, plus I might need to know. In case of, I don't know, an emergency?"

"And what are you going to do, run?" Duncan asked.

"No, you're right," Jo said. "We're going to the place I should have realized he'd be. Holt Manor."

Shay's stomach dropped. It was obvious, in retrospect, but it was the last place she wanted her friends and brother to go.

"The murder mansion?" Gideon asked.

"Where Finnias died?" Duncan stared at her. "You think that's a good idea?"

"It's where he is," Jo said. "There are no better ideas."

"I meant, bringing Finnias, to where he died," Duncan said. "That sounds like a bad idea."

"If it helps, it's not a murder mansion anymore," Rahim said, not even batting an eye at the mention of murder. Shay was starting to wonder what kind of vet he could possibly be. "They do weddings there."

"Once a murder mansion, always a murder mansion," Shay said. "Wait, really? Weddings?"

"It's beautiful," Rahim said. "I had a client get married there, she showed me the pictures."

"Wow," Shay said. "Max, you want to get married in the murder mansion?"

"Sure, we can do a themed wedding," Max said. "But if Archibald did murder Finnias there, and who knows how many other people, wouldn't it be a place of power for him?"

"Exactly, which is why I'm calling everyone I can think of," Jo said. "I know not all of you have any sort of magical ability, and I know this is asking a lot, but I've thought about it a lot, and where he is largely immune to traditional methods of ghost removal, the only plan I have is throwing everything at this until it sticks."

"We're with you." Rahim put a hand on her shoulder. "We'll get Arlo back. It's going to be okay."

Jo nodded. The front door opened. "That'll be Rose. We should get going, it's a bit of a drive and we only have tonight."

Shay answered the door for Jo and to her surprise immediately got a hug. Rose's perfume smelled of lilacs, despite her name.

"Heard you had an ordeal yesterday," she explained. "I'm glad you're okay."

"As okay as I can be," she said. "Glad you could make it."

"Me, too."

Everyone was getting ready to leave and she couldn't do anything, not even load things into the cars. It left her hollow and antsy, but she squashed it down.

She'd promised Max.

Duncan smacked her back on the way out and she punched his shoulder.

Max gave her one final hug. "We'll be back soon. Stay safe, okay?"

"Safe as houses," she said. "…Safe as my bedroom."

"Good." They kissed the top of her head with a loud, obnoxious noise, ignoring her tone, which was probably for the best. "Mwah. I'll keep you updated, okay?"

"Yeah," she said. "Okay."

She was left alone in the empty shop, listening to car doors close as the sky blackened.

Chapter 22: Star Power

Thay cleaned up and changed her own sheets.

It was a challenge with Becky in the room, but she didn't want to be completely alone.

She took a picture and sent it to Max. They responded with a thumbs up, but they were quiet despite her replies. They must have been working on a more solid plan and she didn't want to interrupt.

Without her, maybe it would even be a reasonable one.

She settled in to be simultaneously bored out of her mind and too on edge to relax until they arrived at the manor. Becky curled up next to her. It was half an hour out of town, according to her phone. She thought about pulling out her ancient laptop, but she'd left it in the living room, and she didn't want to go downstairs unless she had to.

She settled for scrolling through videos on her phone, but it didn't take long to find Vic's recent upload. Ignoring common sense, she read through comments. A large chunk of them were trying to debunk it. Her favorite ones called her a bad actress.

"Cheers, Shay, you're a star," she murmured to herself.

The video played out, the screaming and crashing, her being thrown into a table. She closed out of the app entirely. She had access to Duncan's accounts, maybe it was time for a night of light reading with Hans Lyman.

He hadn't texted her. She wasn't surprised.

She opened the book. Duncan had gotten a whole thirteen pages in. There were a lot of "therefore" and "that being said", plus a plethora of "be that as it mays" were already making her head swim. Sentences backtracked on each other and some of them referenced books and papers she'd never even heard of, and a cursory search didn't turn any of them up. She tried to scan for something about hearts, but if it was mentioned in the beginning, she didn't find it.

She wasn't sure she was taking in any information at all.

Something thudded above her.

The only thing above her was Jo's room in the renovated attic space. She stared up at the ceiling with trepidation. Becky's head jerked up, her ears forward and alert.

Another thud. It sounded like something was tossing Jo's furniture around.

A set of angry and fast footsteps thundered down the stairs.

Shay scooted to the middle of the bed and pulled her knees up to her chest.

The doorknob rattled, the door banging in the frame. Becky hissed and dove under the bed.

She thought the cat might have the right idea.

Her lamp flickered and died. A moment later her phone joined it. The only light in her room for a moment was from the streetlamp outside, cold white throwing the shadows of tree branches in sharp relief against her bedroom floor and walls.

Mist rolled in under the door, thick and low to the ground. She shivered and yanked the blanket up over her legs. A blue light glowed in the hallway, shining through the gaps around her door and gleaming on the wood floor. It rattled again, fiercely.

Something slapped against her window, and she screamed on instinct. It left a dark residue on the glass.

It took a minute to psych herself up, but she tossed the blankets off of her and dashed to her dresser, grabbing the wolf statue and tucking it up against her chest.

The lights came back on and the temperature went back to normal. She breathed out, slowly.

The phone rang and it made her scream again.

"Of course." She checked her phone, but it hadn't been magically revived with the lights. If Lichfield had been trying to sell something, he should have started with a ghost proof phone. She would have paid a lot of her non-existent money for one of those.

The phone was still ringing. She cautiously opened the door. The hallway was normal, except the picture across from her door was askew.

And of course, until Jo got a new phone, the only one was an old rotary monster tucked behind the counter.

While she drew up the courage to dash downstairs, the ringing stopped.

She leaned against the door frame. Maybe it had been a customer, and they'd call back when they were open. She could plug her phone in and no one would ever know she'd missed a call she was supposed to pick up.

The ringing started up again.

"Okay, you're a big bad necromancer," she whispered to herself. "You got this. It's just one flight of stairs. And three rooms. Two where you've been attacked. Yeah."

She shoved the room guardian in her pocket. If she was lucky it would act as a portable ward.

Her luck probably wasn't about to get any better.

She ran down the hall as the thuds in Jo's room started again. She grabbed the wall and practically fell down the stairs in her haste to get down. Something dashed through the hall behind her, but she didn't dare turn to look. It grabbed her ponytail and yanked her back. She shrieked, her socked feet sliding out from under her. She fell hard on the stairs, sliding down half the flight.

Something giggled.

"Oh I hate this I hate this I hate this—" She clambered to her feet and jumped the last three stairs. She landed poorly and ran right into Jo's armchair, falling in the seat for a moment. The ottoman slid across the floor, legs catching on the rug and flipping over.

"Is that you, you stupid poltergeist?" she yelled. "I'll kick your ass!"

A shimmer in the air slammed her back into the chair. Another giggle, this one close enough it lifted her hair around her ear.

"Shay, Shay, come and play," a little girl's sing song voice floated through the air. "We're going to have so much fun!"

"Not likely!"

She pulled herself out of the chair. The living room was dark and full of hazards, but she navigated her way through. The poltergeist kept shoving furniture in her way and laughing when she hit it with her knees and hips. She was going to be even more of a singular huge bruise.

The kitchen was dim and lifeless. Something banged a cupboard shut. A drawer rattled open. The light above the kitchen buzzed to life, the volume increasing until the bulb exploded.

She reached the shop and slammed the kitchen door behind her. It wouldn't stop a ghost, especially not the poltergeist, but it was the only defense she had. She dashed to the counter, but the phone had long since stopped ringing.

"Great." She stared at it. "Fantastic. Wonderful. I love my life."

Another cupboard door closed violently in the kitchen.

The phone rang again and she jumped.

She breathed for a second, trying to calm down. The phone rang again. She picked up the receiver, hoping it would be Jo or Max. "Thank you for calling Spellbound, my name is Shay, how can I help you today?"

She cringed. They weren't even open.

"Is Jocelyn available?" A woman asked.

She recognized the voice, but couldn't pinpoint from where.

"No, sorry," she said. "She's out on a job. I can take a message?"

A sucking intake of breath. "I'm actually outside the shop. Is anyone in?"

"Oh, yeah, lemme get the door." Shay put the phone down and scrambled to the door, unlocking it and pulling it open. She could remind whoever it was that they were closed and send them on their way.

A car door out at the street closed and someone walked up the path to the steps.

Shay remembered where she knew the voice from as she stepped into the light. "…Taylor?"

It made sense. The poltergeist was in the kitchen. Of course the spirit charmer was there.

Except Taylor wasn't the spirit charmer, unless she'd gotten herself possessed again. She was simply a person who had been in the wrong place at the wrong time.

In theory, anyway.

"Shay?" Taylor stared at her. "What are you doing here?"

"I work here," Shay said. "Should be asking you that."

"Oh." Taylor nodded. She'd cut her hair in the week and a half since she'd been possessed by the spirit charmer. It fell just above her shoulders. "I really need to talk to Jo. Or…or anyone, really."

Shay closed the door behind her. The cold bit through her thin sweater and socks. The sounds had stopped in the kitchen, but she didn't trust it enough to go get her shoes. "I'm anyone."

Of course, she wasn't particularly good at talking to people. She'd made Max cry just a few hours before.

"Sure." Taylor nodded. "I guess you…know about this stuff?"

"I know a few ghost things, yeah," Shay said. "I don't know what Jo told you…"

"Not much, about you," Taylor admitted. "She just gave me some things to keep me from being possessed, and said I could call anytime, but I didn't until tonight…"

If she had things to keep her from being possessed - and of course Jo would be thorough - then it couldn't be the spirit charmer. Shay hoped, anyway. She didn't seem possessed to her. Just like someone who really needed to talk.

"Well, I can see ghosts. So yeah, I can talk about them." Shay kept it simple. She didn't need to explain her whole deal to just anyone. "But…I can talk about other things, too. Obviously. Anything you need, really, I'm a good listener-"

"Good. It's my family," Taylor interrupted her, as though the words were bursting to get out. "They've been really strange, lately. Especially my mom. I don't know what to think. I'm scared I'm being paranoid, but what if I'm not?"

"Family is uh…difficult." It was the perfect opportunity to know more about the Stevens family and their connection to the spirit charmer, but tricking Taylor into spilling the beans when all she wanted was someone to confide in felt awful. "What do you mean, weird?"

"First it was about the library, about how they needed to…do something there?"

Shay went cold. "When?"

"I don't know, a few days ago," Taylor said. I don't know what they planned, but they started talking about Holt Manor. You probably know it as the murder mansion. It's run by an outside company, but they brought it back into the family and stopped holding events there a while ago. It's weird, they were never interested in it before. I know something is up. Are you sure you can't get a hold of Jo?"

"…I'm a little more positive we need to." Shay's stomach sank down to somewhere around her toes. "Because she's headed there right now."

"What?" Taylor went impossibly paler. "Are you sure?"

"Completely," Shay said.

"They said something was happening there tonight, you don't think…?"

Shay dashed inside and snagged the address book, hurrying back to the porch.

"Can I use your phone?" She held out a hand.

"Um. Sure." Taylor pulled it out of her purse and handed it over.

Shay dialed Jo's number. A pleasant, mildly robotic female voice answered. "We're sorry, this call cannot be completed as dialed."

"Wait, crap, she lost her phone," Shay said. She called Max, the only number she had memorized.

Straight to voicemail.

She tried every number, but no one answered. All of them went to various voicemail messages. She didn't let a single one play all the way through.

She leaned against the doorway, one hand over her mouth to keep what little of dinner she'd had down. She managed to breathe. In. Out. Maybe their phones were dead, sucked dry like hers was. Maybe they'd all turned them off as part of Jo's plan, and no one had told her. Or they had, but her phone was already out of commission by then.

Or something horrible had happened, and they were all hurt, and she was at least forty minutes away by car and didn't have a driver's license. She was definitely willing to drive whatever car had been left behind, but she didn't like her chances of getting there without getting horribly lost.

"Shay?" Taylor sounded concerned. "Is this…is this the spirit charmer again?"

"Most likely," Shay admitted. Dread filled her chest, leaving very little room to breathe. "Or at least she's part of it. I have a bad feeling."

"Me, too." Taylor bit her lip, clearly deciding. Finally, she gave Shay a serious, hard look. "I know you don't know me, and the only time we really talked I…wasn't myself. But will you go with me to the manor? Just to check. I just want to make sure everyone is all right."

Shay considered, for a moment. She'd been attacked by the poltergeist, or something too close for comfort. For all she knew, Taylor was possessed again. She hadn't been able to tell before, and she realized she didn't know Taylor well enough to actually know.

It could be a trap.

It was a trap, for all of her friends, and they'd walked right into it. She'd let them go without a fight, and they'd stumbled into something horrible.

She had to do something. She had no idea what, sleeping through the night and relaxing most of the afternoon couldn't have been enough rest, if Lichfield was right.

But what else could she do?

Max needed her. They wanted her to sit this one out, but she wasn't going to let anyone get hurt just so she could be a little safer.

Maybe she was a wannabe hero type.

Or just very stupid.

"All right," Shay said. "Let me grab my jacket."

Chapter 23:
Inherently Unsafe

"So...Jo gave you things to keep you from being possessed?"

Shay winced at how awkward it was, but she needed to say something. They'd been driving for ten minutes, and Taylor hadn't said a word. She hadn't even turned on the radio.

"A necklace, I wear it all the time," Taylor explained. "And a few sachets. I keep one in my car and one in my house. What about you? I assume she gave you something."

"I can't be possessed," Shay said. That she was pretty certain on. The spirit charmer could have saved a lot of time by just possessing her.

"Oh. Must be nice."

"Yeah, ghosts just kick me around instead."

Taylor's shoulders hunched. "…Sorry."

Shay mentally punched herself right in the face. She was trying to start a conversation, not make things worse. "It's fine. I mean, I think getting possessed is probably worse."

"Maybe," Taylor said. "So…if you can't get possessed, what's the bath salt for?"

"It's anti-ghost salt, actually," she said. She'd raided their entire stock before leaving the house, hoping a line of salt at the door to the shop would keep it from being destroyed. She'd glanced into the living room, and it might as well have snowed with the sheer number of doilies scattered across the floor.

"Really?" Taylor didn't sound impressed.

"Tried and tested in the field," she said. "By Max, they um, they saved me from a ghost, once."

The bag crinkled when her grip tightened on it. She let it go and smoothed it out.

Taylor patted her shoulder, glancing at her. "It's going to be okay. Maybe they don't have reception up there."

"Yeah, we're probably freaking out for nothing." Shay didn't believe it for a second.

They'd left the city behind, the car climbing steadily into the hills. They were golden during the day, but it was so dark the only thing visible was the road in front of them and the occasional clump of yellow weeds.

Shay turned on the radio.

Static, followed by a garbled voice that she could almost understand. The hairs on the back of her neck rose. She punched it off.

"Yeah, sorry, that hasn't been working." Taylor was way too calm about horror pouring out of her car stereo.

"Uh, yeah, no problem." Shay leaned back in her seat, suppressing a shudder.

It didn't take long to get into a narrow, winding ravine. Strands of thick pine crowded in close on either side. They turned a corner, full of scraggly trees reaching out for the car.

"You didn't tell me why everyone is here," Taylor said. "As far as I know, they didn't get permission, and it is still private property."

"I don't know," Shay admitted. That hadn't actually crossed her mind, but she'd done plenty of the entering part of breaking and entering through the years for Max's show, sometimes when they asked her not to. Usually when they asked her not to. "If they got permission, that is."

"And the reason?" Taylor asked.

What did Shay have to lose? If Taylor could help, she needed to know what they were up against. "One of our friends was kidnapped, so they're saving him."

"Kidnapped?" Taylor's voice cracked. "And they think he's at Holt Manor? Why on earth…"

"It wasn't like, a human kidnapping," Shay explained, which sounded worse, even to her ears. "It was a ghost. A ghost took him."

Taylor breathed out. It was a little shaky. "Right. Okay. A ghost took him. Was it…?"

"No, not her," Shay said, quickly. "His name is Archibald. Jo is good at scrying, she said that Arlo was there, so…Arlo is probably there. She knows her stuff. Um."

"Okay, so, a rescue mission." Taylor let that information sink in for a moment. "You didn't go because he would…kick you?"

Shay shrugged. "Something like that? And I was holding down the fort. Anyway, we need to be ready to face him, so the salt. I don't know if it'll work-"

"You just said it was field tested," Taylor reminded her, giving her a brief side eye, but most of her attention stayed on the road. Shay supposed she should be happy Taylor hadn't wrecked the car. Or told her to get out. Or any of it.

"So…he's a special kind of ghost?" Shay knew she was not doing a good job of explaining things. "That's why he kidnapped Arlo, he's using him like a battery I think, and normal things aren't working against him, and we don't have time to figure out another thing, so…just be on your guard. I'll take the lead. If we're lucky you're right, and they just…no reception, or…"

She was rambling. She pressed her mouth closed.

"Yeah." Taylor nodded. "Probably just that, and not a crazy ghost kidnapping people."

Shay hadn't wanted to think about Max getting kidnapped, but it sprinted to the forefront of her worries. If Archibald took Max, she didn't care how burned out she was, or how dangerous things got. She was going to destroy him.

The house came into view, saving her from further conversation.

A few lights out front had been turned on, highlighting the massive hulk of the house.

They pulled into the large, circular driveway, next to Gideon's empty car.

Taylor turned off the car. The heavy silence of a November night pressed in around them.

"So um. What do we do? Go inside?"

"Don't have a better plan," Shay admitted, holding the bag so tightly her fingers ached.

She had her salt and Taylor dug her satchel out of her glove compartment. It wasn't enough, Shay knew it wasn't. If a team of well equipped witches and ghost hunters and whatever else hadn't been able to take Archibald down, she doubted her and Taylor stood a chance.

She had to try.

They walked into the entrance together. Taylor tried the door but it rattled uselessly. She frowned and punched a code into the panel next to the knob, but it didn't beep.

"I guess we'll try the back entrance," Taylor said.

"I don't like this," Shay said. With time the anger that had flash burned her reason away started to die down, replaced with a horrible, cold dread.

"Neither do I."

They walked down the steps, their shoes crunching on the gravel.

Shay glanced behind them, but the trees were dark.

She turned back to the house and a ghost was right in front of her.

It was a woman wearing a high-necked dress. Her face was so bright Shay couldn't make out any details.

She didn't want to. She held up a bag of salt, fumbling with the seal. It didn't want to pull open.

"Crap." She backed away. The ghost didn't move. Her skirt flowed around her ankles. "Oh crap, okay, we gotta go."

"What?" Taylor turned and cringed. "Oh, god."

They backed away slowly, towards the corner of the house. The woman stayed where she was. Smudged blue shapes gathered under the trees.

"I hope this back door is close because there are a lot of ghosts," Shay said.

"We're close," Taylor promised her. They reached the door and Taylor tried to enter her combination into the pad, but it was the same as the front door.

The woman stood at the corner of the house.

Her skull flashed through the brightness of her face.

"I don't mean to be a major downer, but I hope you have another idea," Shay finally got the bag open with shaking fingers.

"What does she want?" Taylor asked.

Shay had no idea. "From my experience? Something bad and violent."

"They must have changed the combination and not told me." Taylor bit her lip. "But…but I know one way in."

"Great! What is it?"

"Through the wine cellar." Taylor pointed to a set of doors, set in an angle in the ground. "It's original to the house, but we made an entrance on the inside."

"Awesome," Shay said. "What if it's combination is locked, too?"

"We don't use a combination for it." Taylor pulled out her keys. Shay kept an eye on the ghost as it advanced to the doors, watching Taylor's back while she unlocked it. The woman didn't move, simply stared at them.

The doors were so heavy it took both of them to lift one.

What little Shay could see looked like a brick-lined throat, sinking into the dark of the earth.

Taylor tried a light switch next to the doors, but nothing happened. She pulled out her phone and turned on the flashlight, bringing the simple wooden stairs into view, edges sharp from the light.

They descended into the darkness. The chill sank into Shay's sweater and she shrugged deeper into her jacket.

They reached the bottom of the stairs.

The flashlight gleamed in crescents on the rows and rows of bottles. Glimmering slivers of blond shimmered in the dark wood grain of the floor.

It would be easy for a person to hide behind the shelves, waiting for them in the dark.

"Be careful," Taylor told her. "Some of those bottles are worth thousands of dollars."

"...Seriously?" Shay asked. "It's fermented grape juice. In a bottle. Sometimes I make wine on accident."

"Some of them are original to the house, they're older than the two of us combined," Taylor explained, which at least sounded better than leaving fruit juice in the fridge well past its expiration date.

"Oh. Really old grape juice. I'll be careful," Shay promised.

They walked down the center aisle. Taylor swung her phone from side to side, but each row was empty, and each time it was a relief.

Towards the back of the cellar the air was frigid. Bits of mist clung to the floor and softened the corners like cobwebs.

"Ghost incoming," Shay said. She yanked open the bag and shoved her hand inside, ready to grab a handful.

The mist converged into a pillar in front of her and the woman in the high collared dress billowed into existence. Shay jerked back from her, but she didn't make any move to follow.

The ghost lifted one arm and pointed, not at the stairs, but at the wall to Shay's right.

"What?" Shay asked.

The ghost pointed again before fading into the back wall.

"…That seemed weird," Taylor said.

"Ghosts don't make sense most of the time," Shay said. It was strange she hadn't attacked, but Shay was grateful. She only had so much salt, and she was pretty sure she was going to need most of it for Archibald. "It's because they're mostly memory, so they're like weird echoes. Just going through the motions. She could have been pointing at something that used to be over there. Maybe it's a Cask of Whatever sort of situation."

Taylor's eyebrows rose. "The Cask of…you think she's bricked in the wall?"

"I mean, it's possible?" Shay smiled in what she hoped was a winning manner. "Duncan was reading a lot of Poe for Halloween."

"Sure, dead bodies in the wall, why not," Taylor muttered. "Let's get upstairs before she shows up again."

"Right, yeah." Shay hadn't looked at the stairs. They were much worse than she expected, a metal spiral leading up to a trap door. "This seems unsafe."

"Probably." Taylor's boots clanged on each step, and Shay winced each time. Her key worked on the trap door. "It opens up into the kitchens. Better than going around, I guess."

"Inherently unsafe," Shay said. There weren't even any grip strips on the stairs. She tucked the bag in her pocket to keep her hands free for the railing.

She expected ghostly hands to reach through the empty spaces between the stairs and grab her ankles, but she made it up without incident. The kitchens were dark.

A howl filled the house. The pots and pans hanging above the kitchen island rattled and hummed, the cupboard doors vibrated. A cold wind rushed through the room. For just a moment, Shay was back in the library basement, being suffocated by dirt.

But she wasn't. She was on the stairs to a wine cellar that were one drunken misstep from being part of a negligence case.

She scrambled up into the kitchen after Taylor.

The kitchen was at the very back of the house, leading into the dining room and several drawing rooms, plus a library, barely lit up by Taylor's phone flashlight.

The sound came again. Paintings tapped on the wall around them, and a few books fell off of the shelves. Whispers hissed from the corners and Shay tried to ignore them, tried not to think about teeth and claws and eyes.

Another howl, louder than the last, and the door blew open. Every door in the house banged and rattled. The wind ripped past her and out through the entryway, stealing her breath for a moment

Shay hurried after it.

She'd seen the entryway before, in a memory. A grand staircase sweeping up to the second floor, surrounded by railings. High ceilings and a chandelier. It had been a beautiful room.

The décor had changed, updated for more modern sensibilities, but the shape of the room was the same.

Most of the paintings were on the floor and the chandelier was askew. The rug had been tugged aside by some great force and knocked over the bench by the stairs and the little table with an old-fashioned phone on it. Salt scattered across the floorboards, hail after a storm.

"Shay?" Duncan stood up from where he was sitting on the stairs, Gideon next to him. "What are you…Taylor?"

"What did you do to this place?" Taylor asked.

Rahim was bandaging up Rose's arm.

Jo and Max weren't anywhere.

"Where's Max?" Shay stalked towards Duncan, like it was his fault.

Duncan shook his head. "Shay, you should go, he's way too powerful, he—"

"Where. Is. Max?" Shay stopped just short of him, tempted to reach out and shake him. "What happened here?"

"The…the ghost, it took them," Gideon told her. He looked physically okay, maybe a little banged up, but his hands were shaking. "They just disappeared, and we couldn't get out…and Finnias…"

The righteous anger Shay thought would consume her didn't come. Despair filled her instead. "…Finnias?"

"He's gone," Duncan said. "He left before…I don't know if we were too close or if the altruistic self sacrificing jerk was trying to save me, but he's gone. I don't know if we can get him back, Shay. Any of them."

She had to sit down. Max was gone. She hadn't been there, and Max was gone. She hadn't been able to do anything to help at all.

"Shay?" Duncan put a hand on her shoulder.

"Where?" Shay asked.

"I don't know," Duncan said.

"Right. I'm going upstairs." Shay stood up. She was shaking, inside and out. She was going to be sick.

She had to keep moving.

"Upstairs?" Rose said. "Do you have a plan?"

"No," Shay said. "But that's where Finnias's landing is, and that's the only way I can think about getting in contact with him. He might be able to help."

"You should go-"

"I'm not going!" she snapped. "He has Max and I'm not going anywhere until I have them back. Do you understand?"

Duncan held up his hands like she was trying to hit him, and she realized she'd clenched her hands into tight fists. "I understand. That's what we'll do. I'm coming with you."

She thought she might cry, her eyes were stinging, but there wasn't time. She wiped at her face with her sleeve, just in case, and turned to go up the stairs.

It was surreal. The walls were painted creamy yellow instead of wallpapered, the carpet was different, and the paintings and light fixtures certainly weren't the same.

But they were the same stairs, leading up to the landing.

No wallpaper, the carpet was different, and the window had a different shape. Square instead of rounded at the top.

She still would have known it anywhere.

Duncan tugged a hand through his hair. "God. Right here, huh? Carpet's different, but… it's been a hundred years. That's normal, right? It's not because…God."

"I don't know." She ran her fingers over where little golden diamonds used to catch the light. "I guess the wallpaper faded."

There was a small table with a vase on it. The flowers in it were fake.

"This is weird, right?" Duncan asked.

"Yeah." She'd never expected to really be there, standing where Finnias had, a century apart. Like she could reach through the years and find him.

Archibald was next to her without any warning at all. He backhanded her, hard enough she saw stars.

She hit the floor, hard, her ears ringing and blood in her mouth. Archibald bore down on her and she barely rolled out of the way, ending up on her feet. The carpet unraveled beneath his feet; the stairs below sagged into disrepair.

She wanted to scream. To force Archibald to tell her where Max was. But the stairs right below her opened up into a yawning chasm, down into the very depths of the foundation and Archibald was still coming for her.

She ran up the stairs.

Her head was pounding and she staggered after a single flight. Archibald was behind her, following at an almost leisurely pace.

"Shay!" Duncan jumped over the hole in the stairs and landed badly on the other side, falling down onto the stairs. Archibald turned and panic flared through her, burning away the pain and the uncertainty. She slammed into him and he knocked her back onto the stairs.

"I don't have time for you," Archibald said.

"You're going to have to make time-"

Archibald lifted one hand and Duncan hit the railing, hard. He looped his elbow around one of the supports, keeping himself from flipping over

"Duncan!" Shay ran towards him, not sure what she intended to do, but Archibald shoved her back up the stairs.

"You have an appointment to keep," he said, calmly. She scrambled up the stairs, not sure where she intended to go, up past the third floor when Archibald barred her way.

The fourth floor opened up into a wide balcony. She pulled a handful of salt out and made the worst line possible across the doorway.

Archibald lifted one hand and dragged it down the air between them, green sparks flying away from his touch. "That won't work for long, but I'm not here to kill you."

"You couldn't if you tried," she spat. A wave of dizziness threatened to take her to her knees, but she stayed standing. "Where's Max? Give them back, right now."

He had the audacity to smile.

"Honestly, Archibald, what are you even doing?" The voice behind her sent a shock of cold up her spine. "We want her help, not to kill her."

"She's fine." He didn't sound sorry. "You can still have your little tea party."

Shay turned around.

An ornate mirror had been placed on the other end of the balcony, mist drifting through the bottom of the frame.

Chapter 24: Decisive Action

"Oh, it's just you." Shay sounded more tired than scared, despite her still pounding heart and the terror laying ice cubes down her spine.

"How rude. I told you that you had until tonight to decide," the spirit charmer's voice echoed out of the darkness. "It's time, Shay."

"I'm not doing anything until you tell me where Max is," she said. "And Arlo and Jo and…and if Duncan is hurt I'll throw your stupid mirror over this railing."

"You are so dramatic," the spirit charmer grumbled. "Fine. Archibald, release the witches."

Archibald looked genuinely surprised. "But-"

"Do it, or I'll tear you into pieces so small you'll never go back together." The spirit charmer hissed. "It's exactly what you deserve."

Archibald gave a stiff little bow and vanished.

"There. I've done my part."

"Is Max really safe?" Shay asked. "And…and everyone else?"

"Yes, the situation is under control. Archibald just got a little big of his horrible head. After you join me, we'll destroy him. Now." A woman flickered into view through the darkness of the mirror. She was pretty, with a narrow face and high cheekbones, hair swept back into a bun. Her dress was high collared with a fitted jacket layered over it. "Let's talk."

Her bones glowed underneath translucent skin.

"Is that really you?" Shay asked.

"It is, my name is Emmaline," she said. Shay had no idea if that was supposed to be significant. Her eyes narrowed and her smile widened. "And you have no idea who I am. Here I thought you did your research. For shame.

"All I need to know is that I don't trust you." Shay ignored the uneasy feeling that she'd seen Emmaline somewhere before. That she should know who she was.

"Oh, you shouldn't trust anyone who says they'll give you the world but hasn't shown you anything," Emmaline said. "That's smart, Shay. You don't know what's coming, but I do. And I can keep you and all of your little friends safe. Isn't that what Max wants? What everyone is working so hard for? To keep little Shay O'Brannon safe from all of the big, bad ghosts because she can't take care of herself. With me, you'd learn everything about your abilities. You'd never have to be scared again. And I can help you with another problem. Starts with an F. Probably important to you."

It was tempting, and Shay hated it. She'd been determined to say no, but that was before she talked to Lichfield. Before she failed Max. She still hadn't seen them. "You tried to kill me."

"I did," Emmaline didn't sound the least bit apologetic. "But you remember, I offered you a deal before I did that. Besides, I had significantly less…freedom, then. But with you, that will change."

"You said you didn't want to tear the veil open," Shay reminded her.

"I don't," she said. "New week, new plan. We both have something the other wants. I have all the knowledge you could possibly need and the ability to keep you safe. And you have the power to help me with a…problem, that I've unfortunately run up against."

"What problem?" Shay asked. "I can't agree to help if I don't know."

Emmaline shook her head. "If we keep talking little Archie is going to keep your friends. Which one? Max? Jo? Tick tock, Shay."

She bit her lip, so hard it stung. The spirit charmer was offering all she needed. Safety, a way to figure out her abilities, an idea of what was coming.

If Emmaline was telling the truth.

"What exactly do you get out of it?" She hated herself, in that moment. She knew Max wouldn't want this, but she didn't know how else to save them. She knew she was just stalling, that she'd already made up her mind to agree.

"You think you're a smart little negotiator, don't you?" Emmaline laughed. It sounded like several people at once, all of them slightly off from the other. Shay thought of the rat king and had to force herself not to take a step back. "You have no idea what you can do. You can make ghosts solid. Not just for you, but for everyone else. All you have to do is be in contact with them. With my help, you might not even need that. And that's just the beginning. You can see magic, can't you? Why can't you manipulate it the way you do ghosts? Do you have any idea what we can do with that power?"

Shay pressed her lips together. It felt like everything was moving too fast. She needed to just say no, but when she opened her mouth, something else came out. "What's coming?"

Emmaline waved one finger. "Oh, something worse than me. There are things much more terrible than ghosts, Shay. You met one of them, didn't you? I can see it all over you. And that was almost tame."

The rats. She shuddered at the memory of their little claws and a hundred bright eyes all around her, hungry and waiting.

"See? We need each other."

"What about leaving a trail of bodies in your wake?" Shay asked. "I'm not…if you're some sort of serial killer…"

"Oh, largely an exaggeration," she said. "But anyone I killed? They deserved it."

Shay looked down at her hands and curled her fingers in, nails pressing into her palms.

Two months. She'd promised Max she would do everything she could to survive, but did she mean this? Did she want to throw her lot in with a murderer?

Would she be able to get Max back if she didn't? Did she really have a choice at all?

She didn't. Emmaline was still attempting to bargain, but Shay had already resolved herself. No matter the cost, she wasn't going to let Archibald use Max like a battery. She couldn't.

"I can help you, Shay. That's a sincere offer. I can help you get Finnias's memories back," Emmaline said. "I—"

Archibald materialized next to the mirror and grabbed Emmaline by the throat before either of them could react.

She choked, her eyes widening.

"Now, honey, how about you stop trying that little parlor trick of yours," he drawled. "You might have wowed the crowds back in the day, but it's been over a century. It doesn't work on me anymore. Time to give it a rest."

The mirror roared.

The noise rose in volume, becoming an incredible, all-encompassing sound. A jet engine going right off in her face. Shay's hair blew back and she held up an arm against the wind howling from the frame.

A skeletal hand burst from the mirror and grabbed Archibald's wrist, yanking him towards the frame. More hands exploded from the surface and snagged at his throat, jacket, and hair. Too many teeth and empty sockets surged from the mirror. Shay screamed but it was a tiny sound in the throes of a hurricane.

"You dare think you can break away from me that easily?" several voices screamed. None of them sounded human. "I can end you! I will!"

"No you won't!" Archibald's voice was, incredibly, louder than the sound. He twisted and with a tremendous crack the mirror's surface shattered, bright white lines against the dark.

Archibald extracted his hand from the mirror and wiped it on the suit coat he was still holding, calmly and methodically.

Shay backed up to the door. It slammed shut before she got to it. The knob didn't move under her hand.

"Ah, Shay." He turned to her. The lights flickered, and Archibald strobed wildly between a stretched out, horrific gray monster in the dark and a man only a few years older than her with perfectly groomed hair and impeccably pressed clothes.

"Are you going to trap me like the others?" It came out much squeakier than she wanted it to. The door rattled behind her, someone was trying to get to her, but even if they did, what could they do?

"No, unfortunately, necromancers can't be used the same way a witch can." He inspected his nails.

"But?" Shay knew he was about to say something horrible.

"But the Emmaline was right, your abilities are extraordinary." Archibald regarded her, carefully.

"What, you're like her? You want me to join you?" Shay tried the handle again, but the cold burned her fingers and she snatched her hand away, curling it up against her chest.

"In a manner of speaking."

She shook her head, loose hair whipping around her face. "No."

"You act like you have a choice." He smiled. "Do you know why Finnias has a hole in his chest?"

A chill screamed its way up her spine.

Lichfield had kept asking her about the heart.

Her voice was shaky, when she found it again. "I have a feeling I'm about to find out."

"Yes, darling, you are."

The coat slung over his arm dropped.

He was holding a knife, long and curved at the end. Its handle was white bone, wrapped with a gauzy black cloth. The edge glowed a brilliant electric blue.

She ducked and half crawled away when he lunged at her, the blade splintering the wood of the door frame. He turned slowly, holding the knife loosely.

"Let's not make this difficult, my dear."

"I am not your dear." Shay's voice cracked, despite her bravado.

Archibald held up his free hand and tightened it into a fist. The glass in the mirror broke further, the glass pulling away from the frame. Shards formed a circle in front of him, rotating slowly.

Shay threw herself to the side when the glass shot at her. Her jacket took the brunt of it, but one piece sliced open the back of her hand and another grazed her leg. Blood splattered on the floor.

She staggered, her hands up. Her left hand burned when she curled her fingers up. She barely felt it.

Archibald advanced on her, backing her into a corner. He raised the knife.

A hand wrapped around his wrist, yanking it back. He turned with a snarl. "You!"

"You bastard!" Emmaline yelled. He slapped her. She vanished.

It was enough to distract him. Shay ran for the door, getting there as it finally banged open, almost hitting her in the face. Rahim grabbed her arm and yanked her through it, slamming it closed and pouring a thick line of salt in front of it.

"That won't stop him." Shay's words were practically a sob. "Is Max…?"

"No one's back, the stairs repaired themselves so we followed you," Rahim said.

Shay tried very hard not to cry. "Duncan?"

"He's safe, he's downstairs," Rahim said. "Just shaken up."

"Your arm…" Taylor moved to help Shay.

"It can wait, we need to get out of here." Shay clambered down the stairs. She would have fallen if Rahim hadn't helped her.

Her jeans were sliced open above the knee and every step was agony. More shards had scored her jacket, some had cut right through. She didn't want to look at her arm, it made her feel sick.

An immense roar filled the stairway and Shay limped faster. She slipped, but Rahim caught her good arm before she fell.

She ignored Duncan and Gideon's questions in the entryway, intent on getting outside. A wind rushed through the house, slamming doors and knocking paintings from the walls.

Max's bag was laying on the floor, the strap ripped. She stopped long enough to pick it up, bundling it under her right arm.

It hurt. More than the cuts. More than anything ever had before, and she could barely breathe.

She had to keep moving. For them, to find them. She didn't care what it took. A deal with the devil, ripping Archibald apart herself…she would do anything.

"Let's go." Rahim's voice was gentle and soothing, and Shay found she could breathe again. She nodded.

The front doors were wide open, letting them out into the night.

Duncan yanked her out of the way and the mirror crashed onto the steps, directly where she'd been standing.

"Geez, Shay, you make him mad?" His voice shook. He had a bruise forming above one eye.

"Something like that." She was shaking, too, and she was so tired, but it wasn't over. It wasn't even close.

"I'm gonna figure out how to be a real necromancer so I can raise that asshole from the dead and kill him again." Duncan had never sounded so angry, checking her arm. Shay had to look away. She didn't want to see it.

"Let's get you patched up before we do anything else," Rahim said. "There's glass in your jacket."

"…Oh, so there is," she said. Everything was far away and soft around the edges. Rahim got her sitting in Gideon's car and helped get her jacket off. Her hand and arm were sliced up, blood already dripping off of her elbow, but she barely felt it. Rahim set to cleaning her up.

In the end she needed eleven stitches. He told her to look away, so she didn't see what he was doing. It should have hurt more, but the thought was vague and far away, and she would rather it didn't.

"You're going to have some scars," Rahim said. "But it was mostly superficial, so no lasting damage."

"I'll tell people I was mauled by a tiger."

"Sounds like a plan." He chuckled, wrapping her up. "There you go. You should get some rest."

"Here." Gideon put a jacket over her shoulders. "It'll be too big, but…better than nothing."

"Thanks." She curled the fingers of her good hand around it, pulling it close over her like a cape.

"Good, keep her warm. I think she's going into shock," Rahim said.

"An evil ghost tried to carve my heart out with a big knife, so yeah, a little shock probably," she said.

"What?" Duncan's voice cracked. "Oh. I am definitely gutting him like a fish. That's…that's what he did to Finnias, isn't it."

Shay nodded. "He…he killed him. For his abilities. Took his heart. Poor guy. We need to talk to him."

"You want to go back in there?" Duncan looked at the house. "Are you insane?"

"Probably, but I don't think we have to." She held out her hand.

"You think we can do the whole wonder twin powers thing."

"We're not twins, but yeah, guess so." Shay was starting to understand why Emmaline thought they'd be stronger together. "Wonder twin powers."

"Activate." He took her hand.

Light poured through the window.

Finnias was there, as she'd hoped. He looked like a corpse, skin gray and hair in disarray. A dark stain bloomed from the gory hole in his chest. He flickered in and out until Shay grabbed his hand, his fingers slick with blood.

"Definitely not a metaphor," Duncan muttered, covering his mouth like he was going to be sick.

"Hey, stay with me," she said. He solidified, color returning to his cheeks.

"Shay?" He sounded awful.

"Where are you?" she asked. "I'm going to save you. I'm going to save everyone."

"He—" Finnias turned away from her. "They'll show you where to go."

"What does that mean?" she asked.

He pulled his hand from hers and they were back in their own time again.

"That was enough fuel for roughly fifty years of nightmares," Duncan said. "Let's never do it again."

The ghost of the woman in the high collared dress formed in front of her, pointing to the trees.

Chapter 82:
Salt and Burn

Shay should have been afraid.

The ghost was close enough if she wanted to it would take very little effort to finish what Archibald started. The cold radiated off her in waves, chilling the November night into something bordering on deadly.

But Shay wasn't scared.

"She's not here to hurt us," Rose said. "She wants to show us the way."

"The way to what?" Duncan asked.

Shay must have been calm because of intent.

Which had never mattered before.

Something was wrong.

"The way we have to go," Rose said.

"That sounds awfully cryptic," Gideon said. They were all far away, things she didn't have to worry about.

She needed to worry about it.

Max was gone, but the thought couldn't sink through a numb buzzing coating her brain in static.

The ghost reached for her. She did nothing to stop it.

Gideon threw a sachet and the woman vanished, like she'd never been at all, the air almost warm in comparison.

"Sorry, was that the right thing to do?" he asked. "Were you planning something?"

"No, I—" She hadn't reacted. Not even a little bit. It was Rahim. She didn't know how she knew, but she was certain. "What are you doing?"

"Trying to figure out where the ghost wants us to go," Rahim said. His tone was completely even and reasonable.

Shay shook her head, trying to fight out the calmness settling over her like a blanket. "You're doing something to me. You're…you're blocking me, or…or making me calm. Stop it."

"You can feel that?" Rahim blinked and took a step back.

Immediately the fear that had been looming over her crashed down, drowning everything out, trying to drive her to be a gibbering mess on the ground. She barely caught herself on the car door.

There were whispers all around, any moment the glints of light would become little eyes glowing in the dark, little claws grasping at her skin and hair, a voice in her ear.

"Hey, woah, I'm sorry." Rahim caught her good shoulder and helped her sit back up. "I'm sorry, I didn't mean to."

Duncan pushed him out of the way, not very gently, and took her shoulders. "Shay. Shay, you need to breathe."

She was breathing, wasn't she? She inhaled and realized she hadn't been, her lungs burned. Her throat was on fire. She gulped down more air, like she'd been drowning.

"Okay, okay, take ten breaths with me, okay? In, and out," Duncan said. "You got this. You're a strong badass warrior princess necromancer, right? You got this."

She laughed, despite herself, and it helped.

It took longer than ten breaths to gain her equilibrium, for her breathing to calm and slow. "Strong badass warrior princess necromancer?"

"Eh, I mean, other than the princess it's basically true," Duncan said. "Too bad, though, a necromancer castle? Aesthetic goals."

"And money."

"Gobs of it."

"You're such a nerd," she said. "Thanks."

"Of course, what good is my own tendency to panic if I can't help anyone else?" Duncan asked. He turned on Rahim, clearly angry. "What was that?"

"I have…the ability to take emotions," Rahim said, slowly. "Jo calls me an empath. Arlo asked me to use it on ghosts a few times, to help them find peace. I take their pain from their past, from their death. It helps them move on, sometimes. I've gotten pretty good at compartmentalizing, I didn't even realize I was doing it. I'm so sorry."

"So, it works on people, too?" Shay asked. Jo had said something similar, once, but it had been about spirit mediums reading people's emotions, not some guy stealing hers.

"Some people, you must be particularly susceptible to it."

"That's awful," she said.

Hurt flashed in Rahim's eyes, but it was gone almost as quickly as she noticed it. "Yes. A little bit. You're feeling volatile, and it's…instinct to help. I can't apologize enough."

"Of course I'm feeling volatile!" She wanted to scream. She wanted to shake Rahim to break through the calm. It wouldn't do any good, but she wanted it, anyway. "My best friend is gone! My boss, my… other boss, and…and he got the spirit charmer, I think. And if he has her, he can control any ghost. He can do anything he wants. He's…he's so strong, and I don't even have…I can't do anything to stop it."

She was not going to cry, even though the sobs were building in her chest and her eyes were stinging. Everyone was staring at her, even Duncan. She forced herself to her feet, putting all of her energy into staying there, even when she wavered. "Whatever, just…don't."

"Understandable," Rahim said, smoothly. If he was hurt by her lashing out, it didn't show at all.

She tried to swallow her anger. It went down like hot coals and burned in her chest.

"Finnias said they'd show us the way." She turned away from Rahim, even though she wanted to say more. Words sharp enough to cut. "He must have meant the other ghosts."

"She was pointing through the trees." Duncan pointed, too. The trunks were closer together on that side of the property. Ghosts stood underneath the dark branches, blue smudges from where she was standing, turning the trees into an underwater cathedral.

She had to get Max back. Max, Jo, and Arlo. No matter what.

"Why, though?" Taylor asked. She'd been very quiet since Shay came back. It must have been horrifically overwhelming. Shay hadn't even introduced her. At least she'd filled her in on who was who on the drive up. Her anger hadn't cooled at all, but she needed to work with Rahim, even if she didn't want to.

"Taylor, uh, is not possessed and is here to help," she said, quickly. "Taylor, you know Gideon and kind of Duncan, this is Rahim and Rose, I told you about them. They're…nice."

"Nice to meet you," Taylor said. "And I mean we know where Archibald is, don't we? He's in the house."

"Yeah, but in my professional ghost hunting opinion, I don't think anything short of burning it down is going to get him out of it," Gideon said.

"Salt and burn the earth," Duncan agreed.

"Of course, I'm not a witch, so—" Gideon shrugged. "Rose?"

"I'm a medium. Which makes me more qualified. Unfortunately, I think you're right," Rose said. "It was quick, but I still got a pretty good read on him earlier. He's very determined to stay in this life, he feels no need to move on. But it's not our house and we don't know where our friends are being kept, or what it would do to him. It could destroy him, but he's shown already he's not site bound. He could leave the area and we'd be back to square one."

"And there's Finnias," Duncan said.

"Too bad, I was ready to commit some arson," Taylor said. "And it is my house—"

"Your family's house," Gideon corrected her.

"Close enough, it's insured, who cares?" Taylor looked ready to set the house on fire with the power of her mind alone. "It'd be better, anyway."

"As much as it pains me to say it, we are not burning any houses down." Shay couldn't believe she was the voice of reason. Under any other circumstances she would have advocated for arson and insurance fraud. But if there was a chance Max was inside, she couldn't allow it. "We didn't even bring marshmallows."

"An excellent point, can't have a bonfire that big if we're not making s'mores." Duncan nodded. "So, what's the plan? Because Jo's plan of 'throw everything and hope something sticks' failed. Really badly."

"What happened, anyway?" Shay hadn't had a chance to ask. All she knew was the aftermath.

"At first it was pretty quiet. We looked around, saw how rich people decorate houses they don't even use," Duncan said. "Jo set down a salt circle in case we needed it. But when Archibald appeared it didn't do much to stop him. Finnias was yanked right out, which was not fun by the way that needs to stop, and Jo and Max were just poof, gone. Not literally poof, but the lights went out, and when I got my candle lit…We threw salt, had candles, the whole witchy nine yards, but it didn't even matter. The salt circle worked well enough to protect us, but in the end, I think he just didn't care enough about us to do much."

Shay swallowed past the surge of panic and despair, used it as fuel for her much more useful anger. "Right, so. What do we do? I'm out and Duncan just deals with memory."

"Yeah and it's not fun," Duncan said. "Trade you."

"Sure, you can have eleven stitches," she said. "Got you beat by seven."

"Not exactly something to be proud of." Duncan ran a hand through his hair. "Finnias is trapped and…I don't know any other ghosts. Could I use Archie's memories against him?"

"Oh yeah, he seems real broken up about carving Finnias's heart out of his chest," Shay said. She put a hand over her own sternum. She had almost been Archibald's next victim.

She wasn't. She was fine, even with her pulse too quick under her fingers.

Would she have ended up like Finnias? No memories, wandering the earth, while her friends were in horrific danger from the power Archibald gained?

If he cut out Finnias's heart, did he still have it? Could she use that?

She didn't know. There were too many variables, too much she couldn't possibly guess at.

"Good point," Duncan said. "The heart of the matter--"

Even she groaned.

"What, too soon?" He shrugged. "Yeah, too soon."

"Something's happening," Rose said.

Every window in the house glowed blue. Bright and cold.

"Hey, just a thought, if he's not site bound are we safe out here?" Gideon asked.

A low sound filled the air, vibrating the gravel on the driveway. Wind whipped into a frenzy, cold and stinging.

Two windows shattered, concussive blasts of sound.

The house was dark and silent.

"He's gone," Rose said.

"I got that one all on my own," Shay muttered.

"Wow, Shay, I know it's bad, but let's rein it in," Duncan told her.

She sighed. "Yeah. Sorry. Well, I'm pretty sure I can tell you where he's heading."

She could just make out the ghost of the woman, right at the tree line, pointing beyond them.

A familiar ridge blotted out the sky.

"Is that…?" Duncan looked at Shay.

"If he left the house, then maybe he's vulnerable. We're going to need everything we can get. Gather up anything that didn't get trashed," Shay put a hand on Max's bag, next to her on the seat. "Taylor, is there salt in the kitchen?"

"I think so," Taylor said.

She got to her feet and only wobbled a little bit. Rahim had bandaged up her leg, which wasn't nearly as bad as her arm. "Great, let's go get some."

"Do you have a plan?" Rahim asked.

She needed him. Even if she didn't want to admit it. "Nope, but I'm saving our friends. No matter what."

Rahim considered her, carefully. He wasn't taking her anxiety, and she realized it must have really been an accident. Most of his patients were of the four-legged variety.

"I'll probably need your help," she blurted out. "Jo's plan was solid, she just didn't have the information she needed. None of us are witches, so…at least he won't be taking any of us. So, if you can distract him…"

"I didn't get the opportunity before, but this time I have a feeling he'll be focusing on you." Rahim seemed to accept her unspoken apology. "I'll do whatever I can."

"That's all I need," Shay said.

Duncan sighed. "Didn't we literally just discuss how we can't do anything?"

"Doesn't matter, no choice." Shay didn't know what the circle was for or what Archibald could possibly be planning. "If he's not in the house, maybe we can salt and burn the circle. If it's still there."

"Works for me," Duncan said. "Glad our plan still involves fire."

"Are you going to share with the rest of the class or…?" Taylor gave her a look.

Shay did her best to explain on the way inside, about the memory and what they'd seen.

The entryway was worse than before - the chandelier was on the floor, the windows in the front were cracked, and there a broken, jagged line drew its way up one of the walls. Taylor winced, but didn't say anything, leading Shay to the kitchen while everyone else gathered up what supplies they had left.

"Why are there seven bottles of cinnamon in here?" Taylor closed the spice cabinet with disgust. "Maybe it's in the baking area…"

"Have you been out here a lot?" Shay asked. She sat on one of the stools. Her head felt like it had been shoved full of cotton to make up for lack of brain cells and she wanted to take a nap and forget the pain.

"I do a lot of event planning for the locations my family owns," Taylor said. "I used to do them here, but…they hired another company, and stopped doing events all together."

"But you were okay with us lighting this place on fire?" Shay asked. "You have a lot of good memories of this place, right?

Taylor sighed, pausing from digging through a cupboard to sit back on her heels. "I do. And bad ones. I know my family's business practices aren't always above the board. I'm not naive. I thought if I was just doing event planning and not the real estate side of things, I would be keeping my nose clean. But…they've been doing things that really hurt people for a long time. I can't keep clinging to the good memories and pretending they outweigh the pain my family is causing."

"What do you think they have planned?" Shay asked.

"Honestly? I don't know," Taylor said. "I know it has something to do with the spirit charmer, but that's it. Being possessed wasn't fun, but I don't even remember it. There's three months of my life are just gone, and I got off easy."

"Still awful." Shay wished Taylor was closer so she could at least pat her shoulder or something.

"Yeah. It was. But it has helped me realize that I was just being a coward." Taylor straightened. "When this is over, I'm going to be your inside person. We'll figure it out together."

"Oh good, I wouldn't want to trick you into giving me information or something, it sounded mean," Shay said.

Taylor smiled a bit. "You're a good person."

"I literally just exploded on Rahim, so maybe not." She did feel guilty about it, after all, even though she didn't want to. He'd almost gotten her killed. She couldn't feel bad about hurt feelings. Somehow, that thought made it worse. "And dragged you into this. And…well, a lot of things, actually."

"I was already a part of this," Taylor said. "I mean, I wasn't expecting to be fighting against an evil ghost tonight but…well. Here we are. But trust me, you're good."

Shay felt a little lighter. "Well, you are, too."

"Thanks, but I was about to say if it was me, I would have ruined my manicure to rip Rahim's face off, so…"

Shay laughed.

"There, see?" Taylor opened another cabinet. "Aha! I found the salt. Lots of it!"

"Great, grab it all," Shay said. "I have a feeling we're going to need it."

Chapter 26: The Circle

Shay didn't have a plan.

But she had to get everyone back tonight, or they might be lost forever. If Archibald disappeared now she might never find him again.

A risk she wasn't willing to take.

They left the house with a few emergency flashlights and candles. They must have made an odd sight, if anyone was driving past, but the night remained quiet. No headlights lit up the driveway.

The only witnesses were the ghosts under the trees.

Shay leaned on Taylor's shoulder as crossed the huge, grassy area where weddings were held. She was the only one closer to her height, and the only person who hadn't been beaten up by a ghost recently.

Yet, anyway.

"Hey, do you know the name Hans Lyman?" she asked, more to keep her mind off of her stumbling and pain, rather than because she thought Taylor would have anything exciting to contribute. Her arm hurt more than before, despite taking pain killers. Rahim said she needed rest, but she didn't have time.

"It's an early pen name for Dr. Robert Lichfield," Taylor said, so fast it was impressive.

"Oh, okay," Shay said. "I mean, I knew, but how did you?"

"Um, I was a ghost hunter, too," Taylor reminded her.

If Shay had blood to spare, it would have rushed to her cheeks. She'd completely forgotten. "Oh. Right. Sorry, it's been…"

"A long week, I know." Taylor didn't sound upset, at least. "Anyway, he's a huge figure in the world of parapsychology. He built a lot of the equipment used by ghost hunters. Why?"

"Just…found a book by him, and it's been on my mind." Shay's phone was still dead, but she knew that even if she could turn it on, there would be nothing form Lichfield. He'd abandoned her to the ghosts. "How did you get into ghost hunting, anyway?"

"When your family owns a lot of property some of it tends to be haunted," Taylor said. "I've always believed in ghosts. I've seen too many things not to, especially when I was a kid. But as for how I joined P.E.I.R.S., back when Vic was first starting out, my dad called him in to check out one of the houses we were trying to sell. We got to talking and the rest is history, I suppose. Not an interesting story. I was fascinated and Vic gave me an opportunity, that's all it boils down to. It helps that my parents thought it was a terrible hobby so it was a bit of rebellion, too. Now, back to why you want to know about Robert Lichfield."

"Well…" Shay figured she had nothing to lose. "I talked to him, and-ow!"

Taylor's arm jerked, jarring Shay. "Sorry! I'm sorry. You surprised me. I mean, you talked to him? Called him up and said 'hi my name is Shay and I thought you might want to talk about punching ghosts'?"

"…Well, I was trying to figure out his book about abilities, so pretty close." Shay realized it had been earlier that day. That the time could be measured in hours. It felt like it should have been weeks ago. "But it was Duncan who got a hold of his publisher. They gave us his number."

"I worked some major library mojo on them," Duncan said. Shay hadn't been aware he was listening to their conversation.

"I thought you asked, and they gave it to you?" Shay said.

"Oh, that, too, but I had to ask in a very specific way," Duncan said. "In a pretending that I was trying to get a hold of him for an interview sort of way."

"So, you lied?" Gideon asked.

"Like a rug, yeah," Duncan admitted.

"What was he like?" Taylor asked, excitement shining in her eyes.

Shay felt bad about letting her down. "Grumpy."

Duncan laughed. "You sure it wasn't because he was talking to you? You have that effect on people, you know."

"You better be grateful I'm injured," Shay said. Gideon laughed, at least. "He answered the phone grumpy. He blew me off, too. He was like 'oh I know let's meet up I can help you' and immediately hung up on me. So overall? A jerk."

"Oh," Taylor didn't sound surprised. "I guess, y'know, he's pretty infamous for being a genius recluse…

"Tay, you know you should never meet your heroes," Gideon reminded her.

"Yeah, you've got a point." She sighed. "Still, if I could get him to sign Malevolent Mysteries I'd be over the moon."

"Malevolent Mysteries?" Duncan sniggered.

Taylor shot him a look. "It's a good book! Still, weird that he agreed to help then just…didn't."

"Yeah." Shay wondered if she should say the rest. "I think…I think he's like me. A necromancer. But I don't think he…I think he might have done something to get it."

"What do you mean?" Gideon asked.

"I think…it has something to do with hearts, and…"

They'd reached the trees and she pulled Taylor short.

There was a path, winding its way up the ridge, and every ten feet was a ghost. They raged from barely there to so bright she could barely look at them, staring at her with empty eyes.

"What do they want?" Shay asked.

"They're leading the way," Rose said.

"Nice change of pace from the usual death murder aaaagh," Duncan said. He shivered. "They all hate him. Archibald, that is. They're tied to him, but they despise him. He wasn't the kindest man when he was alive. He had…many faces. Many different ways he presented himself to the world. For some, he was a good man. For others, a monster. In death, only the monster remains. They all want you to stop him, more than they want to be physical again. And they want that a lot."

Shay didn't like how any of that sounded. "Ominous."

"Little bit, yeah," Duncan said. "I'm getting snippets of things. He came here with Finnias, to stop something. The spirit charmer…Emmaline?"

"Right," Shay nodded.

"Yeah, but there was something happening, something worse than her, and they had to join forces with her," Duncan said. "A ritual, I think. They stopped it. Sorry, no one here saw it directly, and it's all fuzzy, and I'm not used to this. I think this is what happened, but…I don't know. Something to do with the circle. After that, there was a party but…"

"But Archibald went on a murder spree?" Taylor hazarded.

"I think so," Duncan said. "Something happened, at the circle. It changed his perspective, made him drop any pretenses of being a good person. It's…it's hard to pick up on it, it's all residual…but he murdered a bunch of people and turned into a really powerful ghost, and they've all been locked up together for a hundred years. So. That sucks."

"And he's been marinating in ghost power juice until Arlo came along?" Shay asked.

"Pretty much," Rose said. "I'm getting the same feelings. Well done."

"Thanks, I put the done in Duncan."

Shay sniggered, even though it wasn't very funny. She didn't know how to feel about Duncan finally embracing his ability, or if he was even conscious of doing it.

"There are a lot of powerful emotions, too," Rahim said. "Anger, fear, sadness…it was a buffet for him."

"And snagged himself a witch for dessert." Duncan nodded. "We didn't stand a chance. We might still not stand a chance. He's more powerful than ever."

"Duncan's right," Rose said. "We need to be extremely careful. If Archibald is at this circle and it drove him to murder, it could do the same for any of us."

"Just so you all know, if you try to carve out my heart, I don't think we can be friends anymore," Shay said. Duncan laughed. No one else did.

"So, we're heading straight into a circle that made someone crazy and got a bunch of people murdered?" Gideon said. "This sounds like a really awful idea."

"Don't have any better ones," Shay admitted.

The conversation didn't so much fade out as curl up and die.

It was a different world under the trees. Fog drifted around dark trunks and slid across the trail. Ghosts stood sentinel along the trail. Shay tensed every time they came to one, but nothing reached out and attacked them.

The trail ended at the top of the ridge.

"Where do we go?" Rahim asked.

"She's going to lead the way," Rose said.

The first woman stood in the trees ahead of them. Shay let Rose take the lead. She didn't want a repeat of what had happened in the car. No matter how much the ghosts were united in wanting to bring down Archibald, she knew she was a pretty tempting diversion.

"I can see a light." Duncan squinted ahead. "Are we really following that? Isn't this how people die in swamps? Following will-o-wisps and getting sucked under the mud?"

"I don't think this area is known for its rich and abundant bogs, if it helps," Gideon said.

"It does help, thank you." Duncan took his hand and Gideon laced their fingers together. Gross. Shay made a face and Taylor giggled, even if it was high and strained. "My first question still stands. Don't these things usually lead you to your demise?"

"I'm pretty sure that's exactly what she's doing," Rose said.

Duncan sighed, loudly. "You and Jo are cut from the same cuddly cloth, aren't you."

Rose smiled, grim in the otherworldly light. "Comes with the territory, I guess."

They stumbled over roots and through thick undergrowth. Shay got a few new scratches, but Gideon's spare jacket deflected the worst of it.

It didn't take long to reach the bottom.

The trees grew right up to the edge of the circle, but the only thing inside was thick, yellow grass up to Shay's knees. The mist that had lit their way, more or less, didn't cross the boundary, stopping where the trees did. Beyond it seemed much darker.

She glanced behind her. The ghosts crowded behind them, for a moment, and faded away into nothing.

"What do we do?" Duncan asked.

"We go in," Shay said.

They walked into the circle in single file.

The moment Shay stepped over the air grew thick and frigidly cold. It was hard to breathe.

"He's here," Duncan said, softly.

Archibald appeared, directly in the center of the clearing. He looked like he was standing in the middle of a cloudy day, but the shadows around him darker than ever.

He was completely solid. The air rippled around him, full of whispers.

Shay handed Gideon a sachet and he threw it at him, hard. Duncan threw one of his own, followed by Rahim.

All three slowed down before reaching him. He plucked one out of the air with a smile. The other two dropped to the ground. "This can't hurt me."

The sachet burst into flame. Sparks and ash floated from his fingers.

"Was this your entire plan, Shay?" he asked. "Throw a bundle of herbs at me?"

"Oh, I didn't have a plan," she said.

Rose threw another sachet at him and Taylor from the other side. He caught the first and the second hit him in the side, exploding on impact.

It was salt, the only thing that seemed to bother Archibald at all.

The first one burned in his hand. He shook his hand and the flames went out. He didn't appear bored anymore.

Rahim stepped forward, eyes closed. A stillness fell over them, the air lightened, the outline of clouds hovering close above.

And turned violently, suddenly dark. Gray and black swirled out from around Archibald, rot spreading through the circle and into the trees beyond, branches snapping and whole trees slumping.

"Enough of this," Archibald snarled. Rahim stepped in his way but he was shoved to the side. He strode forward, knocking everyone back into the grass.

Except for Shay.

He grabbed her collar and hauled her close. The jacket yanked on her arm and and she cried out in pain despite herself, her leg threatening to buckle underneath her. Archibald's face was inches from hers, his eyes unnaturally bright.

"You." His voice hit a low register that sent panic immediately pooling into her stomach. "Did you really think you could defeat me? Without the spirit charmer? Without your witches? I am more powerful than you could ever imagine and I will have what I have been owed all this time!"

She clawed at his wrist. It was so cold it burned her fingers.

Blue light streamed from outside of the circle, the ghosts being pulled into Archibald, circling around her and adding to the light surrounding him. Until it was bright. Until it was too much.

A horrendous tearing sound filled the clearing. An explosion of misplaced air knocked Shay onto her back. Archibald's disembodied hand was still twisted around her jacket collar. She slapped it and it dissolved into blue mist.

Someone was screaming her name.

There was a tear above her, right where Archibald had been.

Chapter 27: Void

A dark space in the air. A two-dimensional rip in the middle of a field, fluttering gently, a curtain caught in the breeze.

Shay tried to scramble away from it, get as far as she could.

A dozen hands shot through the tear. They burned white and cold, so bright it hurt to look at them.

They wrapped around her arm and shoulders, freezing against her skin. She screamed and tried to fight them, tried to dig her heels into the dirt. All she managed to do was wrench her bad arm.

There was nothing to save her. She was vaguely aware of Duncan reaching for her, but he'd never get to her in time.

She was yanked through the tear.

All she had time to do was screw her eyes shut. Finnias told her not to look the first time. She wasn't going to fail him again.

She plunged into cold beyond imagining. The cold expanded in her chest and wrapped her in an embrace, like needles of ice were being driven into her skin. She couldn't breathe. She could barely think. She tried to turn, but she didn't know which way the tear was, how to get back.

She had to open her eyes. She sent a silent apology to Finnias, wherever he was.

At first it was dark.

Change came slowly and all at once. She could have been floating in a galaxy. A sea of clouds and stars. Cold lights glowed dimly all around her, the mist ebbed and flowed in waves, curling around her. Glimpses of things, lives that had ended, surged up through the mist and vanished again. The shape of a house with a single light on, the glint of water, the trundling headlights of a far-off car shining on a silver thread of road.

Each point of brilliance was a life. The scenes were indistinct and muted. A bridge, an ocean, a tower, a castle. Their shapes faded in and out of her awareness. Something fluttered near her head, a rush of wings. She turned to follow it.

And everything else fell way.

A bright, blue light shone through a gap in the clouds. A moon of impossible color. Heartbreakingly beautiful. If she had any breath left it would have been taken away.

Tears floated around her, sparkling jewels rotating around her in her own solar system.

Nothing hurt. The cold was gone, too, the light a point of warmth in an endless, jumbled expanse, promising an end. A rest.

No more ghosts. No more fear. The light was all that was left, and it wanted her there. She'd never been so welcomed in her entire life. She moved closer and the light grew brighter, more crystalline.

Her glasses frosted over, blocking her view, and that was all it took to make her hesitate.

She didn't want to be there. She needed to get out. She wrenched herself away from the light, looking wildly for the exit, though she had no idea how she'd see it, or even what it would look like. She thought she saw yellow grass, a stand of trees, and she willed herself towards it. She couldn't have gone far. She just needed to move.

Movement.

The lights, shining so brightly just a moment before, faded to dying embers. The fog moved in, thick and syrupy. The fear settled back in her chest.

Something enormous blotted out the stars.

It was immense. Bigger than anything had any right to be. It filled the space around her. All its attention focused on her. She felt the shift of a hundred eyes, invisible in the darkness. It wrapped all around her and she was studied from every angle.

'Finally,' the voice was everywhere and nowhere all at once. It was the wind in the trees, the crash of the ocean, a single scream of fear abruptly cut off. It boomed through her, echoed in the recesses of her mind, dredging up every bit of fear she'd ever felt. She screamed and tried to cover her ears, but it didn't help. She was a single breath of air against a hurricane. 'I've waited so long.'

Each syllable hurt, tearing into her and trying to shake her apart into a million pieces.

She was going to die here. Even if she could breathe, even if it wasn't cold, the voice alone was going to kill her. The fear clawing another useless scream from her throat would stop her heart.

"Shay!"

A familiar voice.

It was enough to bring her back to herself as a hand closed around hers.

The noise stopped.

She was standing on Finnias's landing, holding his hand.

The void was gone.

Golden light streamed through the window, warm and gentle. Motes of dust danced slowly in the sunbeams.

Finnias wasn't the horrible corpse from before, but a scared young man, not much older than her, as alive as she was. Holding her hand tightly enough to hurt.

The pain jolted her into awareness and the rest of her body followed suit, reminding her of all the abuse she'd put it through in the last few days.

She hadn't been breathing in the void and she took in a deep gasp of breath. Her lungs expanded and burned. She relished that pain, too. She thought she would never feel it again.

"Thanks," she finally managed.

"We can't stay here," Finnias said. "Archibald will be here soon, and…and even if he wasn't, you can't hold this for long. I told you not to look."

"I know. I'm sorry. I couldn't find the way out." She laughed. It was surprisingly only mildly hysterical, but it turned into something that wasn't a laugh at all and she had to stop, or it would take over her whole chest. "I'm so sorry, Finnias, I'm supposed to save you, and here we are—"

Her leg buckled and she fell to her knees. He crouched down in front of her.

"You're hurt." Finnas fingers on the side of her face were soft and warm. "I don't know how to help. Once I let go—"

"I'll be right back where I started, yeah," she said. Her voice was breathy and high. The spots were back, swimming across her vision, threatening her with darkness. "Which is…really, really not where I want to be."

"Definitely not," Finnias agreed. "If I could hold onto you without coming here…but with the tear…"

"Yeah," she had nothing else to say.

He looked at her, helplessly. "I can't help you. Not like this. I'm sorry, Shay."

"Hey," she said, squeezing his hand back as tightly as he was holding onto her. If it hurt, if he noticed any change at all, it didn't show on his face. "It's okay."

It wasn't okay. She was twenty-one. She had a million things she still wanted to do, and she'd already wasted so much time.

She was just a kid. She still hadn't grown up in any of the ways that mattered.

And she was going to die.

Finnias would have to let go of her hand, and she would die. Crushed by the void or killed by whatever tried to hold her there.

Max was going to be so upset with her.

Her breath hitched at the thought. Would they be okay? Had she done enough to save them?

All she could do was hope they were free, and the tear would close without her, or the witches would figure it out.

It was the best she could do.

"It's not," Finnias squeezed her hand tighter. "This is not okay."

"It is, it's all right," she said. Everything she had done would simply have to be enough. She choked out another laugh. Her cheeks were warm and wet. When had she started crying again? She didn't think she'd ever stopped. "Maybe we can hang out. Since I'll be. Y'know."

Her breath caught again, and she couldn't say anything else.

She wanted to live so fiercely it hurt deep in her chest, more overwhelming than any of the scrapes, cuts, or bruises she'd accumulated.

Finnias didn't say anything. He pulled her forward so she could rest her forehead against his chest. He wrapped his arm around her, carefully keeping their hands together, and held her there.

She returned the one-armed hug, as tightly as she could, and tried to hold in the sobs threatening to spill out of her. The back of his vest was silky. He didn't say anything when she rumpled it, bunching it up in her fist.

Any moment Archibald's footsteps would herald his eternal walk up the stairs and Finnias would have to let go before he played out his death again. Any moment her will and energy would give out and it wouldn't matter what Archibald wanted.

At least she wasn't alone.

"Thanks for being here," she murmured against his vest.

He leaned his head against hers. "I'll always be here for you."

He pushed her back after a moment, and nodded, jerkily. His eyes were deeply sad, but it was more. Something she couldn't begin to place. She hadn't known him long, but she had a feeling he was about to do something risky.

"Finnias—"

The room went dark and the cold rushed back in like the tide.

And she was lying on the ground, surrounded by grass, stained gray and encased in thick frost. She coughed, her chest was tight, every breath a stab.

But she was alive. She heard footsteps and someone crashed through the grass next to her, kneeling down.

"Shay!" Duncan helped her sit up. "Oh my god, how…are you okay?"

Finnias's hand was still tightly around hers. He wasn't freezing anymore. His hand was a strange sort of solid, like it was sculpted from glass.

"I'm okay," she choked out. "I gotta close that. I gotta. There's something in there."

Long, sickly pale fingers, larger than she thought possible, reached through the opening and curling around the edge.

"Now!" Rahim yelled, and Taylor and Rose closed a salt circle around the tear. The fingers retreated. She didn't think it would hold, not for long.

The dark and rot around her melted away, the grass turned yellow again, spreading in a ripple around the circle and hitting the trees. They creaked and groaned, their needles shivering.

The tear rippled and expanded, filling in the shape of the circle, held open by the fingers of something larger than any ghost she had ever encountered.

She couldn't be sure it was a ghost at all.

It still wanted her, to yank her back into the tear. It reached for her and the salt barely kept it contained, sparking and flaring a sickening shade of green and yellow.

Finnias pulled Shay to her feet. He was more solid than he ever had, more real, as if his presence from the landing was bleeding into the blue she was used to. He nodded at her, and held a hand out to Duncan.

"...What's going on?" Duncan asked. "Why can I see him?"

"We're going to need your help," Finnias said. His voice echoed oddly, as if he was speaking from far away.

Duncan hesitated, but took his hand. "Oh. That's…that's cold. And weird. But yeah, okay, help. What are we doing?"

"We're going to close the tear," Shay said. Finnias glanced at her. His eyes glowed brighter than the rest of him, like newly minted coins.

"How are we going to do that?" Duncan's eyebrows rose. "Didn't you lose him and almost die last time? This seems much much worse."

"Just follow my lead," Finnias said. Shay nodded, and after a moment, Duncan returned the gesture.

The three of them stepped over the line of salt.

Chapter 28: Endings

They stepped into daylight.

Heavy gray clouds covered the sky. Snow gathered around the circle. The grass inside was gone. The bare, hard packed dirt was coated in a thick layer of glittering frost. The trees were dark and bare, each branch encased in ice.

The tear rippled.

"This…is where. No, when we fell, after the tower," Duncan said. "A memory. We're in a memory."

"This is where it all started," Finnias said, his voice normal and no longer echoing. He was solid and looked alive, but there was still a hole in his chest. "Where…someone died here. And someone else decided to take more lives. It has to end here, too."

Shay tightened her grip on his hand and held up her left hand, even though it hurt. She could work through the pain. "Let's finish it."

They stepped forward as one.

A hot pulsing filled her chest.

Finnias once told her that all ghosts wanted to be alive. They wanted to feel something, anything.

Maybe that was all that made her different from a ghost. She wasn't just existing, She wasn't a memory. Some leftover from a life not fully conceived.

She was a possibility, and she was going to burn as brightly as she could.

A scream echoed from the tear. The sound echoed over snow covered hills. The ice on the trees cracked, each one a gunshot.

"What is that?" Duncan asked.

"I don't know," Finnias said, not taking his eyes off of the tear. "Something old. Something…I think I've faced before. Shay has, too."

"The thing from the void," Shay said. Finnias nodded.

Max had talked about demonic entities before.

It was the only words she had to describe what crawled its way out of the tear.

It could have been a siphon, or something even older and more dangerous than that. She didn't know.

It was huge, even with its head bowed low it was three times her height.

It had eight arms, the puckered skin pale with disease and covered in red marks. It dragged a bulbous body behind it, swollen belly scraping against the ground. Its face had no eyes, just old silver scars, surrounded by matted and dirty white hair that trailed on the ground. Too many sharp teeth lined its wide and gaping mouth, stained red around the lips.

"Oh, sick," Duncan muttered. "How do we beat that?"

"We don't have to beat it, just shove it back in," Shay said.

"Sure, yeah, that'll be easy," Duncan said. "Big demon spider. Just scoop it up in a cup and toss it out the door."

"Easier if you have a piece of paper," Shay agreed, ignoring his sarcasm.

Archibald stepped through the entity.

His skin was gray, his eyes dark holes and his mouth a stretched, comical parody of what it used to be. He was too tall, stretched thin and desiccated. Ribs, sharp and curved, jutted out of his skin and the tattered remains of his vest. His arms dragged behind him, knuckles bumping against the frost. His fingers curled up, ending in sharpened bone.

He swung one arm and the siphon moved with him, an enormous hand with too many fingers bearing down on her, nails dark and serrated.

Blue fire blazed around her fist and she hit it, hard. The hand exploded into glittering particles and the fire lashed up the arm. It fell from the rest of the body, turning to ash and floating away on the wind.

Archibald shrieked, his own arm going up in flames, burning right down to the shoulder.

The face trained on her, a dark and diseased tongue rolling out of the open mouth. The marks on its arms opened, revealing hundreds of red rimmed eyes.

She staggered. One punch might have been all she had in her. The long night had taken its toll. The bandages on her arm were stained red and dizziness washed over her in a wave.

"Keep it together," Finnias said, softly.

"We don't have to take out that thing," Duncan said. "Just him."

He ran forward. Archibald swung out at them, but they were too close. Duncan used his free hand to grab his shoulder.

They were all standing on the landing, together. Archibald was no longer tall, simply a shriveled husk of a man, his bones sticking out of him, his skin stretched tight over his skull, his eyes hollow, dark pits. The carpet wore away under his feet. His arm had been burned away, the skin scorched red across his shoulder. He wrapped a skeletal hand around the nub.

Shay stepped forward, ready to bash Archibald's pathetic skull in. "Where's Max?"

"Darlin', I'm afraid I don't know who you're talking about." The drawl was more obvious than ever, thick as honey. "If you mean the witches, they'll be free soon enough. You've ruined me."

Shay could have collapsed on the stairs right then. Max and Jo were free. They would be okay, they would have to be.

"And you killed Finnias here," Duncan said. "And for what? More power? You're just a ghost now. You both are. It didn't even matter, in the end."

"I controlled the demon," Archibald spat. A few of his teeth plinked on the floor. His skin cracked and peeled around his mouth. "Did you see? We never had to force it back, Finnias. We could have controlled it. We could have had everything. You could have been everything! I would have followed you to the ends of the earth, but you just wouldn't listen! You wouldn't do anything! Emmaline was right, after all. You'll never amount to anything, never do anything, because you're too scared."

Shay jerked at the mention of the spirit charmer.

Finnias didn't react to the name. He glanced down at the hole in his chest. When he looked up again, his expression was sad. "I don't remember you, or anything you're talking about."

"You will." Archibald chuckled.

"Do you have his heart?" Shay asked.

"I did, once, in every sense," Archibald said. "But now I have nothing. They're coming back, Finnias, and they'll bring your heart. And when you remember everything, you'll know I was right. You killed us all, and it's going to happen again with these two brats and all their horrible little friends."

"Yeah, yeah, you told him so," Shay stepped forward. Blue flames surrounded her fist, but she knew it wouldn't last. "Who's coming?"

Archibald laughed, his ribs rattling together. "You'd really choose her over me?"

"Yes," Finnias said. "I would."

"Then I suppose that's all there is," Archibald bowed his head. The last of his hair fell to the ground in thin, wispy coils. "All we are is a memory, and you aren't even that. I don't know what you are. Maybe it's for the best."

"Who's coming?" Duncan repeated.

"I'm not going to tell you," He grinned, tight and rictus. "Are you going to stand there all day threatening me? You'll never get your little coven back if you don't destroy me."

"Do it, Shay," Finnias said.

Shay nodded. She limped forward. Archibald made absolutely no move to attack her, just kept standing on the stairs. She had a feeling that all the fight was out of him, so she simply placed her fingers on his collar bone. He let out a sigh, like he'd been holding his breath for a long time.

Blue flames consumed him, so quickly they were only there for a moment.

Ashes rained down slowly, twisting and twirling like dust motes. Everywhere they touched the landing disappeared into bright light, burning, sparks hitting the edges of an old, worn photograph. It disintegrated around them.

They were standing back in the field.

The tear was gone.

Duncan let go of Finnias's hand and Gideon grabbed him into a hug, so tightly his feet were off the ground.

"Woah!" Duncan hugged him back and laughed. "Glad to see you, too!"

"You were gone for ages," Gideon said. "I thought…but you're okay. And… everything's okay, right?"

"I think so," Duncan said. Gideon kissed him on the cheek with a loud, smacking sound.

"Ew," Shay said.

Duncan laughed. "Wow, okay, I want to talk about that later, and apparently I need to disappear more often, but my sister is right there."

"Oh, who cares?" Gideon asked.

"I care!" Shay protested.

Gideon ignored her. "You will absolutely not disappear more often."

"Yeah, okay, I'll do my best. Safe Careful."

Gideon finally looked at her. "Oh, Shay, you're bleeding."

"…So I am." She stared at the bandages around her left hand. They were soaked through with red. Finnias let go of her hand and backed away.

Rahim used gentle fingers to check Shay's wrist. "Looks like you popped a few stitches."

"Oh. Yeah. Probably." She stared at the bandages. They were red. "Is Max—"

"We'll patch you up back at the house," Rahim said.

"Sounds perfect," she said. She glanced at Finnias. "I'll need a second."

"Of course," Rahim said. "Duncan, you're next."

"I'm fine," Duncan protested.

"He's gotta make sure you have all of your shots before you start dating anyone," Shay said.

"You're the worst," Duncan told her. "The worst sister."

"I can live with that," she said.

She wanted to see Max so badly it ached, and surprisingly she felt nearly the same about Jo. She wanted to meet Arlo. They had to be back at the house.

But she needed a moment to get her bearings. A second to breathe. She was scattered and unfocused.

She'd almost died.

The sky above the hills was paler, the faint light painting the world in shades of indigo.

The blue hour.

It was the blue hour, and she was alive in a field with Finnias, who was more solid than she'd ever seen him. She breathed. It was cold and she'd never been happier to be freezing.

The ghosts from the path stood at the tree line.

"They want to thank you," Finnias said. His voice was quiet, but he didn't sound as distant as he had before. If she didn't look at him, he might have been as alive as he'd been in the memory.

She wasn't sure what it meant. Or if it meant anything at all.

"They're free now?" she asked.

"Thanks to you," Finnias said.

"And you." She waved at them.

They disappeared, one by one, fading into the shadows until only the woman was left. She held out a hand to them before she was gone, too.

Finnias was still next to her.

"You're not going anywhere, are you?" she asked, her voice small. She knew he was a ghost, that moving on was probably better for him, but she felt like she'd just met him. She wanted to get to know him.

"I don't think so," Finnias said.

"You gave up your landing, didn't you? Back in the…in the place. What we saw were Archibald's memories," she said.

"I did." He nodded, looking to the horizon, towards the sunrise. "I thought it was important. That if I stayed there, or…or at least kept it, my memories would return, that I would know who I was. But I suppose there was nothing there but my death. It was an empty place. In the end, saving you was more important."

"You could say your heart wasn't in it," Shay said.

Finnias covered his mouth with one hand, but she could tell by his eyes he was smiling.

The first rays of the sun rose over the hills, painting the tops of the trees yellow and gold.

"I think I'm ready to go," Shay said. "You coming?"

"Of course." He nodded. "Wherever you need me, I'll be there."

"Sounds like you plan on haunting me now," Shay said.

"Ghosts need to be anchored to something," Finnias said. "Usually to a place, or a memory. I was tied to my death. Now I'm tied to you."

It should have been alarming, but it was strangely right. Maybe it was a necromancer thing. Maybe it was a her thing. She couldn't honestly say which it was, but she found she didn't mind at all. She held out her hand and he took it. His fingers weren't much colder than hers. "Sounds good to me."

Chapter 29: A Quiet Moment

Picking her way back to the house took Shay significantly longer than getting to the circle. Rahim hurried ahead to make sure the witches returned okay, but everyone else stayed with her.

She honestly appreciated it.

Bushes grew thickly on the side of the ridge, snaking treacherous branches and roots over the path they'd taken the night before. Exhaustion weighed Shay down by the time they got to the top. Duncan made her sit down. She wanted to get to the house, she had to know if Max was okay, but she supposed taking a tumble down the other side wouldn't do anyone any favors.

"Are you sure you're okay?" Taylor asked.

"Peachy," she said.

"Peaches and plums," Duncan said.

"The whole fruit basket," she agreed.

"We're a bunch of fruits, at any rate," Gideon said.

"Obviously." Rose looked at Shay. "Is the ghost following us Finnias?"

"That's him," Shay said. She wasn't sure what everyone else saw, but he still seemed solid and real to her, standing just below them on a rock jutting out of the side of the ridge. "He's with me now."

"I see," Rose said. "Be careful."

"Of what?" Shay wasn't sure she should ask.

"Just…be careful."

"Are you saying he isn't safe?" Taylor asked.

Finnias sighed and folded his arms. "Well, I certainly don't want to possess you."

Duncan looked like he might laugh. No one else reacted. Shay was pretty sure they were the only ones that could hear him, which was probably for the best. "It's okay. We're friends."

"That is not what I said."

Jo had once told her ghosts weren't her friends, and she'd meant Finnias specifically, but Shay was starting to think Jo wasn't the authority she'd assumed she was. She'd thought other people had all the answers, but maybe no one did. They were all stumbling through as best as they could. With ghosts. And life.

"Hey Donuts, are you…all you again?" She was pretty sure she knew the answer already.

"Feels like it," he said.

"Seems like it to me, too," Rose said.

"All right, no longer a baker's dozen. Go team."

The path wound down the other side of the ridge to the house, a dark spot in blue shadow. Taylor made sure

Shay didn't roll down the hill, but Shay had a feeling Finnias would keep her from falling too far.

Cold sunk into her jacket and her arm throbbed.

It was a beautiful morning.

The moment Shay left the trees Max ran over and swept her into a hug. She hugged them back as tightly as she could, but she must have winced a little too much because they pulled away, quickly. She made a noise of protest, keeping the fingers of her right hand curled around their sleeve.

They were really there. Tears pricked at her eyes, and she didn't even try to stop them when they made her vision blurry.

"Oh, Shay." They cupped her face.

Their voice was the best sound in the world. She wanted to stare at their face forever, even if it was tear stained, their hair sticking up where they must have shoved their hand through it. "You're really here."

"I'm really here." Max rubbed their hands on her shoulders. "Your arm..."

"Looks worse than it is." She wasn't sure if that was true, but she didn't care about it. "You're back, that's what matters. I was so scared you were gone and...you are okay, right?"

"Am I okay? Shay, I say this with all the love in the world, but you look terrible." Their face crumpled and they were dangerously close to crying.

She glanced down at herself. Her clothes were torn and bloody, her jacket ripped, and the bandages around her hand were dark and stiff. "...Okay, yeah, a little bit worse than usual. But you are okay, right? He didn't hurt you?"

"I don't remember any of it," Max said. "One minute I was running into the entryway, the next I almost punched the family vet in the face."

"Oh, that would have been a little awkward," she said.

Max laughed, but it was strained and tight. "What happened? I tried to keep you out of danger but here you are—"

"I'm sorry to break this up, but you are aware of that ghost, right?" A voice she didn't recognize asked.

Shay hadn't even noticed Jo and a large, red-haired man who must have been Arlo walking up to them.

"Should I be offended?" Finnias rose an eyebrow.

"Woah!" Max took a step away from Finnias, clearly noticing him for the first time. "That's…is that?"

Shay had to crack a smile. "This is Finnias. Hi, um, Arlo. I'm Shay. And um. Glad you're okay?"

"You're the one with the ghost touch." Arlo glanced at Jo, who completely ignored him to check on Shay, looking up and down, wincing when she saw the blood.

"That's Shay," Duncan said. "Punching ghosts. Like the one who had you! Totally annihilated him. Just bam."

"I didn't punch him?" Shay wasn't even sure what she'd done. Archibald was definitely some kind of gone, if the witches were back, but Shay wasn't sure what that meant for a ghost. She'd never really stopped to consider it.

Whatever happened, he'd deserved it.

But she thought at the end he was ready to go, anyway.

"Psh, tomato, tomahto. Potato potahto."

"We live in Idaho, you know it's potato," she argued. "And I didn't-"

Duncan ignored her. "It was rad and you all missed it. Luckily, I'm here to tell you all about it. My name's Duncan, by the way, nice to meet you finally, Arlo."

"Nice to meet you, too." Arlo was paler than the photos on Jo's phone, the shadows under his eyes darker, but otherwise he was the same. "Jo has said basically nothing about you.

Jo ignored him entirely, checking Shay over. "Oh my god, Shay, I told you to stay at the house."

"Yeah so about that, the poltergeist was there, and uh…might have trashed your room." Shay winced. "Sorry?"

"I don't even care about that right now," Jo said. Shay was sure she would care a lot, later. "Do you need a hospital? Emergency clinic?"

"I'm fine, Rahim can stitch me up again-"

"Stitch you up!" Jo exclaimed.

"Again?" Max added. They looked like they were about to shove Jo out of the way.

Arlo put a hand on her shoulder. "Jo, let her breathe. So, I was gone for three weeks and you start a…wayward house for ghost afflicted children?"

"Something like that." Jo hugged Shay, tightly. Shay hugged her back. She was really glad she was okay. She'd been so focused on Max, she'd barely had room to realize she was incredibly worried about Jo, too

"Jo adopted me," Shay explained. "She's my big sister now."

"Then I'm a terrible big sister. I'm so sorry." Jo ignored Arlo. "I wanted to keep you out of it, and…and my plan failed pretty badly."

"Now you can't make fun of my plans anymore," Shay said. Jo laughed, weakly. "Seriously, it's okay. We took care of Archibald, I think my ghost banishing powers are working again, and we saved Finnias. Might have trashed two houses. All in a day's work. And hey! We're all okay."

"I think I'll be the judge of that," Rahim said. "Not with him. You. And my judgment is you are very much not okay, and we need to get you back to the house."

"Oh, I'm fine," Shay said. She took a step forward and her legs chose that moment to buckle. Luckily, there were a lot of people not willing to let her fall. She leaned heavily on Max, blinking dizzily. "All right. I concede your point."

"Max, can you carry her?" Rahim asked.

"Sure can." Max gave her a piggyback ride the rest of the way to the house, though she was sure she could have leaned on them and been fine, she didn't complain. Max smelled of coconut and lavender. They were warm, solid, and present. She might have held on too tightly, but they didn't complain.

They were really there.

"Wait," she said when they got to the steps. "Set me down, I need to talk to Finn."

"I'm objecting to that nickname." Finnias had been quiet, up to that point.

"Object away." Shay knew she'd probably wear him down, eventually.

"You can do that now?" Max and Jo asked her at the same time.

"Surprise?" She sat down on the steps, mindful of the broken mirror frame. "I don't think you should go inside."

"I agree," Finnias said.

She nodded. "I'll stay close to a window or something. Or you could meet me at home? Well, the shop."

She wasn't sure when the shop had become home, but it was.

"…I don't believe I can stray far from you," he admitted.

"Oh, car rides are going to be interesting," she said. He smiled. "Have you ever even been in a car outside of Duncan? Holy crap, you're so old."

"Thank you, Shay, I appreciate it," he said.

"I know." She looked down at the remains of the mirror. The broken pieces reflected the sky, the frame mangled. "Emmaline is still out there, isn't she."

"Who?" Max asked.

"The spirit charmer," Shay said. "We had a more formal introduction."

"What on earth happened while we were out?" Jo asked.

"Um, a lot. Duncan likes talking, he can tell you," Shay said.

"I do, in fact, enjoy talking," Duncan agreed.

"She's still out there," Finnias said. "I don't know where. I believe she's going to be…persistent in getting you on her side, but I couldn't tell you her plans."

"Yeah, no thanks," Shay said. Finnias's surprised but grateful look was enough to cement her decision if she hadn't already made up her mind.

In the light of day, the wreckage of the entryway was much worse than she remembered.

"Okay, this isn't great," Taylor said. She looked like she might cry. "What do I even...how do I fix this."

"We'll help you put it back together," Gideon offered. "Pretend the rest was an earthquake."

"Except for Shay," Rahim said. "Max, help me get her to this side room."

"Right." Max nodded. They got her situated on a couch near the window.

She grabbed Max's wrist before they left. "You can stay."

"I was just going to get my bag-" Max started.

"It's in Gideon's car."

"Nevermind." Max sat next to her.

"I'm going to numb you out a bit," Rahim warned her. "Is that okay?"

"Doesn't it hurt?" she asked.

"The point is for it to not hurt-"

"I meant you," she cut him off.

"Oh." He blinked, like no one had ever asked him before. "It's not my pain so...it's easier to manage. Though usually I'm just doing it with a dog that needs an anesthetic, and they feel pain in an entirely different way..."

"But for people? Ghosts?" Shay asked.

"Depends on the pain, depends on the person," Rahim said. "With you, I honestly don't feel much, so I was surprised it was so effective. I really am sorry. About earlier."

"It's okay," Shay said. "Sorry I blew up."

"You were well within your rights to do so," Rahim said. "But I appreciate the apology. I'm still very-"

"If one more person apologizes to me, I'm going to kick their teeth in."

Max snorted

"Ah, yeah, please don't do that, my teeth are gorgeous," Rahim pulled up a chair in front of her and began unwinding the bandages. Even though the weird static overtook her, she buried her face against Max's shoulder. "It's not as bad as I thought, you're lucky."

"Doesn't feel that way most times," Shay said.

"Maybe you just have good luck in small doses," Rahim suggested.

"I didn't have to clean, so you might be right," she said.

He chuckled. "Okay, once I'm done, you are resting, and no buts. You're staying on this couch before you head home, and when you get home, you are going to get some rest. Okay? And if it starts to hurt more or look worse, you get your butt to an urgent care. Got it?"

"Yeah, okay," Shay said. Rahim gave her a sharp look. "I mean, yes. Of course. I will take a nap, Dr. Ahmad."

."I'll make sure she does," Max said.

"Good." Rahim stood up. "Now, relax. Max, I'm glad you're okay, make sure she doesn't move."

"Thank you," Shay said.

Once Rahim left she told Max, haltingly, what happened. Some of it was hazy, outside of the void. The rift? She wasn't sure what it had been. A precipice between life and death, holding moments of memory. She did her best, but the words wouldn't form when she tried.

"That's terrifying," they said, quietly. "Are you…?"

"I'm all right," she said. "It was kind of like a dream, it's fading. I don't think people are meant to go there, y'know? I can't even describe it, now. Not really."

"Yeah." Max squeezed her, gently. She was leaning against their shoulder.

"And…and I get it," she said. "Being scared, wanting to protect someone. Because I couldn't get a hold of you, and I got here, and you were gone and…"

"I'm all right," they said.

"You are now." She took a deep breath. "I have a point. Sort of. I don't want to pretend things are okay because things are calm now. I know you're scared, and I am, too. Believe me, I understand. But I promise, I'm not giving up. If it's me against the world, it had better be you, too."

"Always," Max sounded a little watery.

"Good. And I don't care what Lichfield or anyone says, parapsycho rock star or not, I'm not going anywhere," Shay said. "I'm not dying, not now, not in two months. You're stuck with me for life. And I'm talking decades. We're growing old and gray together. We'll be sitting on a porch in rocking chairs in fifty years yelling at parked cars to slow down."

Max laughed. "You promise?"

"I swear," Shay said. "I have a lot of people depending on me. And…that's okay, because I depend on them, too. Especially you."

Max took a deep breath. "And I depend on you. For a lot more than you probably realize. I was so scared to lose you…I'm sorry."

"Nah." She held up her good hand to silence them. "I won't follow through on my teeth kicking threat because it's you, and I know your braces were astronomically expensive, but you said I don't have to be sorry, and same goes to you. You never have to be sorry with me."

They finally really smiled, their entire face softening. "What if I say something mean?"

"If you're saying something mean I deserve it," she admitted.

"Got it." They took her good hand in theirs, letting out a shaky breath.

"Hey. I love you," she said. "You're my best friend, and there's no one else I'd rather be here with. I wasn't kidding. You're stuck with me forever. You got that?"

"Yeah, I got it." They smiled. "I love you, too."

"Good, you better, I'm amazing," she said.

"Yeah," they said, without a hint of sarcasm. "You really are."

She ignored how warm her face was. "And you're amazing, too."

"I know." They grinned.

They sat together for a little while. The pain was back, but she found she didn't mind so much.

It meant she was alive.

Chapter 30: Omen

The answer to car rides ended up being Finnias wasn't even aware they were happening. Shay forced Gideon to stop driving several times, just to check he was still there. He appeared every time, acting like no time had passed at all, only slightly put off by different surroundings. Shay wasn't sure how that worked, if he saw the world as it was, or something else entirely.

He didn't seem negatively affected, so she got back in the car, even dozed for the last ten minutes.

The house wasn't nearly as bad as Shay feared.

A few cupboards were hanging open in the kitchen, the table had moved across the breakfast nook, and some of the lighter furniture had been shoved around the living room. There were a few doily casualties, but if Jo was broken up about them, she hid it well.

"Ugh, poltergeist residue over everything," Arlo said. "Jo, you weren't kidding about the wards being wrecked. This is a mess."

"Sorry," Shay said. "My bad."

Arlo shook his head. "Don't even worry about it. I'm going to set up brand new wards. This is good. Great, even. Fresh start."

"A fresh start for when you've had some rest," Rahim corrected him. "You were gone for three weeks."

"Yes, okay." Arlo patted his shoulder. "Let's do your room first, Shay."

"Can you even hear me?" Rahim asked. "I swear, you can hear ghosts, but nothing else."

"Is someone talking?" Arlo asked. Rahim smacked him on the shoulder but didn't stop them from heading up the stairs.

"Can you make an exception for Finnias?" She glanced at him. He'd shown up the moment she got out of the car, the sun shining through him like old, wavy glass.

"I shouldn't have to," Arlo said. "You're anchoring him. Any wards that protect you should protect him, too."

"Good," Finnias said.

"Aww, Finn." She smiled at him.

He gave her a very pointed look. "I don't trust you to stay out of trouble without me. I was gone for a week and you almost died."

"That's fair." She nodded. "I have Max, too, you know. They're like 95% of my impulse control."

"Honestly, I'm surprised they can say no to you at all," Finnias said. "You're lucky they repel ghosts or you wouldn't have survived for so long."

"Wait, they what?" Shay asked.

"Oh, that makes sense," Arlo said. Experimentation showed he could hear Finnias, distantly, but enough she didn't have to constantly relay everything he said.

"They repel ghosts, normal ones, at any rate," he explained. "I can only be around them for so long because of you."

"What?" Max asked. "What about me?"

"You repel ghosts," Shay said. The dismay on their face was comical. "Oh my god. Oh my god that means we could have gone to every haunted place in the whole valley and we never would have seen ghosts if this hadn't happened. Ever."

"Are you kidding me?" Max's voice cracked. "I put literally hundreds of hours into a ghost show, and I was never going to catch anything?"

"I'm sorry, this is devastating, but you have to admit it's a little funny." Shay tried not to laugh. She wasn't entirely successful, but the giggle she let slip out could have easily been part of the cough she tried to disguise it as. Max clearly didn't buy it for a moment. "Hey! You kept me safe for ages, you can at least be happy about that?"

"I'll be happy when I'm done mourning." Max sulked. "Hundreds of hours, Shay. Hundreds of them. Wasted."

She patted their shoulder. "It wasn't a waste. We had fun, right?"

"Yeah, we did." They sighed.

"And I believe in ghosts now, so you accomplished your true mission."

They gave her a flat look. "Oh, that was my true mission?"

"Obviously?" She grinned and their expression turned and exasperated shade of fond.

"Yeah, hi, still here," Arlo said. "If you were doing that without any training, you've got a lot of potential, kid. A few weeks of training you up and you're going to be a great witch."

"…Okay, that makes it sort of awesome," Max said. "A little bit. I'm still upset, don't get me wrong. I need three to five business days to get over this."

"Well, we're ordering pizza for dinner. Lunch? I hope it helps some," Arlo said. They reached Shay's room and he stopped, putting a hand to the doorframe. "Wow, Max. You did this yourself? It's pretty strong. You're already a great witch."

"I'm pretty sure you're just trying to make me feel better, but it is working," Max admitted.

"Told you," Shay said. Finnias slipped into the room after her easily and some of her anxiety melted away. As long as Max or Finnias was there, she wouldn't have to be afraid. The tear, and everything after, was starting to sink in. She'd nearly died, and without Finnias she would have.

She owed him her life. Being an anchor to keep him grounded was the least she could do.

Even if Jo was right, if Finnias wasn't her friend, not really, she found it didn't matter at all.

"Hey, what happened to the house guardian?" Max asked.

"Oh! I grabbed it, I hoped it would help, and maybe it did." She'd completely forgotten about it. It came out of her pocket in three separate pieces. "Aw, it broke. Sorry."

She had no idea when it had happened. When she'd fallen on the stairs from the poltergeist? When Archibald backhanded her on the stairs? Or maybe when she'd been knocked around in the void.

She needed to sit down and not move for a few months, if only so she'd stop being one, giant bruise.

"Not a big deal." Arlo held out his hand. She tipped the pieces into his palm. "Should probably set up a new one, anyway. Let it get acquainted with you."

"Yeah, I bring that funky necromancer vibe." She finally sat down on her bed and could have cried. She was exhausted. She wasn't sure she'd even have the energy to change into pajamas.

Arlo nodded. "You kinda do. Max, you want to come help me pick out a new house guardian? I trust your judgment."

"Really?" Max perked up. "Sure! Shay, go rest."

"I'm going," she waved them off.

Once they were gone it took all of the energy Shay had left to get up, close the door, and grab a change of clothes. "You're awfully quiet."

"A lot of noise tends to drown me out," Finnias said. "I'd rather conserve energy."

"And just talk to me? Finn that's so sweet," she said. "What about Duncan?"

"I think we've said all that needs to be said to one another, for the time being," Finnias said.

"So, you're still mad about the whole head sharing thing," Shay said.

Finnias huffed. "I am not annoying. Or old."

"Yeah, okay, grandpa." She grabbed the hem of her shirt, but couldn't bring herself to yank it over her head. She knew Finnias was a ghost, logically he didn't care about her state of dress. She wasn't the most logical person. "You're not going to creep on me, are you?"

"No." He sounded offended. "I'll leave the room if you want me to."

"I do, you don't want to see me naked, you'd die again," she said. Finnias rolled his eyes. "One minute and…I'll tap on the wall, or something. Sound fair?"

"If you must."

"I must," she said. "I really must."

He faded through the wall into Jo's office.

It would take some getting used to, but she was willing to put in the work.

Finnias was next door. Max and the rest of her friends were downstairs. She was surrounded by people who cared about her. People who needed her.

It was nice to be needed.

She had a purpose again. Maybe it wasn't clear, but the spirit charmer was planning something, and if Archibald could be trusted at all, something else was on the horizon. She would have to be ready for it.

Being in pajamas was something close to heaven. It would have been better with a shower, but she could barely keep her eyes open, she didn't think she could stand long enough to scrub her hair one handed.

A movement out of the corner of her eye gave her enough adrenaline for several showers, but it was only a dog out on the sidewalk.

"Dammit, I really need to get on Jo's case about those curtains," she muttered. The dog stared up at the house. There was something horribly off about it. It was too thin, the shape all wrong. Unease tickled its way up her spine. "Move along, puppy, we have enough weirdness here."

The dog stood up.

It wasn't a dog.

It was a blackened skeleton, vaguely canine in shape.

She staggered back from the window when it stepped forward. It was in her bedroom, towering over her, its vertebrae scraping the ceiling. She fell and scrambled back, pulling the stitches in her hand.

The inside of its ribcage glowed, the light pulsing, and shadows wrapped around it in the shape of a dog, the light piercing through in a galaxy. Its eyes shone so brightly it hurt, but she couldn't look away. Cold fingers wrapped around her wrist. She couldn't move.

And it was gone, as if nothing had happened.

"Shay." Finnias repeated. "Shay, look at me."

"Finn?" She was shaking. He was crouched next to her, his hand around her wrist. "What was that?"

"Nothing good, I'm afraid." He helped her to her feet. "I'm not letting you out of my sight from now on."

"You're going to be a creep?" It was a stupid thing to say, but it was the only thing she could think of.

"If I must," Finnias said. "I can't be sure, I'd need to…I'm fairly certain that was a death omen."

"Ah." She sat down on her bed, hollowed out and too tired to really let anything sink in. "So that means creep time."

"We need to tell Jo."

"Right." She looked out the window. The dog wasn't there, just the bare branches of the tree outside, carving lines into the pale November sky. "I'll get on that."

Acknowledgements

I loved writing this book, but I never could have done it alone, and I have a lot of people to thank!

First and foremost as always to my beta readers, Brooklyn and Jennifer, for cheering me on and reading through the very weird first draft.

To Yoko and Katie for their continued encouragement.

My sister, Emily, for reading the first book (even though she's not a reader!) and being excited about this one.

To everyone in my writing groups, who laughed at my terrible jokes.

Carmilla, for being so enthusiastic and for the amazing cover, and just wonderfully supportive all around.

My roommate, Colleen, who stoically endured many a rant.

To Cloaked Press for believing in the first book, and for all of your hard work making this book come to life!

A special thanks to my incredible Cindy, for giving me fun facts, helping me work out details, suffering through me losing character references, and giving me great advice.

And of course, to everyone who read this book! You're all amazing, and I couldn't do this without you. Please remember to review (it really helps!) and to join me for book 3, Night Terrors!

About the Author

A. Lawrence made a joke about Ghost Punch one day and decided to fully commit to the bit.

They live in Idaho, where long stretches of roads through nothing but hills of yellow grass and abandoned cabins have always inspired them.

When they're not writing, they are drawing or being forced to relax by their geriatric and demanding cat.

Tumblr: akidoodles
Instagram: akidoodles

www.ingramcontent.com/pod-product-compliance
Lightning Source LLC
Chambersburg PA
CBHW050742190726
48285CB00005B/1493